YUCCA MOUNTAIN
DIRTY BOMB

To Janet Presley —

A tall tale —

Wendy

Also by Wendell A. Duffield

NONFICTION

Volcanoes of Northern Arizona:
Sleeping Giants of the Grand Canyon Region

Chasing Lava:
A Geologist's Adventures at the Hawaiian Volcano Observatory

Poems, Song Lyrics, Essays, and Short Stories by Nina Hatchitt Duffield:
An anthology edited and annotated by Wendell and Anne Duffield

From Piglets to Prep School:
Crossing a Chasm

FICTION

When Pele Stirs:
A Volcanic Tale of Hawaii, Hemp, and High-Jinks

YUCCA MOUNTAIN DIRTY BOMB

A Novel

Wendell A. Duffield

Wendell A. Duffield

iUniverse, Inc.
New York Lincoln Shanghai

YUCCA MOUNTAIN DIRTY BOMB

iUniverse books may be ordered through booksellers or by contacting:

iUniverse
2021 Pine Lake Road, Suite 100
Lincoln, NE 68512
www.iuniverse.com
1-800-Authors (1-800-288-4677)

With the exception of the person referred to as President Forty-Three, the characters in this novel are creations of the author's imagination. Some background information is based on historic events that are recast within a framework of fiction. All happenings beyond the date of the book's publication are obviously the products of the author's imagination.

Cover Photo: Phreatomagmatic eruption of a new volcano (subsequently named Ukinrek) on the Alaskan Peninsula, 5 PM, April 6, 1977. The billowing dark cloud is a mixture of shattered pre-eruption rocks and new volcanic ash, blasted out by steam explosions that were triggered when molten rock encountered groundwater. Public domain image by photographer Richard Russell, provided courtesy of the Alaska Department of Fish and Game.

ISBN: 978-0-595-44203-4 (pbk)
ISBN: 978-0-595-88534-3 (ebk)

Printed in the United States of America

ACKNOWLEDGMENTS

From the time I first began to develop the idea for this novel, I realized that I would need and want sound advice and other forms of input from a variety of bright people. Friends and colleagues stepped forward when asked, and to all of them I shout a loud thank you. My barrister friend Peter Baird assured me that the probability of being hassled by a particular easily recognizable character in the book is extremely low. To paraphrase Peter: *In the Pantheon of those who criticize President George W. Bush in print, you are a wee insignificant activist.* Peter, also a novelist, put me on a path to begin writing engaging dialogue. Michael Eastman helped steer me from saying foolish and incorrect things about the radioactive material so central to the story. Whether they realize it or not, Dick Fiske, Greer Price and John Sass led me to believe that my "Yucca Mountain" friends and colleagues in the U.S. Geological Survey and the Department of Energy will not be too upset to read about the fictionalized destruction of their beloved repository. The advice *"Lighten up folks. It's just a novel."* fits here. Kevin Schindler taught me to calculate the phases of the moon and the positions of constellations for future dates. Bill Jackson helped me understand the in-and-out water balance of Lake Mead and how long it might take to quickly drain that lake should the need arise. Michael Ort helped keep my descriptions of volcanism, most especially phreatomagmatic volcanism, within the realm of the possible. Nancy Riggs served as another volcanism referee, and convinced me that sweet likeable characters can be more fun to read about than a _ _ holes and rogues. Jim and Sharon Lammers sacrificed time during a vacation in Hawaii to critique the manuscript. Louella Holter added whatever editorial polish the novel carries, and helped me develop some balance in my description of the politics behind the story of selecting Yucca Mountain as a potential storage site for radioactive waste. Most importantly, my wife Anne has forgone tons of play-and-enjoy-life time by allowing me to create a part-time widow as I wrote. I take full responsibility for any errors of fact … and for flights of fancy that may seem excessive to some readers.

PROLOGUE

Del Playa Drive
Isla Vista, CA 93117
January 1, 2030

George and Susan Shanks

Dear Dad and Mother,

I feel a bit silly writing to you, knowing that there's no way you can read what I want to tell you. But I'm putting these thoughts down on paper anyway, as part of a healing process that I'm sure you would approve of.

I can already picture Mother's head nodding in agreement, with Dad sporting an "I-knew-this-would-eventually-happen smile" in the background.

The healing is for me, so simple logic tells me it's a selfish act ... the kind of behavior I'm trying to rid myself of. But I also know that you would understand that this selfish act is aimed at something much loftier than self-gratification. Enough said about that. All three of us will never forget our last supper together and the life-changing advice you gave me that night. I wish I had recognized the value of your words sooner.

As an enticing starter about the new me, you would be proud to hear that you are the grandparents of twins. And yes, I did this the right way by marrying the mother of these lovely kids before putting her in a family way. So you see, my childishly immature bachelorhood pursuit of the three Bs is a behavior of the past. Heather is beautiful, patient, understanding and intelligent. She's a UCSB prof. She and I have named the boy George and the girl Susan. For the next few months, I'll be the stay-at-home, warm-the-milk-bottle, diaper-changing dad while Heather continues to teach English composition at the university.

I can sense Mother's head nodding again!

You wouldn't believe the glut of money that continues to fill our family coffers from my novel (been in the top ten of the *New York Times* bestseller list ever since getting into print!) and the follow-on movie about the volcanic disaster of three years ago. Much of that income goes to the Geology Department at the university. Their gratitude has landed me the role of Adjunct Professor, with an office next door to that of the Dean of Sciences. Did you ever imagine in your wildest fantasies that your son would occupy a position of such academic prestige? There's even a large shiny bronze nameplate on my office door announcing BARNABUS SHANKS, PhD.

Whoa now! Be careful Mother, or you'll sprain your neck.

Heather and I keep enough of our royalty income to raise your grandkids in a style you would like. The rest goes to various charitable and social causes, of the sort you would approve. I volunteer most of my free time to such worthy activities. During last year's food drive for the needy of Santa Barbara, I collected the most edibles of all participants. And I was presented the Big Brother of The Year award for Santa Barbara County in 2029. The bottom line is that I have finally learned to be a giver, rather than a taker … and I'm enjoying it! I've even been able to give our country some help, maybe. That possibility needs a few more years to play out.

I don't want to sound maudlin and teary about this inner conversion of mine, but the new me feels greatly rewarded by helping others. So you see, that last-supper advice you served up was probably the healthiest dish I've ever been offered, satisfying for both the mental and physical appetites, though I didn't realize it at the time. I'll always regret that it took me so long to digest your information and get on the behavioral diet that you had in mind for me from early childhood. (I apologize for the lengthy and not very well crafted food metaphor. I'm practicing to improve my writing for a second novel that's rattling around in my head.)

Thanks for sticking by me for so long during my three-Bs years … for having faith that I would eventually grow up. I think you'd now be proud of the "one unique thing" you left on Earth.

Hugs from Heather, your grandkids and me. We all love you. We can feel you looking down toward us to receive our messages. I'll write again soon. Be happy.

Your son,
Barney

1

A WAKEUP CALL

*A **wakeup call** more akin to taps than to reveille.*

7 AM EST, Sunday, August 15, 2027:

"You about ready hon?"

Graying, middle-aged Sean Conklin gazed into a bathroom mirror at a wrinkled freckled face while clipping a fiery red bowtie to the too-tight collar of his starched white shirt.

I'm gonna hafta start a diet soon. Or buy some new clothes. I hate this gettin' old, soft and pudgy. I oughta hit the gym more and the fridge less.

He emitted an ornery Irish grunt and picked up a comb.

At least I still have my hair.

"Almost," came the reply from the bedroom.

Margaret was humming *Too-Ra-Loo-Ra-Loo-Ral* while slithering into a form-fitting size seven blue sheath. Yoga class and daily jogs in Central Park paid clear visual dividends. Her long mane of hair was glistening auburn, thanks to the chemical industry.

"Let's get going, or we'll be late again," Sean said, exiting the bathroom.

The Conklins were about to walk to Upper Manhattan's Saint Olno's Cathedral for early Mass, before packing a picnic lunch and catching a shuttle bus to their favorite Long Island beach to enjoy what was promising to be a stunningly pleasant late summer day. The bedroom radio was tuned to National Public Radio.

Their plans for the day were shattered when the announcer shouted: "Ladies and gentlemen, I interrupt our morning weekend edition newscast to advise you that a powerful volcanic eruption is reported to have totally blasted apart the mountain in Nevada where the nation's stockpile of high-level radioactive waste is stored. A cloud of eruption dust is being windblown toward Las Vegas as I

he4	YUCCA MOUNTAIN DIRTY BOMB

speak. This is all we know about the situation at the moment. Stay tuned for updates as more information becomes available."

The Conklins were seasoned New Yorkers who had watched much of the twin towers horror of 9/11/2001 unfold through an apartment window.

"Here we go again," Sean said. He shrugged drooping shoulders as he and Maggie looked at each other in partial disbelief.

In silence, they changed into comfortable sweatsuits and plopped down in front of a TV set, where they would remain for the entire day. Consumption of nothing but caloric and fat-saturated junk food would make Sean's collar even tighter when he put on the white shirt to go to work on Monday.

6 AM CST, Sunday, August 15, 2027:

"Yumm! That's such good food you prepare, Emma."

Olaf Christiansson and his wife were finishing a hearty breakfast of bacon, over-easy eggs, hash browns, pancakes, toast, milk and apple juice … all products of their family farm. Emma mopped up residual deep-orange egg yolk from her plate with a piece of whole-wheat toast. Olaf downed a second large glass of fresh milk, and wiped a white mustache from his upper lip with the back of his hand.

Through a kitchen window, they watched the sun rise above the eastern horizon of a flat southern Minnesota landscape. Olaf had six hundred acres of oats that he should harvest today, once last night's dew was evaporated, or perhaps lose the crop to strong wind and heavy rain forecast for tomorrow.

"About an hour of sunshine should dry the oats enough for me to get the combine into the field, Emma. I'll be out there all day. Please put an extra sandwich in my lunch pail."

Though loyal Lutherans, church attendance would have to wait a week. In farm country, pastors quickly learned to accept the fact that crops come before God when an entire year's efforts are at risk. As Olaf often reminded Reverend Roske, "Maybe Jesus worked his magic of feeding the masses with a few fish and a couple loaves of bread. But years of life on the farm have taught me that I need every scrap I can harvest for Emma, me and our boy to scrape by."

The monotone of a Chicago voice from a radio perched on the corner of their massive pine kitchen table droned current market prices for oats, barley, wheat, and other grain crops.

"Did ya hear that, Emma? If that price holds for a few days, our oat crop will easily keep the family farm going through another year."

That idea triggered a creative thought as Olaf sipped his coffee. Maybe there's a bit of magic in the air today. Once the oats are harvested, I can buy Emma that fancy new bagless vacuum cleaner she's wanted ever since seeing it in the Sears catalogue.

Yah, having the vacuum would tickle her pink. And that'd solve the annual riddle of what to get her for the wedding anniversary.

I'd better order that machine soon. The ad is on the next page of my butt-wipe down in the barn.

All thoughts of harvesting today for financial security tomorrow disappeared when the radio monotone became agitatedly animated. "Ladies and gentlemen. I've just received word that a violent volcano in Nevada has blasted its way into the nation's storehouse of radioactive waste. A cloud of volcanic ash is drifting toward Las Vegas at this very moment. No other information is available yet. Stay tuned for updates."

Olaf and Emma piled dirty dishes in the kitchen sink and switched to TV news. Church and harvest would both be postponed today. With luck the weather forecast for tomorrow would be wrong.

Their son Ingvar had just recently traveled to Las Vegas, where he would begin college at the University of Nevada later in the month. Olaf and Emma spent the entire day trying to contact him by phone. Connections were either impossible to complete, or their calls simply went unanswered even after tens of rings. The parents were deeply worried. They felt helpless.

5 AM MST, Sunday, August 15, 2027:

"What a perfect vacation so far, sweetie. People travel from all corners of the world to enjoy what's just a day's drive for us."

James and Janette Brady were exhausted from a long arduous hike, but too excited to sleep. They were camped on a sandy beach of the Colorado River at the base of the Tanner Trail into the Grand Canyon. The moon was down, and they wouldn't see the sun for another hour. The only sound was that of flowing water, on its journey from Colorado's Rocky Mountains and Wyoming's Wind River Range to the Sea of Cortez. The welcome octave-spanning melodies of canyon wrens would soon be echoing off sheer rock walls.

"Can you believe we've got this whole place to ourselves! I never thought we'd be alone down here."

The Bradys lay on their sleeping bags, holding hands. They gazed into a cloud-free star-studded sky in awe of a nighttime scene that was impossible to enjoy in their brightly lit home city of Denver.

They had saved up mad money and vacation time for a year to be able to make this, their first Grand Canyon hike possible. They weren't about to waste time sleeping in the presence of a landscape so grand. Still, they were slave enough to their city habits to pack in a radio for its soothing sounds of classical music during a game of star identification. Playing the role of amateur astronomers was their favorite dark-sky hobby.

James squeezed Janette's hand.

"Look straight up, Netty. There's Perseus. See its brightest star Algenib beaming out from the belt?"

He lifted her hand with his and pointed.

"The one right there."

Netty remained quiet long enough to add to a palpably growing romantic mood.

"That's a neat star alright, lover, but my favorite in Perseus is still Algol.

"Remember why?"

"Aaah. Maybe."

"Cripes. You don't remember. That's the name of our college yearbook, numby.

"The place where we met while stargazing during a party in the arb."

"Oh. Yeah."

Jim turned to face his partner and nodded. Thinking again about those halcyon undergraduate days prompted a satisfied uuuuumh as his right index finger began to suggestively stroke her left palm. She welcomed the gesture.

"Netty. We've been talking about starting a family. Maybe tonight should be the night. I'm tired of wearing these damn rubbers. They always snag pubic hair."

He squeezed her hand. She responded in kind.

"The author of our Hikers Guide claims that the Grand Canyon is the cradle of more pregnancies than any other place on Earth. We could beef up that statistic."

Jim sidled closer and pronounced the romantic-sounding name of yet another heavenly body, over the rising sound of Netty purring, as the Summer concerto of Vivaldi's Four Seasons was abruptly replaced by the worried-sounding voice of a radio announcer.

"I interrupt this program to advise you that a violent volcanic eruption has burst through the Yucca Mountain storage site for the nation's radioactive waste in Nevada. A gritty ash cloud that might be radioactive is being blown downwind, away from Yucca." This fairly unbelievable story was repeated with added advice. "This is not a civil defense practice exercise. This is the real news."

As professional meteorologists, Jim and Netty knew that downwind in this case meant eastward, maybe directly toward them. "Damn it!!" reverberated off canyon walls in repeated shattering of a quiet lovers' mood. Hormones ablaze or not, they jumped up, quickly stuffed camping gear into their backpacks, and began the long steep trek back up the Tanner Trail. Their dream vacation and thoughts of starting a family in the Grand Canyon were early victims of a potentially lethal nightmare.

4 AM PST, Sunday, August 15, 2027:

"God, I like working with these Braeburns," Will said while polishing one on his pant leg.

"They're hard to bruise, and they taste a hell of a lot better than what we used to raise. We should've got rid of our Delicious trees long ago."

It was the height of the apple harvest at the Cranson family orchard near Yakima, Washington. This time of year was round-the-clock work for Willis, Thelma and their sons Alan and Don. Six green-card-carrying Mexican nationals provided seasonal help.

The routine was to pick by day … wash, sort, and box by night. Two Cransons plus three of their Latino helpers fleshed out daytime and nighttime crews. Will and Alan were part of the night crew, working beneath the bright lights of the packing shed. Loud radio music helped keep them awake and alert. An additional jolt of alertness slapped them across the face when *La Cucaracha* ended in mid chorus. They stopped work.

"We interrupt this program to report that a violent volcanic eruption has occurred right up through the radioactive waste stored underground at Yucca Mountain in Nevada. A huge volcanic ash cloud is drifting southeastward and it's considered dangerous. Though not yet confirmed, officials warn that the ash might contain some of the radioactive waste. This could be lethal if any of the grit is ingested or simply settles out in your environment. Stay tuned for updates."

"Ya know, Alan," Will said, "you're too young to remember the St. Helens eruption of nineteen eighty. Your mother and I sure do, though. That was a gut-wrencher for us."

"Yup. You've told me about those times, Dad. More than once."

"We watched our land get covered with what looked like fluffy snow. The damn stuff sure didn't melt, though.

"We thought we were seeing the end of the world. At least the end of our world of running an apple orchard. We darn near gave up and left. And we'd just started the business."

Silent remembering followed.

"We eventually made out okay. Might be different for folks downwind of Yucca Mountain. At least Thelma and I didn't have to worry about the possibility of that radioactive crap."

They went back to boxing apples.

"The way it turned out, that eruption was a blessing. It almost wiped out our nineteen-eighty crop. But the ash was great fertilizer. Next year we had the best crop ever. More than made up for the lean pickins the year before."

"I know, Dad."

Will looked up through a skylight.

"I guess that eruption was God's gift. With a little of Job's testing thrown in."

Will turned to look toward his Mexican crew, their backs to him across the room, working at the washing vat and sorting tray.

"Hola, amigos," he shouted. "Vengan aqui."

He translated the news into Spanish, and the night crew of five went back to washing, sorting and boxing … to the loud brassy radio sounds of mariachi trumpets.

The safety and livelihood of the Conklin, Christiansson, Brady and Cranson families would not be directly impaired by what was happening in Nevada. But these ordinary middle-class Americans, like all thinking citizens, would never forget where they were and what they were doing on August 15, 2027.

The horror of that day would prove to be as memorable as the December 7, 1941, attack on Pearl Harbor, the assassination of John Fitzgerald Kennedy in Texas on November 22, 1964, the suicide airplane attacks on New York City's Twin Towers and the Pentagon on September 11, 2001, and the terrorist toppling of the Gateway Arch at St. Louis on May 14, 2015, the two-hundred-eleventh anniversary of Lewis and Clark's departure from that spot to explore the Louisiana Purchase.

An inward-looking nation living in fear of violence by a few unpredictable sociopathic terrorists, ever since the 9/11/2001 attacks, was reminded of a far more powerful, less controllable, and sometimes destructive force with which citizens daily share their lives.

2

CALCULATING THE ODDS

"This month's Geotimes takes a look at some big problems of predicting natural hazards. Prediction is as much art as science." From an editorial in a monthly news magazine for professional geologists.

December 2000:

Vincent Gordon reached back to check the collar of his open-neck shirt ... smooth. He looked down to inspect the crease in his khakis ... straight. He harrumphed to clear his throat and opened the door to the meeting room. The place was full and abuzz with conversations among seated neighbors. He strode in to take control.

Before opening the formal business of his panel's final session, though, he decided to circulate among observers who occupied the back half of the room. As usual, these folks outnumbered the panel. Most had attended so many of the earlier meetings during the past eighteen months that Vincent knew them on a first-name basis. They included members of the Fourth Estate, ordinary citizens of the thirty-sixth state, and career employees of Nevada. Representatives of federal agencies and companies involved in projects dealing with radioactive waste were present too.

He headed for the front row, center, knowing who would be there.

"Hello Brad. How are you today?" Vincent followed the greeting with a firm handshake.

"Doin' fine, Vince. And you?"

"Great! Just great! I always look forward to working with this panel. A bunch of brilliant men."

"Yeah. Real smart. And real slow. I'm hopin' to finally hear your brilliant bunch's results today. Been a long time comin'."

"Thorough analysis takes time, Brad. Be patient."

Brad was a young geology professor at the University of Nevada's Las Vegas campus, where he taught eager students about the wonders of volcanoes and the rocky products they erupt. His unofficial job assignment, dumped on him from above and eating into what he preferred to do, was to follow, analyze and critique the Gordon panel's deliberations about Yucca Mountain. A university colleague would fill in today to teach Brad's class about igneous petrology.

"I think you'll be quite interested in what you hear. Maybe even surprised. Stay alert."

"I'll try to. So, what is this? Your tenth panel session in almost two years? Hell, I'll be gray before you finish."

Vincent was unfazed by Brad's complaints.

I know this guy wants an instant answer, but I'm working for a higher authority that understands what goes into sound science.

Whatever it was that Brad would learn from Vincent later today, he would report it to his university dean, whose summary would ascend several levels of state bureaucracy before landing on the governor's desk by sunset. The state's congressional delegation would have the information on their Washington desks when they arrived for work the next morning.

Employees and elected officials of Nevada were always in search of information to bolster their unending efforts to keep Yucca Mountain free of the nation's nuclear waste. Nevadans argued that they already had plenty of that poisonous stuff mixed in with their desert sands from above-ground nuclear weapons testing from the cold war years. Enough was enough. It was past time to fight back, rather than lay back and continue to get shafted.

The diverse population of Nevada cooperated on a workable NIMBY strategy in the fight to keep the innards of Yucca Mountain untainted. Republicans, Democrats, Libertarians, ranchers, bordelloists, and survivalists alike were in lock-step opposition to using Yucca the way the Department of Energy proposed.

Outsiders accused Nevada of being unpatriotically selfish in fighting against nuclear storage on their turf, though the lineup of other states volunteering to take in the highly radioactive crapola was shorter than the nose on a pug.

Vincent nodded to a rep from Nevada's environmental agency seated behind Brad, and moved on.

"Hello Linda. Hi Cal. I'm glad you two could escape D.C. for our last PVHA session."

The acronym for Probabilistic Volcano Hazards Assessment was familiar to all present.

Linda and Cal were career employees of the Nuclear Regulatory Commission, an agency that would eventually decide whether or not the Yucca Mountain project would get the green light for storing radioactive waste there. Green would see the care-taking of Yucca pass from the DOE to the NRC, a major handoff of the responsibility baton.

"Good to be here and see you again, Vince" came the joint response during handshakes.

"With my job in a city where secrets circulate faster than scandalous rumors," Cal said, "it's relaxing to visit a place with the reputation for keeping a lid on confidential stuff."

Today's panel session was at the Pink Palace Hotel in Las Vegas. Though still early morning, outside gaudy neon lights, persistent hawkers, and alluring hookers tempted visitors into a variety of gambles. This was vintage Vegas: The city that never sleeps. The city of *What happens here stays here.*

Pink textured cloth covered the walls of their meeting room. A dozen wall-mounted life-sized mirrors invited egotists to admire themselves. Rotating ballroom lighting fixtures dangled from a thirty-foot-high ceiling. The room was wired for sound-and-light shows, off for the moment. Like all other available meeting rooms in Sin City, the atmosphere was far more appropriate for loud liquor-saturated parties than serious discussions of volcano science. But Vincent and his panel wanted to gather close to their geologic patient, so Vegas was the only choice available to these earth doctors.

Linda nodded agreement with Cal's comment about leaks and added, "Now honestly Vince, will you be sharing the panel's final result with us today? Or will it be another of your more-study-needed teasers? We've been run through that wringer enough."

Vincent grasped Linda's hands in a reassuring gesture.

"We've done it, Linda. Just wait and see. I won't practice Washington's pastime of selective leaks. You and everyone else in this room will soon know the panel's result. This windup session should be brief."

Vincent acknowledged employees of the DOE, the agency that paid him to guide the panel's business, as he made his way to Sam Donovan, reporter for the *Las Vegas Clarion.* In deference to non-smokers, cigar-loving Donovan sat in a back corner near the room's only exhaust fan, enveloped in a pall of burned Cuban tobacco.

"Hello, Sam. I bet you're here looking for another big story."

Vincent kept the proverbial ten-foot-pole distance between them.

"Greetings my friend. Yeah, I'm always in the market for an attention-grabbing piece," Sam said through a raspy cough. "After sitting in on so many of your panel meetings for months, I think I deserve hearing something special to write about. Gotta maintain my reputation you know."

Donovan was a bald, paunchy, drooped-skin seventy-year-old, whose insatiable taste for cigars had produced yellowed fingers, brown-spittle stains down shirt fronts and damaged lungs. He was a beloved Vegas legend, warts and all. Years earlier, he had endeared himself to the city and state by coining what Nevada adopted as its mantra ... *The Yucca project is no laughing matter!* The youngster Donovan had feasted on a diet of the cartoon character Popeye, whose trademark chuckle had left an indelible impression on a mind as malleable as damp clay.

Donovan initially built his professional reputation on reader-devoured salacious stories about the two-minute weddings for which Vegas was famous. He was at one time purported to be the only serious competition for the *National Enquirer*, in part because he religiously followed up on the torrid matrimonial pieces. His descriptions of divorces printed above the fold on the front page of the *Clarion*, practically before wedding champagne bottles were empty, were as popular as those of initial matrimonial bliss. Bread and circuses. Give the common reader what he wanted ... stories that made his life seem like a raving success, even if it really wasn't.

Donovan's take on Yucca Mountain paralleled his human coupling/uncoupling story formula ... an early love affair gone bad between Nevada and the federal government. The creation of the Nevada Test Site and all of its cold war nuclear testing had been fine with state officials. It brought buckets of federal money into their coffers when Vegas was but a small cow town and the rest of the state was nearly deserted.

That was now ancient history. Donavon was at the Pink Palace hoping for a controversial outcome from Vincent's panel. He longed to fit the panel's conclusions into the mold of his juiciest wedded bliss/hateful divorce story. He was ready to cap the piece with a motto from his home state of Minnesota—*It coulda been worse, ya know.* The barely-able-to-read masses would love it.

"Stick around til the end today, Sam. You might go home with something tasty to feed your fans. Just try to keep the facts as facts."

"Gimme something to work with, and I'll write a prize-winning piece."

Vincent glanced at his watch.

"Excuse me. It's time to get the business underway."

He walked to the other end of the room, where his panel of ten experts sat, chatting, around a U-shaped table. Vincent positioned himself at the U's opening, in front of a small lectern on wheels. One hundred eighty pounds of six-foot, well-preserved middle-aged male took charge.

"Gentlemen, it's time to get this final meeting started."

Ten of the nation's most talented volcano scientists stopped their chitchat and focused on their leader. They came from academia, government agencies, and the private sector. All carried the title of PhD. Many possessed honorary degrees and prestigious science awards, bestowed in recognition of their outstanding professional accomplishments. A Bowen Medal here. A Walker Citation there. Two were members of the National Academy of Sciences. One had visited the White House Rose Garden to accept the National Medal of Science from a president who had barely managed to earn a Bachelor's degree.

They had been selected from a slate of seventy qualified candidates. Their collective judgments of all things volcanic were said to reflect that of the entire national, perhaps even international earth science community. Cynical detractors liked to point out that a conclusion based on the pooled judgment of a small sample often proved to be misleading. With a cumulative age of six hundred fifty years, not even the doubters could reasonably argue that the panel lacked professional experience.

"Betty." Vincent waved to a helper standing near the door.

He had just counted bottles of chilled spring water distributed around the table. There were nine.

"Be sure there's enough cold drinking water for the panel members."

Most were gray-haired or bald, and all had devoted their entire careers to the study of volcanoes. Whatever the volcano question might be, at least one panel member was an expert for that topic.

The lack of females reflected a general paucity of that gender in the earth-science profession. There were appropriately qualified women in the nation's workforce, and they tended to be brighter and more productive than their male counterparts simply because they had to be better to be in the game. But geology had long been an old-boys, all-boys club, and that wasn't about to change for something as important as helping to safeguard the nation's stockpile of radioactive waste.

Vincent watched Betty place a liter of Evian in front of Dr. Clark.

"Good. Now we're ready.

"Gentlemen. It's been my privilege to work with you. To guide you through the process we call elicitation. Hell of a word, that, isn't it, that you've come to know so well."

Vincent positioned his wire-frame reading glasses professorially low on an angular aquiline nose.

"You've done our country a monumental service by determining the probability of a future eruption disrupting Yucca Mountain."

The sound of his deep voice resonated throughout the room.

"Yours was not an easy task, and you can expect plenty of discussion, including dissent, of the results."

He gestured toward the back of the room.

"For starters, you and I know that the people behind me will have a variety of reactions."

The measured meter of his speech projected a religious fervor.

"But by whatever higher power you may wish to swear on, you can justifiably say that you did the most thorough and mathematically rigorous evaluation possible."

His students, as Vincent thought of the panel, were soaking up this praise. With a PhD in the science of earthquakes, Vincent was actually one of them. But because of his special ability to guide peers through seemingly impossible exercises in the field of assessing natural hazards, he spent more time as *Mr. Elicitation* than as a researcher. Were he to stoop to carrying business cards, they might read "Give me marching papers and a panel, and I'll produce defensible results."

"You should feel proud. And you must be exhausted."

He extracted a monogrammed handkerchief from his hip pocket and dabbed at his forehead.

"I wish I could continue to work with you. But the business of our panel has concluded. Today marks the end of the PVHA project. I'll miss working with you guys."

He tucked the handkerchief back in its pocket.

Vincent would also miss the substantial consultant fees that had flowed into his pockets from the DOE coffers. But he'd soon backfill that void. His reputation as *Mr. Successful Elicitation Man* had spread internationally. Next week he would be in Tokyo to lead Japan's PVHA panel as they tried to select a safe underground site for storage of their radioactive waste.

"Let me remind you that during the past year and a half you attacked your mission with zeal. You left no rock unturned, figuratively if not literally. You agonized to pin down the ages of volcanoes that have erupted in the Yucca Mountain region during recent geologic time. You analyzed and reanalyzed the charts and maps of our science, looking for evidence of aborted eruptions that might have been sneaking up under the mountain."

Vincent ran his left hand through a thin cover of short red hair.

"Your understanding of that past volcanic record guided you to foresee what Vulcan has planned for Yucca's future."

He made individual eye contact around the table, left to right.

"And need I remind you that the past record is alarmingly thin?"

"Amen! No!!" echoed around the pink walls of the room.

"In spite of that you have come to a conclusion about the suitability, or lack thereof, for Yucca Mountain to become the place for the nation to bury its inventory of high-level radioactive waste."

Vincent moved to the lectern, grabbed a blue bound report and held it overhead.

"We've come a long way together."

But first, Vincent had had to educate his highly educated panel.

◆   ◆   ◆

The Year 1999: The business of the PVHA panel's first meeting was about to get underway. Social preliminaries of handshakes and how-do-you-dos were wrapping up. Panel members knew each other well from decades of professional interactions. Their leader Vincent Gordon was the unknown of the PVHA team. An atmosphere of curiosity tinged with a bit of anxiety silently enveloped the meeting room.

"Let's get right to our business," Vincent said. "We have a lot of ground to cover in the coming months."

"Dr. Clark. I know from your bio that you are a geologist who specializes in the arcane field of geochronology. You are a world-recognized expert in determining the age of a sleeping or extinct volcano. The exact time that it erupted."

Clark nodded.

"In addition to your years of research around the Ring of Fire belt of volcanoes that surrounds Earth's largest ocean, you have studied Vulcan's children of the American Southwest. Some of your field work took place right here in the Yucca Mountain area."

Vincent continued, his eyes locked on Clark.

"In fact, your published results state unequivocally ..." Vincent raised a copy of that report above his head and slowly rotated through three hundred sixty degrees so that everyone in the room had a chance to see the title page. He pulled his glasses up into reading position and brought the paper back to eye level.... "that the youngest volcano near Yucca Mountain, the one called Lathrop, erupted eighty thousand years ago. As we all understand around this table, that's only moments ago in a world nearly four point six billion years old. Such a young Lathrop Volcano might be bad news for the future safety of Yucca from another eruption."

Clark nodded his agreement and wondered what motive might lurk behind all this praise.

"Now … are you positive that this age of eighty thousand years is correct? Having confidence in the age is absolutely critical to our deliberations. It is almost certainly the most important single bit of data that bears on the panel's eventual findings about what to expect for future volcanism here."

Vincent pushed his glasses back down his nose and paused long enough to make eye contact, one by one, with his students.

"Please tell us about this cutting edge age-dating research of yours. Explain to us how you came to such a firm conclusion."

He turned toward the back of the room.

"I imagine that some of our public attendees will also be very interested in your explanation. Take all the time you need to explain your work on Lathrop."

Clark rose to take the floor.

"Yes. Yes, you're correct. Lathrop is the youngest volcano near Yucca Mountain. And I have great confidence that the age of eighty thousand years, the one you just read from my publication, is accurate."

The target of an unwavering stare from Vincent, Clark cleared his throat, uttered a few uumhs and straightened papers on the table in front of him. Body language spoke a dialect of unease.

Vincent let him brood.

These experts think they know it all. It's time for them to be students instead of teachers. I have a key lesson to teach the panel, and Clark's going to help me do it.

He watched Clark, silently asking to hear more.

And more there would be. First though, three years of Clark's professional life replayed in his mind.

What's with this guy? Does he think I do sloppy science? I busted my butt on that project. I spent weeks in the hot desert sun searching out the best samples to work with. How many times did I climb that damn cinder cone anyway, in search of the Rosetta stone? Three steps up and slide back two in that loose crap. How many miles did I put on my aging legs, zig-zagging across the rubbly lava flow looking for rocks that hadn't suffered chemical rot from sitting out in the Nevada desert since eruption? Those were heavy-sweat days. I've got a permanently gimpy ankle to remind me of that work.

Back in my lab I took meticulous care in processing the samples. Preparing them for chemical analysis that would reveal how long their natural radioactive clocks had been ticking since eruption triggered the onset of their timekeeping job.

I wonder if Vincent appreciates the irony that these timekeepers rely on the very stuff that our panel is supposed to help protect the nation against?

Once I had the chemistry in hand, it was simple math to calculate the age of the samples. So simple I had one of my students crunch the numbers.

Then I got my story into print. The first two journals rejected the paper, because a couple of my jerky jealous colleagues gave negative reviews. The editor of journal three did the right thing, though. He relied on reviews of colleagues I suggested.

Recalling this long rough road and its occasional shortcuts to results and publication gave Clark pause about the level of confidence in the words he had used in his final conclusion, "… the age of Lathrop Volcano is almost certainly 80 ka," ka being jargon for thousands of years old.

Maybe instead of "almost certainly" I should have said "about," or "roughly," or "in the vicinity of." Maybe I should have checked my student's calculations. Maybe hand picking friendly reviewers isn't the way to go in the search for truth. Maybe Vincent is on to something about the scientific enterprise that I haven't appreciated during my four hectic decades of research and publish, publish, publish … or perish.

A nauseating wave of uncertainty splashed across Clark's mind as his consciousness returned to the Pink Palace and Vincent's facial expression of anticipation.

"Well, of course, there's the possibility that my lab instruments included a little plus-or-minus error … you know, a little uncertainty. That's understood by all of us in this kind of research.

"It's almost impossible to analyze the same rock more than once, even with the same machine, and get the exact same answer. Like people, gages and such have bad days."

Vincent was smugly pleased. The rest of the panel was paying close attention, silently, probably recalling some of their published proclamations that may have been stated more strongly than the evidence supported, and glad to not be in Clark's hot seat.

At the back of the room, a reporter from the *Las Vegas Clarion* was noisily scribbling copious notes.

"There's a chance that a sample of lava I analyze is weathered so the age I determine doesn't tell us when the lava was erupted."

Vincent smiled in approval of what he was hearing, head bobbing in a yes gesture.

"I use more than one technique to deal with this situation. If one radioactive clock in a rock has gone bad, a different one can still record the right age."

If Vincent knew how to laugh, he would. Instead, he silently shouted QED, letters his calculus professor at Berkeley had written on the blackboard at the conclusion of each problem-solving demonstration.

Clark seemed not quite ready to fully accept his role in Vincent's *Quod Erat Demonstrandum* exercise. He was tired of being Vincent's poster boy for what's weak this week in science.

"On a lighter note," Clark said, "the recap of my work on Lathrop reminds me of an entertaining story I once heard on late-night TV. It went like this."

Panel members looked puzzled, wondering what path their colleague Clark was about to lead them down.

"During a hike, this guy told his buddy that the age of a volcanic pinnacle they were walking past was exactly one million two hundred thousand and seven years. Friend asks how he could be sure. The guy says that seven years earlier on a trip to this very spot, a geologist told me that the rock was one million and two hundred thousand years old."

Clark paused briefly and finished with "Do the math, my friends! Remember that I published that age for Lathrop Volcano back in 1990. We must add nine years to the published eighty-thousand-year result."

Clark sat.

Vincent broke an uneasy silence. "Thanks for sharing your Lathrop experience with us, Dr. Clark.

"So, panel, in the end, mountain hike tale notwithstanding, what can we honestly say about the eighty-thousand-year age, or any of the other published eruption ages that we have to work with for volcanoes near Yucca Mountain?"

Vincent was now the twenty-first-century version of a Greek philosopher gently leading students to a logical conclusion in the comfortable shade of an Athens agora, if the Vegas environment of gaudy flashing neon and the non-stop clanging bells of one-armed bandits can be compared to serene ancient Athens.

"We can say that we've done our best with the rock samples and analytical tools available to us, and that we believe the result is as accurate as humanly possible."

Clark raised his right hand and bobbed an extended index finger up and down as though making a critical point to students back in his classroom.

"In fact, my published conclusion about Lathrop is in error by some amount that's hard to define and quantify. Maybe I should have said more about that in the paper."

"Exactly!" Vincent said. "Exactly! Probably in error by some amount. QED! All of you listen up. Never forget that phrase. It describes the essence of our task."

"We have to accept the fact that even the best science is neither perfectly precise nor perfectly accurate. And having accepted that somewhat unsettling truth, we must apply our considerable expertise … and don't be shy about the fact that you are the best in your field that the nation has to offer … to determining the probability that an eruption will compromise the waste storage site.

"Probability analysis, gentlemen … this is our lever in support of a defensible conclusion about the hazard that eruption poses to storing waste at Yucca Mountain. In the end, we will not arrive at a single yes-or-no answer about the hazard. But we will determine how probable it is that an eruption will occur at Yucca Mountain during the coming years."

Vincent knew he sounded preachy, even didactic, but this performance was more for the public audience than for the panel. He maintained eye contact with panel members as the volume of his voice rose to a muted evangelistic fervor, about as close as he ever came to losing his cool. Under a large tent at the edge of an Iowa cornfield, he might have been a calm Elmer Gantry striving to seduce doubters into joining his flock … mellow wisdom-sharing Greek philosopher turned sales-pitch evangelical.

"Given the nature of our task, I think it's most appropriate that we meet here in Las Vegas. Each casino in this city banks on being profitable by knowing the probability that a gambler will lose at his or her game of chance during any given try. Probability is the name of our game, gentlemen. And uncertainty in our scientific knowledge feeds directly into determining that probability."

Vincent turned toward the back of the room. Public observers were paying close attention. The period for their questions, which would come soon, might be longer than he had anticipated before completing his primer on uncertainty in science.

I hope my lesson won't generate news stories that paint our science as uselessly uncertain. There are plenty of people who would like to draw that unfounded conclusion, but I expect I'll be able to handle any public doubters of my panel's work.

♦   ♦   ♦

With that introductory lesson etched deeply in their minds, the panel members toiled singly and as a group for the following seventeen months to define and review all types of information pertinent to their task, always keeping in mind that all of that information was flawed, was carrying a degree of uncertainty … fuzzy ground they had to somehow bring into useful focus. Vincent seemed to present appropriate lenses whenever the emerging scientific picture began to appear uncomfortably blurred.

During the final month of their task, Vincent summoned panel members one by one to Science Solutions LLC headquarters in San Diego, where each was interviewed in a way that required him to make a chain of decisions that led to his final answer for the probability that eruption would disrupt Yucca Mountain.

The setting and execution of the interviews were not unlike those for a crime suspect grilled in a police interrogation room. The room was small and circular. It had no windows and was dimly lit, by a single overhead lamp. Walls were bare and gray. In short, there were no unwanted sensory distractions.

The scientist sat alone in a folding metal chair of church social discomfort, across a small table from Vincent and his staff. They numbered from one to three, came and went at unpredictable times, and posed question after question in bland monotone voices. With no coaching. With no hints of approval or disapproval.

"Just answer the question, please," was all they said.

Sessions were filmed and taped by hidden recorders. There was no hiding behind the closed doors of the interview room.

The interview was called elicitation, to give it the friendly face of coworkers simply eliciting answers to their questions. But the process didn't seem so friendly after two back-to-back eight-hour days of the drill. Academic panel members were especially uneasy subjects. They were used to grilling their students this way, but not being in the hot seat themselves.

"So, Dr. Warren," Vincent began on the morning of the first elicitation. Two of his facilitation colleagues encased him like quotation marks on their side of the table. "we see that you have chosen to analyze geologic evidence restricted to a circular area ten miles in radius, centered on Yucca Mountain. To get started, please tell us how many eruptions, and of what ages, have occurred within this area?"

Warren knew that there was no single simple correct answer, even though he would have glibly reported definite numbers in a paper for publication that he might have written before being subjected to what panel members had dubbed "the Vincent uncertainty principal." His answer today to this and a host of related questions carried a range of possibilities that could be graphed in the form of a roughly bell-shaped curve. The top part of a bell shape spanned a relatively narrow range of possibilities that included the most-likely-correct answer, the answer that Warren would have reported in the hypothetical paper for publication. The right and left tail-end edges of the bell covered less likely, though possible ages that were also part of today's answer. Some bells stood tall and narrow. Others were low and broad. Many were lopsided. And so Warren's elicitation proceeded, bell shape after bell shape as batteries of questions were posed and answered. Warren's mind was abuzz with bells by the time he finished.

During his elicitation, Dr. Clark created a bell shape for Lathrop Volcano, indicating that even though the top of the bell centered on eighty thousand years, the number he had earlier committed to print, the tails of the bell indicated a ten percent chance that the volcano was no older than fifty thousand years and a fifteen percent chance that it was older than one hundred thousand. The seed of Vincent Gordon's lesson about uncertainty in science had germinated and taken root in the mind of Professor Clark. There was no weeding out this fact. He actually found comfort in his newly adopted uncertainty; in the academic competition of publish or perish he now had the makings of a new paper … one that would point out that Lathrop might not be exactly eighty thousand years old, and why this was so.

Thanks, Vincent. I may owe my next promotion to you.

And so it went. Each expert answered a set of questions, including the when, where, and how many of past nearby eruptions … questions whose answers were cast into probability curves that led to a prediction about what was likely to happen in the future. In the end, Vincent and his staff compiled the results for each panel member and combined the results into a final group result. Consensus in the form of yet another bell-shaped curve was attained by mathematical manipulation.

◆   ◆   ◆

Today at their final meeting, none of the panel members knew the results of their elicitations. Vincent was a contemporary O. Henry, playing his audience like a master maestro, tantalizing them up to the last page, paragraph and sentence of his story. Would the panel's efforts end on a single high note, pleasant harmony, or a dissident cord?

Vincent gripped the sides of the lectern.

"Let's see. Where did I put that page of final results?"

He shuffled through a stack of papers as though he might have lost the key sheet. Clark, Warren and the others squirmed impatiently in their chairs, experiencing the anxiety of a student waiting for the teacher to return his final exam.

"Here we go. By the way, I have copies of the complete report for each of you and extras for observers in the back of the room."

Vincent raised a single sheet of paper above his head and looked out over his students.

"I have this memorized. Bottom line. In your composite expert opinion, you have concluded that there *are* one point six chances in ten thousand that an eruption will disrupt the Yucca Mountain waste storage site during the coming ten thousand years."

A din of discussion erupted among the panel members as soon as Vincent used the verb *are* to describe their result. By now they knew this guy as an anal's anal who prided himself on correct grammar, as much as he prided himself on his choice of clothing and personal grooming. His use of the plural verb could mean only one thing.

"One point six, gentlemen," Vincent repeated.

At the back of the room, Cal Strephammer and Linda Planktz made a quick exit to phone the somewhat surprising finding back to the home office in DC. It looked as though the baton of responsibility for overseeing Yucca Mountain would not be passed to their agency anytime soon, if ever.

Brad and his Nevada colleagues shouted "Yes!" Brad jumped up and fetched a copy of the report from Vincent.

"Beer is on me!" He and fellow Nevadans headed for their favorite watering hole.

Donovan scribbled notes as fast as his stained arthritic fingers allowed.

Vincent kept his focus on the panel.

"Your reaction to the final result is what I expected, gentlemen. The probability exceeds the permissible level. By sixty percent. The real bottom line is that the Yucca Mountain site must be abandoned because of an unacceptably high volcanic risk.

"I have a plane to catch. This panel is dismissed."

◆   ◆   ◆

Las Vegas Clarion

YUCCA MOUNTAIN FAILS VOLCANO HAZARD TEST!!

By Sam Donovan

In a surprise finale to a nearly two-year-long study to determine the probability that a volcanic eruption will impact Yucca Mountain within the coming ten thousand years, a panel of the nation's most talented volcano experts concluded that the odds of this happening exceed the acceptable limit set earlier by the National Academy of Sciences and adopted by the Nuclear Regulatory Commission.

As published in the panel's final report, presented publicly yesterday by Dr. Vincent Gordon who coordinated the study, the probability exceeds that limit by sixty percent.

This panel was convened at the request of and funded by the Department of Energy, the federal agency that for decades has championed the idea of storing the nation's high-level radioactive waste in the bowels of Yucca Mountain. The volcanic hazard study should finally put this idea to rest.

Since billions have already been spent by DOE to prepare Yucca for waste storage, including the drilling of a huge access tunnel into the mountain, this reporter suggests that some of our tax dollars be salvaged by burying the DOE champions of the Yucca project in that expensive tomb.

Years earlier yours truly coined the phrase *The Yucca project is no laughing matter.* I now rescind that sentiment.

So fellow Nevadans, I encourage you to get out, party, and yuck it up!

◆   ◆   ◆

A less biased story on the panel's conclusions appeared the following day in an East Coast newspaper. This in-depth analysis noted that the panel's final result was an average of the results of ten individual panel members. Four of those individual results fell within the acceptably safe limit of probability. The other six fell far enough into the unacceptable field to pull the overall average to that side.

Across the country confusion reigned. It seemed that the final answer was either yes or no, depending on how a proponent or opponent chose to deal with Vincent's bread-and-butter lesson about uncertainty in science. There would have been much less uncertainty filling the airwaves if the entire bell-shaped curve of the final result had resided on one side of the fence between acceptable and unacceptable.

A political cartoon in a Midwest newspaper showed ten men sitting on Yucca Mountain sketched as a fence. Each leaned forward with his head in cupped hand to mimic the pose of Rodin's *Thinker.* Four of their butts hung over the side labeled NO PROBLEM. The other six hung toward NO GO. The cartoon caption read RETURN OF THE MUGWUMPS.

3

POLITICAL SCIENCE

*"**Oxymoron: noun**. A combination of contradictory or incongruous words (such as, sanitary sewer). Something (as a concept) that is made up of contradictory or incongruous elements.* Merriam-Webster

"I still don't understand the politics," Warren said. "We bust our butts on the Yucca project, and our conclusion is ignored. Why'd we bother? Where's the logic?"

Several of the Yucca panel experts welcomed in the year 2001 by gathering over a cold quaff in San Francisco a few weeks after their work in Las Vegas had wrapped up.

"Get your head out of the academic clouds," Gary of the private consultant patch said. "You gotta admit that our answer to the big question wasn't exactly clear cut. Hell, it was four of you professor types that hung your butts on the no-problem side of the fence."

"Yeah. But that's not how this elicitation stuff works. So what if a few buns said Yucca is okay? It's the average of all backsides that counts."

"I agree with Warren," Clark said. "But we can complain and moan all we want, and the fact is that the final decision on Yucca wasn't ours. Never was."

"Remember the lofty speeches and promises made during the campaign run-up to last year's election?" Warren said. "The man who's now our prez said he wouldn't give Yucca the go-ahead unless that decision was supported by sound science. By the best science, I think he said."

"Sure, I remember," Clark said. "And his opponent promised that if elected he'd never ever allow waste to be stored at Yucca. No matter what the science said."

"Get real you guys," Gary said. "Both the elephant and the donkey probably were lying. Shit, they just wanted Nevada votes in their election tallies. Do you really think they gave a crap about our fancy elicitation exercise? We were window dressing for political sham."

Gary's cynicism proved to be on target. By 2005, President Forty-Three declared that Yucca Mountain was indeed suitable for storage of the nation's high-level nuclear waste. He proclaimed that the process of application for approval of such storage could go forward. Accordingly, the Department of Energy began to prepare a draft of the application that year. Following a review reflective of the oxymoron "government efficiency," approval was granted by the Nuclear Regulatory Commission several years later.

All the while, that awkward probability of a volcanic impact to Yucca Mountain virtually leaped from the pages of the Gordon-panel's final report, for those who bothered to read the document. President Forty-Three was famous for his lack of interest in reading ... anything. He was also known to stay the course once he chose a course. He greased the skids to help the oxymoron *political science* trump true science for this issue of such national importance.

◆   ◆   ◆

December of 2005 once again found several of the PVHA panel members gathered at a San Francisco watering hole.

"Ya know, our prez never has shown much interest in exercising his gray matter when it comes to science," Warren said. "I've heard he believes that politics is science. Says his college alma maters offer a major in political science. Says that since he's the county's top politician, his call on Yucca must be based on the best science.

"Best science, BS!"

Warren gulped a couple swallows of ale to ease his rising blood pressure.

"Have you heard him rant about this political science crap? What an oxymoron! And damn it. I'm embarrassed because that poli-sci label is in every fucking university catalogue ... and I'm part of the university system!"

They all raised glasses, shouted "hear, hear" in unison, and did their version of bottoms-up drinking. Ale was spilled by shaky hands. Misty burps emanated from the throats of sexagenarians and septuagenarians all around the table.

"Speaking of morons ... I mean oxymorons," Professor Grant said. "I've heard it said that our compassionate conservative prez gets clearly confused about his Administration's zero deficit as he snacks on jumbo shrimp and fresh jerky washed down with an icy hot drink from a plastic glass."

That pronouncement temporarily silenced the slightly tipsy group of Presidential critics. Sawyer was the first to react.

"Nice try at creating the longest string of oxymorons in a single sentence, my learned colleague. You might win this year's prize, except that this prez presides over a deficit that wants to challenge the mathematical concept of infinity, not cuddle up with zero."

Clearly confused or not, President Forty-Three's decision set in motion the completion of the construction of the underground storage chambers at Yucca Mountain, followed by the transportation of the nation's radioactive wastes to their burial places there … both in record time. A few canisters of the waste were ejected from their eighteen-wheeler flatbeds during a rollover along Interstate 5 in central California. A couple more skidded from their railroad cars into the adjacent pine forest of northern Arizona. But none of these errant canisters burst, which the DOE touted as a point of pride in canister design.

A transportation process that was expected to take twenty-five years was completed in seventeen, disproving the notion that the phrase "government efficiency" is always oxymoronic. The access doors to the burial tunnels were locked in 2025. Yucca Mountain began to heat up as one hundred forty thousand tons of radioactive waste played its game of fission in closed space.

Within weeks of closure, some of the heat appeared as hot springs issuing from the flanks of Yucca. The heavy rainfall of Nevada's new climate percolated through the mountain's myriad cracks and fractures, picking up heat along the way.

Though long since retired to the Texas task of cutting brush on his ranch, a prideful President Forty-Three requested that one of his favorite souvenirs from the early days of his reign be dusted off and hung above the now-closed main entrance to the underground workings.

A fellow Republican, the current President, number Forty-Six, honored the request by ordering that a resurrected banner proclaiming MISSION ACCOMPLISHED be hung at the north entrance tunnel to the underground storage complex.

4

THE ODD COUPLE

Hank: Look. We have to have a plan, agreed?
Barney: Agreed.
Hank: Okay. What do you think the plan should be?
Barney: Hey. I already did my part. I agreed.

Lines adapted from Neil Simon's Odd Couple II

October 17, 2025:

"Yeah, Connie. I'll meet you at the beach in a half hour or so. I'll pick up some brews and snacks on the way. Why don't you and the gang get a fire going," Barney said.

He listened briefly.

"Hey. Don't go all blubbery on me.

"Yeah, yeah. I miss you too.

"It's only been a week.

"I've been busy. You know, as in b u s i n e s s busy.

"Okay. We'll do something special tonight. How'd you like to come back to my place after the beach bash?

"Now you're sounding like the Connie I know.

"Really?

"Be careful what you say over the phone. Big brother might be listening.

"See you soon."

Barney made the smacking sound of a juicy kiss and laid his cell phone back on the floor.

Barney Shanks was a geologist, better known around his home turf as a surfer's surfer. He'd been born and raised along the southern California coast and by age two had taken to water like the proverbial duck … though this duck came with a surfboard rather than webbed feet. A generation earlier, his would have been the poster body for the Beach Boys.

By age twenty, he'd successfully conquered the most challenging waves that the coastal surges of Hawaii, Tahiti, Australia and South Africa had to offer. And he had enjoyed a raucous and extremely sybaritic social life along the way, ever happy to entertain and be entertained by bikini-clad beach bunnies who invariably gravitated toward a classically handsome and athletic California hunk.

Today, at age forty-five and for the first time counting those years as his physical stamina and physique began to plateau, he kept pursuing his watery fun-filled life, albeit at a slowed pace. His staging center was a two-bedroom fixer-upper that he owned in Isla Vista, a ten-minute saunter from his college alma mater. His south-side location on Del Playa Drive came with an expansive view of the Pacific Ocean and its changing moods. Barney reasoned that living by the sea where he was surrounded by UC Santa Barbara students of an infamously party-oriented town would keep him forever young in spirit, if not in body. So far that reasoning had been on target.

In spite of preferring fun over responsibility and honest-to-god labor of the sort that whittled away at the health of his working-class parents, the growing-up Barney harbored a serious side, too. It's just that that ship was so firmly moored that it rarely left its berth. Still, with native intelligence that helped define the upper fringe of the IQ scale, Barney realized that he couldn't sail through life as a one hundred percent playboy. His high-octane intellect nagged him with the notion that pure fun had its limitations.

There was also the money problem. His playboy lifestyle didn't come free. Broads, boards, and international travel costs mounted quickly and hugely. His proud blue-collar parents bankrolled their only child through his undergraduate education and then bid him an independent adult life beyond that scholarly hurdle, as they concentrated on tending the family-run flower shop in nearby Carpenteria.

"We just can't sell enough red roses on Mother's Day and anthuriums on Valentine's Day to support your lifestyle," Dad explained. "We'll always be here for you, but now you're on your own as far as money goes."

"Understood, Dad. I'll keep you and Mom posted."

With those few words and B.S. sheepskin in hand, Barney knuckled down to earn a PhD in geology at UCSB as a compromise path to making a livable wage. Though geology wasn't lucrative in the way medicine and law could be, pursuing earth science would allow him to keep his feet wet, playing while working.

He specialized in the various ways that water and molten rock interact when mixed, and gave his graduate school studies a volcano-hazards-and-how-to-mitigate-them twist. The National Science Foundation was more than keen to provide financial support for such a critical national concern. The violent eruption of Mount St. Helens in 1980 had reminded the nation that not all of the country's volcanoes are in Hawaii and Alaska. More recently, earthquakes had begun to rumble beneath Mount Rainier, triggering concern that a rocky slurry might be shaken loose from the slopes of this looming giant pile of rotten rock and bury thousands of homes and their inhabitants as it sloshed its way to the outskirts of Tacoma.

The same autumn he enrolled to begin his PhD program, a "super volcano" called Yellowstone and an only slightly less than super one in California called Long Valley got restless. If either of these blew, mankind might be forced to reconsider the wisdom of living in the northern hemisphere. All of these earthly rumblings of Vulcan were more than enough to grease the skids for NSF funding to slide towards Barney's thesis proposal. His money problem was solved.

Barney's research required visiting places where lava flows had recently spilled, or were actively spilling into water. A surfboard was standard field gear that helped him discover new wave-riding challenges while studying to become a world expert in an erudite topic called phreatomagmatism. *P h r e a t o m a g m a t i s m!!* Barney loved that word, even if only a handful of earth-science specialists were the few people who knew what it meant. The sound conveyed a musically poetic image as it flowed off his tongue. And it sure as hell impressed those in need of impressing as he advanced his professional and personal agendas.

Being a UCSB student of phreatomagmatism had helped him become a legendary folk hero at a young age. The first wave of such fame washed over him during a trip to Iceland to study what happens when a volcano erupts under a glacier.

"Phreato Meets Magma! Melted Ice Versus Molten Rock! Geology Grad Student Barney Shanks to Visit Iceland's Grimsvötn Volcano" announced the lead story of the UCSB *Daily Nexus* the week of Barney's departure.

His current squeeze Janet drove him to the Santa Barbara airport, where he bid her farewell with false bravado. He was absolutely terrified of flying, but for this trip there was no alternative that wouldn't take days instead of hours.

Cruising at thirty-five thousand feet on his connecting flight from LA International, Barney tried to personally commandeer the entire nerve-soothing inventory of a beverage cart. A pert twenty-something flight attendant named Sally refused that request, but somewhere over the eastern seaboard she helped him relax by granting a seven-mile-high tryst in the aft lavatory.

Two hours later, Barney deplaned, flight shakey and testosterone placid, at Keflavik International Airport.

"I hope to see you on the return flight to LA, Mr. Shanks," Sally said as he bid her goodbye while stepping from plane to passenger ramp ... something connected solidly to mother earth.

"Ditto. My return flight is scheduled for two weeks from today, and I'd appreciate help then in conquering my fear of flying."

"I have the formula for that."

"Yes. You sure do. Til then."

Barney walked down a ramp whose walls were decorated with posters of volcanoes, glaciers, geysers, wild mountain rivers, miniature horses, and barren rocky landscapes decorated with colorful puffins ... advertisements for a country of outdoor activities.

Customs was a brief formality.

"Anything to declare, Mr. Shanks?"

"Nope. Only unusual stuff is my surfing gear."

"Surfing? Here in Iceland?"

"Watch the news. You might be surprised."

"Yah sure, Mr. Shanks."

The click of a machine stamping a page of his passport was followed by a cheerful "Welcome to Iceland."

Barney rented a four-wheel-drive Toyota Land Cruiser. He packed his personal trappings and field gear into the copious baggage space of Japan's best and embarked on his research adventure.

Six hours later, he was leaning against the warm hood of his rig, parked near the seaward margin of a huge glacier called Vatnajökull. A wide vegetation-free gravelly plain sloped eastward from the edge of glacial ice for a few miles, to where the land disappeared beneath the lapping waters of the Atlantic.

Barney popped the door on the luggage compartment and started to recheck his field gear. The road from the airport had been washboard rough.

A farmer rode up on his Icelandic pony. He dismounted.

"Hello sir," Barney said. "I hope I'm not trespassing on your property."

"No. Not at all. Not much here of value anyway, is there. Just a lot of barren ground."

They shook hands, Barney's nearly crushed by the huge callused paw of this hard-working man.

"I'm Sven Isacsson. Fourth-generation farmer of that place over there."

He pointed southwest to buildings clustered at the base of a tall black cliff of lava. The surrounding land was an emerald green pasture being enjoyed by Sven's cows, sheep and ponies.

"Nice to meet you Sven. My name is Barney. Barney Shanks."

"What's got your interest here, Mr. Barney?"

"I'm a geology student from America. From California. I came here because some of your geologists think a volcano is melting part of that glacier."

Barney motioned toward the broad snout of Vatnajökull.

"They say they expect a flood of meltwater to wash across the gravelly wasteland where we're standing. Soon."

Sven nodded a silent yes.

"But they aren't sure when. I came to watch the flood and get some information to use for my student project. I can only stay a week or two. If something's gonna happen, I hope it's before I have to head home."

"I think you won't be disappointed, Mr. Barney. My family's been here long enough to see many of these floods."

Sven briefly pressed his right index finger to the side of his nose. "My nose tells me the next one is overdue."

"Your nose?"

"Yah. My nose."

"Hmmm. Your nose."

"My animals get jittery when one of those floods is coming. Nervous gives them the runs. Stinks worse than rotten mackerel!" Sven pinched his nostrils shut and created a "Phew!" facial expression.

"My father Isac said it happened with his animals. Same thing two more generations back. I think our critters know more than you geologists."

Sven looked back toward his house. "Mr. Barney. I think you should do your waiting at the edge of my pasture. The floods never get there, ya know."

"Thanks Sven. Good advice."

"Maybe you could join Helga and me for dinner tonight. She's never met anyone from California."

"Sounds fun, Sven. Generous of you. What time?"

"Seven o'clock."

"See you then."

Sven mounted his pony and headed home. Barney backtracked to Sven's pasture and pitched his tent on soft grass.

Dinner that night was simple, hearty, and washed down with Sven's home-brewed beer. Conversation was mostly about California, as experienced by Sven and Helga through rerun programs they'd seen on their satellite-dish TV.

Barney spent the following three days at camp, waiting and hoping … wondering if Sven's animals really could sense the eruption of two-thousand-degree molten rock busily creating a large lake covered by the glacier.

Sven rode by Barney's camp every day. He smiled, nodded, and pinched his nose shut, head tilted back.

On day four it happened. Water gushed forth along the base of the ice sheet, flooding the rocky landscape between glacier and ocean. Barney retrieved his field gear. He pulled on a well-padded wet suit, donned a high-impact helmet, extracted a hollow aluminum surf board from its travel case, walked to the edge of the surging flood, pushed off and mounted the board. Astonished, Sven and Helga watched from the safety of their pasture.

Barney rode the rock-choked comfortably warm floodwater to and into the chilly Atlantic. Media volcano groupies in a hovering helicopter captured this unique ride in startling moving images. A fishing trawler seined Barney and board from the briny. His public and professional fame ballooned overnight.

Following a week of national festivities in recognition of the "Brave-as-a-Viking" California geologist, Barney left Iceland with a framed certificate of honorary citizenship and an engraved state invitation from President Gutrudsdóttir to return when another eruption of this sort occurred, as it surely would.

When he boarded his flight at Keflavik, he was disappointed to learn that Sally had been reassigned to a domestic route. Her replacement was male. Barney's tired body was in need of a bit of rest, anyway, which was helped along with a half dozen gin and tonics once airborne.

Within days, back at his UCSB student office, he had finished typing up the findings of that research adventure and published the manuscript under the title of "Fluid Dynamics of an Icelandic Laharic Jökulhlaup: A Firsthand Account," startling the stodgy world of geology.

That was only the first of several similarly unconventional, bizarre, and cutting-edge phreatomagmatic studies by Barney. But those exploits were then. Today, middle-aged Barney was a relatively reserved private consultant whose surfing adventures were secondary to pleasing money-paying clients more interested in the antics of volcanoes.

At the moment, he was nestled deeply into his favorite beanbag chair, thinking about heading to the beach and Connie.

His business phone interrupted dreams of past frolics, volcanic and personal. Barney rolled right to reach the source of the noise. He cleared his throat and projected his most professional sounding voice.

"Barney Shanks of Volcano Studies, LLC. How can I help you?"

"Hello Barney," was followed by a pause overprinted with the whirring and clicking sounds of an office at the caller's end of the conversation. "I'm so glad that I caught you at home."

It was the soft, high-pitched, all-business voice of Henry Thomas, Barney's part-time partner in science. The two of them shared a flood of money from the Nuclear Regulatory Commission for the study of volcanoes and earthquakes in southern Nevada. The project paid Barney ninety percent of his monthly income.

That fact and the sound of Henry's voice pulled Barney's mind into serious business mode. He scrunched into a more upright position in the bag of squeaky plastic beans. He pictured his all-business partner sitting in a CEO-ish office chair atop two thick elevator pillows to raise his small body to desk level.

"What's up, Hank?"

"Nothing particularly special, Barney. But it is time to remind you that we need to visit the field area where our instruments of science are gathering information that keeps the NRC happy enough to continue funding us. You still remember, don't you? A monthly field check is one of the promises we made our government sponsor."

This was vintage Hank. Right to business. None of the how's-your-surfin'-and-love-life questions that a relaxed friend would ask. And of course September seventeenth was the day they had embarked on their most recent field visit.

"Sure. Sure. I remember that pledge. In fact, I was just sittin' here with my cell phone in hand, thinking of calling you. So … uuuh … should we meet at the same place as last time out?"

"Yes. Exactly. I'll see you at the Lathrop Cafe tomorrow morning at eight o'clock for breakfast. I'll have maps that show the locations of recent earthquakes. Nothing big has hit, but we can look for tell-tale patterns. Be sure to bring copies of the latest interferometric synthetic aperture radar surveys, so we can check for possible ground swelling." Having heard the same message from Hank each month, Barney pulled the phone away from his ear.

My god. I wonder if this guy ever comes down off his high academic cloud? Even a casual phone call ends up sounding like a classroom lecture. I'd love to hear a little plain street English from him from time to time.

"Yes, sire. I'll bring the data of InSAR," Barney said, saluting a phantom superior as he spoke. "I'm not as unorganized as you think." *I'll download and print out the images as soon as this conversation is over.*

"And Barney. This time bring rain gear. I'm tired of supplying you with the basics of field work in Nevada's new wet climate. Your mental image of the place seems to be irretrievably stuck in the dry desert of the twentieth century."

Hank was right. Barney could still not get his mind to accept the fact that rapid climate change had turned a once arid and wind-blown desert into a verdant green countryside of rivers, streams, lakes, and hillside springs. Even the world's most talented climate experts who had been vocal about the onset of rapid climate change during the waning 1990s had been shocked at accelerating worldwide glacial retreat and practically overnight switcheroos, from desert to rainforest and vice versa, depending upon one's location relative to the new patterns of Earth's atmospheric and oceanic circulation. Gore's *An Inconvenient Truth* had got most of the big picture correct back in 2006.

"Remember our little memory trick? I say *PUB*, a word dear to your life style. And you reply …"

"*Poncho, Umbrella, Boots*" Barney said. "Okay, okay. Tomorrow it is … eight o'clock at the Lathrop ptomaine palace. Til then, adios amigo. Give that cute wife of yours a hug for me."

Barney grudgingly rolled out of the beanbag embrace and headed for his stash of field gear in the garage. He'd have to hurry. He wouldn't take time to let Connie know about the change in plans. She'd be mad as hell. Maybe even want to drop him.

Plenty more fish in my sea. I'm ready for a new taste. Connie's getting kind of pushy, anyway.

He phoned his parents.

"Hello Dad. Good to hear your voice, too. Look Dad, I won't be able to join you and Mother for dinner tomorrow. Business calls. I have to go to Nevada for some field work."

Barney listened impatiently to a disappointed voice.

"Yeah, I agree. It seems like breaking your invitations is a habit of mine. It's just, you know, the way my life's going these days.

"Sure. Let's try to connect next week. I'll let you know when I get back to town. Give Mother a hug for me.

"Bye. Gotta run."

Barney was facing a challenging ten-hour drive to make the rendezvous on time. The Lathrop greasy spoon was about an hour north of Las Vegas. Meanwhile, Hank, who lived in Pasadena, would fly his private plane from the Burbank airport tomorrow morning, well rested after a relaxing night's sleep cuddled in the embrace of his barrister bride, Bonnie. She did love her man.

That's a good thing, Barney mused. She could splat Hank against the bedroom wall like a soggy rag if she chose to.

Hank had long ago stopped offering to pick up Barney for the flight to Nevada. He knew that Barney was fine with surfing any raging flood caused by the old battle between lava and water, and that he had recently even talked of designing an asbestos boat so he could paddle down one of those tame Hawaiian lava rivers on its trip into the Pacific Ocean.

An unusually enthusiastic French geologist named Krafft had proposed this kind of exciting river trip three decades earlier, but had been overrun by a blast of ash from an erupting Japanese volcano before he could try the hot wild float. Krafft's unrealized river adventure was the sort of experiment that Barney dreamed of trying.

"But," he explained to anyone who would listen, "airplane travel is way too dangerous for my taste."

Three days of field checking passed smoothly. All seismometers were intact and functioning. InSAR maps were boringly bland.

Before returning to their home offices, Hank and Barney stopped by the observation post atop Yucca Mountain where a work crew kept tabs on what was brewing underground in the waste-storage area. They compared notes. Both the big picture and the local scene were serene.

5

A GREAT COUNTRY

Is this a great country *or what! I screw up royally and as a result land a cushy job.* Deep philosophical thinking by Roy Bates.

October 17, 2025:

"God bless America, ..."

Roy Bates was deliriously happy and singing a cappella with all the volume and emotion his lungs and vocal cords could muster.

"... land that I love."

Roy was seated near the center of a small thick-walled building. He glanced over his muscular right and left shoulders before continuing. He wanted to feel beyond-doubt certain that no one else could hear his attempts at music. He was alone, but was so embarrassed about his pseudo-tenor voice that his knee-jerk reaction was to look for listeners.

"Stand beside her, and guide her ..."

He loved to sing, but he had never been invited to fill musical roles for staged events at Puckney Public School. Ditto for pageants at the Puckney Baptist Church. He was always the large silent guy, standing expressionless in the background. His singing as a student had sounded like the aria of a bullfrog with laryngitis and aging had not mellowed that croaky sound.

"... through the night ..."

At the moment, he was so uncontrollably happy that he best expressed his feelings by singing, mellifluous or not.

"... with a light from above."

Roy raised his fists overhead and added a loud "Hooray!!" The shout echoed loudly as it ricocheted off the thick concrete walls of his work space.

I'm so dang lucky to live in America. The land of opportunity. The country where we all have equal rights. On second thought, maybe those rights weren't quite equal for everybody back in the old home town.

Roy had grown up in the dirt-poor coal mining country of West Virginia, where skin color carried some restrictions on this equality notion once the anthracite dust was washed away. His unmistakably Caucasian skin came with a full complement of rights. He'd cashed in more than once on the color-code system as practiced in Puckney. And now skin color had helped him escape the life of poverty and poor health that continued to consume so many people in Appalachian coal country. Meanwhile, his whole-lot-smarter high school football teammate Frank Jones was stuck back there, forever black.

If it hadn't been for a bad rubber my senior year, I would've gone down the same grimy path to early death that took my daddy and grandpa.

The earlier generations of Bates had worked underground as virtual slaves to the owners of Cyrus Energy Company in Logan County. Both had died of black lung disease long before reaching the golden norm of American life expectancy.

What a weird mix of bad and good luck I had back then. All wrapped up in a little crinkly package, Roy mused in a rare fit of thoughtful reflection.

He was a doer, not a thinker.

That was plain bad luck I had with Wanda on the front seat of my old Ford at the Park & Purr.

As Puckney's star athlete, Roy had been a natural match for Wanda, the school's sexiest cheerleader. He'd already done his way through the rest of the cheerleaders, one by one. He'd saved the best for last, just like he used to save the frosting on his mother's chocolate cake until the okay but second-rate stuff underneath was gone.

Roy and Wanda had gulped down a few beers and were watching a rerun of *Debbie Does Dallas* when raging hormones overtook them both during the same torrid scene. Kissing and stroking as they watched Debbie's incredibly athletic sexual antics wasn't satisfying enough. Primitive urges displaced rational emotions that might have otherwise lasted beyond their increasingly lingering tongue-twisted French kisses. Finished, they had redressed and then marveled anew at Debbie's stamina and devil-may-care attitude.

Roy squirmed in his chair. He tugged on his pant legs to ease a tight feeling higher up.

Damn. I still get hard just thinkin' about that night.

Roy and Wanda had thought they practiced safe sex. They had gone through all the cautionary steps their biology teacher described in class. Two months later they knew better. Wanda had cried and said she really loved Roy. That had set him to thinking hard about their pickle.

I never shoulda listened to Lee's advice when he told me to tuck my Trojans up under the dashboard, wedged above the back of the glove box.

Lee had grinned like a Cheshire cat when he told Roy "Dad never ever found my rubbers stashed there. They were out of sight and always in easy reach when an opportunity and somethin' else rose up. It's the way to go, buddy."

All those miles I put on the Ford over rough roads must have rubbed a hole right through the package.

Had that happened sooner, Roy might have been a five-time impregnator, five being the number in Puckney High's cheerleader squad. As with his first four conquests, time for a balloon-blowing inspection hadn't been in the cards as he and Wanda shed clothing on their frenzied passionate path to coupling.

It had been her first time … one that she and Roy would never forget, for more than one reason.

The good luck I had with that leaky rubber came when I decided to marry Wanda.

The one bit of daddy's advice that always stuck with Roy was "Be man enough to take responsibility for your actions. If you make a mess, you clean it up."

His marrying decision had triggered a crashing domino effect of serious thoughts … including thoughts about getting a job that would support a family.… a job other than the coal-dust dead end that had claimed the past two generations of Bates men and would likely take his friend Frank.

Roy took to reading want ads in the *Puckney Times*. One job opening lured him to Tyson's Corner, Virginia, for an interview with Beltway Security Systems.

His two hundred pounds of coordinated muscle topped with a handsome tanned face and a blond crewcut had been a perfect fit for BSS.

They shook hands and exchanged names. They sat on opposite sides of an oak table in a large room whose walls were decorated with photographs of selected American presidents, interspersed with images of the flag and well-known scenes from the country's many wars.

The interviewer looked Roy over like a judge might do with livestock at a county fair. He asked a few simple questions about Roy's family history and upbringing. He smiled, stood, and reached across the table, hand outstretched.

"You're just the kind of man we want, Roy Bates. Strong, young, dependable, clean-cut, and from hard-working mountain stock. Job's yours if you want it."

"I sure do."

He called in a tailor who measured Roy for a green khaki company uniform.

"Roy Bates will be embroidered in red across the left chest pocket."

He pushed some papers across the table.

"Here are two copies of your employment contract. They spell out your salary, a health insurance package to be provided by BSS, your vacation time, and other things like that. You can sign now or have your lawyer examine the contract first."

"I'll sign," Roy said. "I trust you. I've never put much stock in lawyers. They just want a piece of the action, whatever it is."

Roy wrote his name on the bottom line and kept one copy.

"Now go fetch your wife from Puckney and report back for work next week."

"Yes, sir!"

I'm *glad* that rubber was leaky with Wanda. She was my ticket out of Puckney. The best thing that's ever happened to me.

BSS had provided housing until Roy and Wanda could save up a down payment for their own place. His starting monthly salary was more than his daddy made grubbing underground during half a year for Cyrus.

"From the mountains, to the prairies, …"

I sure crossed a long stretch of prairies to get to my work place here up on a Nevada mountain.

"… to the oceans, white with foam."

On a day off I'm gonna drive to California and see the Pacific. Always dreamed about that when I was stuck back in Puckney.

"God bless America, my home sweet home. God bless America my home sweet home."

The eerie silence at the end of Roy's singing was a glum reminder that the only downer part of this job was that he wasn't home. He wasn't able to get back to Tyson's Corner nearly enough to reconnect with Wanda and the two kids … Troy the boy and Helen the younger girl. Roy missed his family and the red-brick four-bedroom house that his BSS salary made possible. He was a grown man. But he was homesick as hell and about ready to cry.

His first four years with BSS had been in the D.C. area. His supervisor had recently promised Roy that he would be transferred back there soon. Roy was now wishing that he had asked for a drop-dead deadline definition of "soon" during that conversation.

Meanwhile, he tried to keep his spirits high by feeding his ego huge servings of the notion that he was a critical cog in the machinery of keeping America safe and secure. The notion was written into his current work description.

Mental back-patting helped salve the loneliness that tore at him. But he wondered how much longer that salve could function before drying to a fragile brittle crust that could break into a million useless pieces.

Roy sighed deeply and began the series of isometric exercises he often practiced as an in-chair workout. He was proud of his athletic body and strived to maintain a youthful level of conditioning. He needed that energy whenever he got back home to Wanda's open arms.

The beads of sweat running off his forehead and down his arms pulled his thoughts from family and home to the trappings of his job. He stared at a massive array of changing numbers and charts displayed across a large wrap-around screen that nearly surrounded him. He scanned that screen from top to bottom, side to side, and ended by focusing on a satellite-synchronized digital clock showing Pacific Standard Time.

All numbers and charts were in the green zone of okay. It was time to push a button to record this mass of information. This was Roy's contribution to keeping the country safe: Watching the huge flickering screen, alone for eight-hour shifts, and pushing a button every few minutes to make the nation secure.

The audible click of the button was muffled by Roy humming *Take Me Home, Country Roads* in time to the faint metronomic rhythm of raindrops splashing on the roof of his workspace.

6

A LOUSY JOB

*"**Work consists of** whatever a body is obliged to do, and play consists of whatever a body is not obliged to do."* From *The Adventures of Tom Sawyer* by Mark Twain.

August 14, 2027:

Roy Bates sat alone at his post. He was bored with his job. The fun, excitement and importance factors had dimmed and gone dark during the past several months. Roy's mind was mired in confusion and drowned in disappointment. The sounds of silence filled the room.

His wrinkled brow mimicked the furrows of recently plowed ground. Why'd I ever agree to this assignment? The family needs the money. But my boss coulda found me somethin' closer to home.

Roy's expression morphed from befuddled to gritted-teeth angry. Damn boss says stick with it or walk. Not much choice there. Same turkey who promised to get me back to Virginia real soon … two years ago. That jerk!

He relaxed his face and shook his head from side to side. Much as I don't trust those slick operators, guess I shoulda had a lawyer check my contract before I signed.

Bored but not lazy, Roy once again scanned the flickering glow of the tall wrap-around screen that displayed numbers, graphs, and codes transmitted from remote dials and gages in the tunnels where radioactive waste was stored.

The screen was Roy's personal IMAX theater. Roy would have preferred the action of a hot romance or he-man adventure to a bunch of ever-changing numbers, chemical symbols and this-versus-that plots of math.

He emitted a drawn-out sigh. Dang. I wish I was back home wrapped in Wanda's arms. Instead, I'm alone here, surrounded by a bunch of blinkin' electronic eyes.

He looked over his shoulder toward the room's only door. These damn lights make me feel like I can't pick my nose or scratch my balls without being watched.

Wouldn't be surprised if there's a secret camera in here somewhere takin' pictures of all this.

Satisfied with the information he saw on the big screen, Roy reached out to a button on the desk in front of him and pushed to record that data at the satellite-linked precisely timed moment of button click. All the information was continuously recorded as digital and analogue files at several places around the country. His employer required the button-push redundancy to document that a real live person was involved with the data gathering. Multiple recording was one of many items detailed in the BSS contract with the Nuclear Regulatory Commission, whose reasonable outlook was that one could not be too careful when monitoring the status of the nation's entire stockpile of high-level radioactive waste.

Button pushed, Roy leaned back in his comfortable padded chair. It was a high-backed executive style on six small roller wheels. The armrests were adjustable. A lever near the left armrest moved a lower-back panel to fit the body's contour. About the only missing pleasure accessory was an optional set of built-in magic fingers that would massage one's upper back at the flick of a switch. His supervisor had nixed the magic-finger option, because such a massage might reduce the alertness of the massagee. His boss claimed that Roy's job called for full-time, wide-awake attention to detail.

Roy closed his eyes briefly and yawned. He stretched his arms to the sound of a deep guttural moan barely audible over the faint hum of electronic gadgets and the muffled splat splat splat of huge raindrops hitting the roof of his workroom.

At thirty years old, he was in peak physical condition in spite of his sedentary job. Carefully programmed calorie consumption, frequent isometrics in the chair, and time-off visits to a gym maintained his trim.

He was wearing sandals, cut-off blue jeans, and a tee-shirt that proclaimed his preference for lite beer. His official company khaki uniform wasn't required at this remote outpost.

He pulled his arms back close to his body and glanced at the Rolex on his right wrist to see that the little hand was on ten and the big hand on twelve.

Crap! A couple miles down the road, folks are havin' a ball in Vegas. I can almost hear gamblers screaming with excitement. And here I am spendin' Saturday night alone ... working a dull job.

Roy was fascinated by the way gamblers behaved. Every one he had watched on his days off seemed to believe that he would strike it rich, in spite of the fact that a burgeoning lineup of profitable casinos, large and small, stood along The Strip as incontrovertible proof that the occasional headline-grabbing large payout to a shrieking customer notwithstanding, the house always wins. Gamblers actually seemed pleased to throw away their money

I'm not gettin' sucked into that trap. I'd end up right back in the dead-end life of Puckney where a big gamble is switching to a new brand of motor oil.

Roy's idea of an okay risk with money was to invest in a diversified portfolio of conservative stocks and bonds offered by no-load mutual funds. He didn't understand the mumbo jumbo of investing, but Wanda did. She handled their money. They had plans for Roy to retire early.

Roy leaned back in his chair and smiled. God I love that woman. I'd probably be underground breathing coal dust if it weren't for her.

Momentarily content, Roy raised his right arm to complete a satisfying scratch of a hairy armpit with the eraser end of a pencil. In boredom, he had chewed the wooden part of the pencil to a stick indented with tooth imprints. But the eraser was functional and tickled his underarm tangle.

Screw those beady eyes that watch everything I do. Just two more hours before my shift is over.

Roy had six more weeks of this mind-numbing repetitive shit called work before a replacement from the home office in Virginia would arrive to sit in the same chair where Roy now sat. Replacements rotated in every six months.

Home-leave time back in Virginia lasted six weeks, providing a fairly generous number of vacation days each year for someone with Roy's skills. His formal education had never gone beyond a post-high school computer course in word processing and some elementary electronics training.

Roy's income for his level of education was substantial, too. He received a six-figure salary, which BSS increased ten percent each year. He was one of many beneficiaries of a federal government obsessed with hiring private security agencies for imagined, created and rarely real threats to the nation's safety. The age of mercenaries had returned ... well-paid mercenaries.

Roy's special contribution to the job was that he paid close attention to details. He was instantly aware when the numbers changed on his IMAX screen. Without fail, he punched the recording button at least six times each hour. He never ever slipped into slumber in his comfortable chair, unlike some of his now-fired coworkers who had.

He slapped his cheeks and sat erect. I've gotta hang in here for Wanda and the kids. We ain't goin' back to a coal miner's life no matter what.

He and Wanda planned to send their kids to college for the education their parents never had ... or had much desire for. College would be a huge financial burden, especially if the kids couldn't be convinced that a good public university in Virginia was preferable to a Midas-priced Harvard or Stanford. Wanda's investment plan was designed to cover whatever the cost might be.

Roy relaxed in his chair feeling confident that as soon as this current work assignment ended, he and Wanda would reunite and successfully fulfill their mutual dreams. They were admired and envied by family and friends trapped back in Puckney. Roy aimed to keep it that way.

Yucca Mountain's just gonna be a forgettable stretch of my life.

He leaked a long satisfying fart. He grinned and flipped dual birds at the flickering screen staring at him as the odor of digested salami permeated the room.

Take that, big brother.

His chair was positioned near the center of a thick-walled steel-reinforced concrete building whose exterior could be mistaken for that of a large WWII bunker on the cliffs overlooking Normandy Beach on D-Day of 1944, if it weren't for the fact that Roy's abode was in Nevada, lacked guns, and didn't have so much as a narrow slit to shoot through even if he had been armed.

Roy was enclosed in a dimly lit cube that measured about thirty feet on a side. The walls of the cube had been built to align with the cardinal directions as accurately as current surveying techniques permitted. He had learned that when the scientists Hank and Barney measured wall orientations to check for possible land movements.

The building was painted gray, to blend in with surrounding rocky outcrops. A door, at the northeast corner of the east wall, was decorated with an international-orange knob to help guide would-be entrants to the only port of ingress.

In a corner behind Roy's south-facing chair was a small kitchen area that provided refrigerated water, other non-alcoholic beverages, and snacks … fuel for eight-hour shifts. The salami supply was getting low. Near the opposite back corner behind a cheap white plastic curtain sat a minimalist chemical toilet stool that served as receptacle for the digested results of kitchen-item consumption.

Roy rubbed his eyes and looked left at a calendar. Fourteenth. Day later than when I looked yesterday. Big effin' deal.

Two years had passed since all the nation's really bad nuclear waste had been delivered to Yucca and tucked in for a major Rip Van Winkle sleep. The amount of this highly hazardous stuff had been about ready to exceed the combined capacity of storage sites dispersed all across the country. A voraciously increasing American appetite for electricity never let up, and had long since soared beyond the capability of any known combination of fossil fuel and alternative energy sources, augmented by what an earlier politician had disparagingly described as the brief feel-good contributions of conservation, to keep the lights on.

Nuclear power plants sprouted like dandelions in an untended Minnesota lawn to help address the persistent gap between demand and supply. The radioactive waste of spent fuel rods had to go somewhere. That somewhere was Yucca Mountain.

Roy's concrete observation post was perched atop the north end of the mountain. Yucca would hardly qualify as a third-rate mesa in the Hopi land of Arizona. But politicians knew the public would feel safer being told that the bad stuff was deep within a mountain rather than in shallow passageways that had been drilled into a low flat-topped ridge of nondescript ancient rocks that geologists called ash.

Almost two more hours of dull routine passed, with eleven more pushes of the human-activated button expertly executed. Eleven forty-five. Roy perked up. His replacement should walk through the door soon.

The squeak of metal hinges and clank of the door banging against the outside wall announced the arrival of Chuck, directly behind Roy's chair. Roy kept his concentration on the flickering screen.

"Hey, Chuck. Welcome to ho-hum central."

"Hi Roy. Damn, it's wet out there," Chuck said as he removed and shook his wet poncho.

"Yeah, I've been hearin' rain on the roof. All's quiet inside Yucca though.

"Come on over and take the controls. I'm more than ready to get out of here."

Roy was about to push the button one more time before relinquishing the throne, when he noticed some big-screen changes on the readout for temperature and air sensors. He pushed the button and focused unflinching at the incoming information as though his stare would push the readings back to normal.

"Hmm. Guess I spoke too soon. Take a look at this, Chuck. This is somethin' new and weird."

They watched together in puzzled disbelief as the temperature number climbed and the tunnel-air indicators changed from a moderately fresh atmospheric mix to the stuff of mild city smog. Nothing like this had happened before during the two years since the entrance to Yucca and its waste had been locked shut.

Roy stood, walked around behind the screen and tapped it, like he would a stuck gage, but to no effect. He returned to his chair and pushed the button several times. No improvement.

"Chuck. Get on the horn to company headquarters. I'll watch the readouts."

Numbers were still slowly drifting away from normal readings.

After talking to a BSS supervisor who resented the midnight call, Chuck described what was happening to a contact at the Nuclear Regulatory Commission. Both listeners were as skeptical as he and Roy were that anything truly harmful was happening in the underground storage chambers.

"My guess is it's a simple problem with electronics," a sleepy Cal Strephammer said.

"Yeah. Sure. Could be," Chuck said.

Wishful thinking was plentiful at both ends of the conversation. The human-nature instinct that a few gages and circuits had gone haywire kicked in with the result that East Coast advice from the top of the NRC food chain was to keep watching and report back in the morning if the puzzling behavior persisted.

Roy yielded the chair to Chuck, but decided to stay beyond his normal rotation time. If nothing else, this glitch gave his boring job a kick of interest.

7

SHAKE

If I could use one instrument of science, and only one, in an effort to understand when a volcanic eruption might be imminent, it would be a seismometer. You see, that molten rock we call magma can't rise to the surface to erupt without causing the Earth's crust to break, tremble, and shake along the way. Paraphrase of a statement by Dr. Robert I. Tilling, one of the world's foremost experts in forecasting volcanic eruptions.

August 15, 2027:

Skeeeeeeeech.

Henry Thomas woke to an increasingly loud fingernails-across-a-blackboard sound coming from a small alarm nearly hidden behind a book on the lower shelf of his bedside table. He reached down into darkness and tapped the off button before the irritating noise also woke Bonnie, softly snoring on the other side of their queen-size bed.

Yesterday had been their twenty-fifth wedding anniversary. They had celebrated that special argentine occasion by downing a bottle of Dom Perignon on their back deck, followed by a wine-saturated restaurant dinner that featured fresh sea bass. Then came the very satisfying demonstration back home that the ingestion of manufactured pharmaceuticals was not necessary for the masterfully successful performance of at least one man over fifty. The pair of satisfied celebrants had fallen to sleep physically exhausted. A dozing-off Bonnie had nearly crushed her diminutive man with a bear hug of complete sexual satisfaction.

Henry Ignacious Thomas had also been a big hit with parents while growing up as an only and precocious child in Berkeley. He was always more popular with adults than with his classmates. Henry found his age contemporaries childish and uninteresting. They found him boring. Henry graduated valedictorian from high school at age fifteen, and hoped for an intellectual challenge in his new surroundings at UC Berkeley.

Henry started a major in math but quickly found it too sterile. He wanted to become an expert in something concrete, rather than develop into a talented manipulator of a bunch of so-called real and unquestionably imaginary numbers.

The middle of his sophomore year, he switched to physics. He was soon depressed by the total focus on a rancorous race to identify increasingly small forms of matter ... mesons, pions, kaons and whatnons ... that permeated that field.

At the beginning of his junior year, he discovered geophysics, where his knowledge and facility with the tools of his two rejected majors could be applied to understanding the materials and behavior of good old Earth ... something he could sample and handle as real physical objects.

As a bonus, he thought it cool to be part of a profession whose earthquake fault named Hayward ran smack dab through the Cal Berkeley football stadium. Hank had attended the tradition-saturated Big Game against Stanford the year when the ground shaking from a magnitude 5.2 temblor on that fault had caused Stanford's star receiver to misjudge the path of a last-second, potentially game-winning pass. The ball bounced off the guy's head and dropped unceremoniously to the ground in the end zone. That experience was the clincher than bonded Hank to geophysics for his entire professional career.

Now a fifty-five-year-old PhD-toting earthquake expert and professor at the California Institute of Technology, Hank Thomas was extremely popular with his professional colleagues and his students. No one seemed to mind that he was a physical wimp, inexplicably married to a robust knock-out-gorgeous woman who was his intellectual equal.

Hank was an animated lecturer, who combined the theoretical study of earth-quakes with plenty of field projects. His research proposals attracted big bucks as predictably as a dropped slice of buttered bread is said to fall on its sticky side. Other researchers of his profession envied his prodigious record of high-impact publications in top-notch refereed technical journals. Graduate students who worked under his tutelage were awash in financial support from his flood of fund-ing, just downstream from the eddy where the greedy administrative hooks of Cal Tech fished out their inflated share of the grants to help keep this place of higher education among the wealthiest in the land.

Hank had begun his earthquake studies with a focus on the world-famous San Andreas Fault, a long and restless break in the earth's crust that slices California into two pieces that are about as different politically as geographically. San Andreas was a convenient target. It sliced across southern California a few min-utes' drive from his office.

Eventually, Hank was drawn to the intriguing study of the earthquakes that are part of what makes a volcano tick. His expanded interest led to a huge grant from the Nuclear Regulatory Commission. In 2024, the NRC had funded Hank to be the lead scientist for monitoring earthquakes and other geologic events that might be precursors to ground shaking and breaking and possibly even volcanic eruptions in the region with Yucca Mountain at its center.

To many observers, he and personality opposite Barney Shanks seemed an unlikely team for the project. Off the job, they didn't socialize. But on the job, they were arguably the nation's brightest shake-and-bake team.

When the ground of southern Nevada shook, Hank's warning buzzer squawked. During waking hours, he kept track of the situation with a hand-held computer that he wore in a canvas holster attached to his belt, the way nerds of their time carried sliderules during the 1950s. This wake-up warning was the first nighttime buzz for the project.

The luminescent dial of the digital clock on his bedside table indicated exactly four minutes after midnight. The clock was linked by satellite to the internationally accepted universal timekeeper for planet Earth.

Hank was a brilliant scientist and a technology junky. At a lightweight five-feet-five, topped with a toothy grin, thick glasses and short blond hair, he looked the part. No one would mistake him for a tight end on the once-again Los Angeles Raiders of the National Football League.

Naked as a newborn baby, he slipped quietly out of the dark bedroom, snapped his fingers to turn on a hall light, and padded downstairs to his office. He picked up a cordless phone and punched a button that dialed one of several numbers important to his research projects. On the second ring, his right ear was serenaded by the familiar down-home lilt of Roy Bates's voice.

"Hey, Hank, what ya doin' up at this time a night?"

Roy's caller ID function was working fine.

"I was just about to call, but now I don't have to wake you and that gorgeous wife of yours."

This greeting was followed by a silence uncharacteristic of the normally fun-loving and loquacious Virginian.

"Hank, uh, the reason I was gonna call is that I'm gettin' some unusual readings on the temperature in the waste-storage tunnels."

As Roy spoke, Hank watched the tracings of earthquakes snake across the screen of his hand-held computer.

"You remember how the temperature rose after the waste containers were brought in and the tunnels were closed off?"

"Sure."

"We all knew that would happen, right? Heat from the radioactive garbage got trapped underground."

"Yes. You've got that correct," Hank said.

"Well tonight the temp decided to go higher and real fast. I mean like forty degrees in the past coupla hours. It's been doin' this since a little before midnight."

Roy paused, hoping that Hank would say something encouraging, which he didn't.

"Either heatin' up is happening, or we've got bad gages. One or two bad ones I could believe. It's happened before. But all of 'em goin' AWOL at once? That's about as unlikely as moonshine bein' legalized."

Or as Republicans voting for higher taxes, Hank thought. Unlikely but possible, remembering a certain read-my-lips promise of a past president.

"Yes, yes. I agree with you about the moonshine."

"And another strange thing's goin' on, Hank. The gages that are supposed to tell us what the air is like underground are showin' more ..."

Silence this time reflected Roy's need to glance at the words printed on a data sheet.

"... carbon dioxide and sulfur gases. It's like somebody shipped a bunch of your stinkin' LA air and put it in with the Yucca garbage."

"Look, Roy. I'm not sure about what's going on underground. But my seismometers are also acting a bit wacky tonight. It was my bedside warning buzzer activated by them that woke me up tonight. We've both got something unusual happening. I'm worried because it seems unlikely that we're dealing with a simple technical glitch."

Hank closed his eyes for a few seconds of silent thought.

"I think Mother Earth is speaking to us, and we need to translate her words ASAP. I'm coming up. I'll be there with you in about three hours. Stay on the job until I arrive."

"Will do."

"I hope you've notified the NRC and your boss."

"Yup. They said to sit tight and watch the big screen for a coupla hours."

"You do that. Meanwhile, give me a call if any big changes occur. No one ever claimed that the safety of that Yucca storage site is one hundred percent certain."

Hank was thinking like the trained scientist that he was. Roy was trying to join in, but was mostly thinking about how his supervisor was going to be really pissed at him if this was a false-alarm glitch that happened on Roy's watch.

"Okay, Hank. I'll stick around til you get here. My replacement Chuck is here with me. We'll stay tucked away in the little concrete outhouse waitin' for ya."

That was Roy's rural West Virginia goodbye. The outhouse label had become so established with the Yucca Mountain staff that the concrete cube was generally called the CO. When feeling clever, Roy liked to say that it was as close to CEO as he'd ever get.

Hank punched the off button of his phone, climbed upstairs to the bedroom and gently shook Bonnie awake.

"Sorry to rouse you, lover."

She pulled him down into a powerful embrace.

"Oh you rogue. Are you ready again?"

Hank untangled himself from her arms and sat up.

"Hold that thought, Bonnie. I have to go up to Yucca Mountain."

"Can't you wait til morning?"

"No. I just talked with Roy Bates, who's on duty up there. Something weird is going on with the monitoring instruments, both his and mine. It may be a harmless glitch. I'll come back as soon as I can."

Hank didn't believe his glitch comment. But he didn't want to alarm Bonnie.

"I'll call you at your office around mid morning to let you know what we've found. Good luck in defending your client against that egomaniac actress Lola. The damn prima donna thinks she's being libeled every time someone prints her exact spoken words. That case should be an easy win for you."

Hank lay down face-to-face atop Bonnie. His toes rubbed her shins.

"Love you. Here's to many more happily married years together."

"I love you too big boy. Have a safe trip. And take care of yourself."

They kissed so passionately that the thick rims of Hank's glasses nearly bruised Bonnie.

She drifted back to sleep before Hank finished dressing. Dressed, he punched Barney's cell phone number. He was about to give up on an answer when the sounds of a beach party and Pacific surf came through.

"Hello partner. What's up with you at this late hour?"

"Sorry to crash in on your party, Barney. But we've got to get up to Yucca ASAP. Earthquakes are shaking the mountain. Started a few minutes ago."

Barney shook his beer-saturated head.

"Really. That's a first for us, isn't it."

"Sure is. I just talked with Roy Bates who's on duty at the CO. He says the sensors in the storage tunnels show the temperature rising and an increase in carbon dioxide and sulfur gases. There's too much unusual stuff happening to be a coincidence."

"Yeah. Sounds like it."

Hank heard Barney hiss a "let go" amid the sounds of female giggling in the background.

"I know you don't like to fly. Besides I want to get up there fast, without a side trip to Santa Barbara. You drive up and meet me at the CO. I'll expect you to be there by mid morning. That's it. I've got to get going."

"Okay. See you in a few hours."

Hank packed some clothes in a canvas traveling bag, made sure his computer was in its holster, walked downstairs and entered the attached three-car garage. His hydrogen-powered Toyota purred as he backed onto a dimly lit Pasadena street. He programmed the dash-mounted global-positioning navigation system to take him to the Burbank Airport. He leaned back for a nap during the few minutes that trip would take. He wanted to be as alert as possible at the CO.

His jet-powered four-passenger Aero Bronco was on the tarmac, ready to go. He strapped himself into the pilot's seat, radioed the control tower and filed a flight plan to the Nevada Test Site. He received clearance to land on a strip near the CO.

Once airborne, he activated the autopilot and grabbed a few more winks en route. The pre-flight weather briefing forecast was for mild turbulence and scattered rain showers. But Hank slept soundly as he crossed the San Gabriel Mountains and the trace of the San Andreas Fault.

He was beeped back to consciousness over Death Valley, about to enter Nevada air space. Five minutes later, amid plane-shaking stormy gusts and raindrops spattering the Plexiglas windscreen, Hank decided to land manually. He reduced power to lose altitude, and lined up with the asphalt strip oriented sixty-five degrees west of north across Jackass Flats, a gently west-sloping plain east of Yucca Mountain. He was headed straight into the wind, avoiding the need to rise to the challenge of a crosswind landing, many a pilot's nemesis. Following one brief tire-screeching bounce, he was back on terra firma.

He taxied to a side ramp where a faded green WWII jeep sat waiting. He was alone. This landing strip was solely for business visits like his ... no services available. He turned his plane into the wind, shut off the whining engine, hopped down to the tarmac, and secured ropes from hooks on the underside of the wings to grommets embedded in concrete anchors flush with ground level.

He threw his clothes bag into the jeep. The driver's seat was wet from blowing rain, but this was no time to worry about a soggy butt. The engine kicked to life with the first push of the metal starter button on the dashboard. Hank pulled the shift lever into first gear, eased up on the clutch pedal, and headed to the CO, perched atop a promontory several miles to the northwest.

He followed the road due west, across Forty Mile Wash. Water was flowing about three feet deep beneath a two-lane bridge. The length of a football field beyond, he turned right onto a twisting angling route up the mountain. He slowed to cross several axle-deep creeks fed by warm springs that issued from higher up the mountainside.

Twenty minutes from his plane, he parked next to the CO, at the corner where the sole port of entry was announced by the orange knob. He sprinted to the door through pounding rain. His first twist of the knob was a reminder that the door was securely locked against unwelcome, albeit unlikely, visitors. He punched a six-digit code into the numeric pad extending from the base of the knob. This time the door swung open when he twisted and pulled on the orange orb.

He shook himself dry like a wet retriever as he walked across the room and extended a damp hand to Roy and then Chuck, standing in front of the display of incoming data.

"We're sure glad to see you Hank," Roy said.

"Ditto, guys. Let's see if we can figure out what's happening."

Hank's trip had eaten up about three hours, door to door, since their midnight phone conversation. Meanwhile, the temperature in the storage drifts had risen another forty degrees. In the middle of their handshakes, it became quakingly obvious that terra was not only hot, but not very firma at Yucca Mountain that night. That part of what was happening was easy to figure out.

8

BAKE

"Experts consider *the Yucca Mountain region one of the least active volcanic fields in the western United States."* From a U.S. Department of Energy Fact Sheet.

August 15, 2027:

The brief sharp snapping motion underfoot that greeted Hank's entry into the CO felt like the mild whiplash of a rear-ender. All three men briefly lost their balance.

"That earthquake was close," Hank said.

Roy and Chuck exchanged a who's-this-idiot glance.

"Hey, doctor," Roy said. "This place's had more than one shake like that since you and I finished talkin' around midnight."

Hank slapped canvas and withdrew his computer faster than a crack gunslinger. He hit the on button and scanned information about the quake.

"Magnitude 3.1. Not very powerful. It came from three thousand feet under Yucca. That's only about two thousand feet below the storage chambers."

He stared at the computer screen and started to nod his head up and down in sync with what was appearing there. Roy and Chuck wondered what was going on in the mind of the wonder-boy professor.

"I'm seeing something we call tremor. It's a steady ground shaking."

Roy and Chuck were shaking, too … shaking their heads in total bewilderment.

"Roy. Chuck. Stand still. Stand very still."

They froze in place, as motionless as two mimes performing at San Francisco's Union Square.

"Now, close your eyes. And *c o n c e n t r a t e.*"

They did as Hank asked.

"Do you feel a vibration? Maybe a kind of tingling?"

They waited long enough to be sure, before opening their eyes.

"Nope. Don't feel a dang thing unusual," Roy and Chuck said in unison.

"Well I feel it. My computer doesn't lie about what's happening." Hank closed his eyes and didn't move. "It's subtle."

"So what?" Roy said. "Why should I give a damn if you feel a tingle and I don't?"

Hank's voice rose as though he was back in his Cal Tech classroom trying to penetrate the obstinate mind of a dense student.

"You should give a damn, Roy Bates, because if we were at a volcano right now, this tremor would mean that magma was on the move underground, prying apart and breaking rocks to make a pathway up to the surface."

Hank exhaled slowly. "That's why we should all give a damn."

Roy shuffled his feet and gritted his teeth, lips closed. He didn't like being preached to by someone half his size.

"It's my theory," Hank said. "My working hypothesis. An idea we should test."

"If you say so doc," Roy said. "I still don't feel any shakin', though."

Chuck nodded his agreement. "Me neither. How we gonna test something we can't even feel?"

Hank had never before felt the ground tremble from magma on the move. Nor had he seen an eruption. But he had read all the technical literature about volcanic tremor. He was as excited and worried as Roy and Chuck were dubious, befuddled and stupefied.

"Roy, contact your BSS colleagues at the Jackass Flats dorm. Have a team of them get ready to enter the storage chambers."

Roy hesitated.

"Do it now!"

"Hey. I don't take orders from you," Roy said. "Those guys will be pissed if I wake 'em up in the middle of the night. And it'll get back to my boss."

"Look Roy," Hank said, trying to contain a growing sense of worry, "we need to get people underground to find out what's going on down there."

Roy stood firm.

"We should do this because the gages have gone screwy. On your watch."

"Yeah but my people told me to just s …"

"I know," Hank said. "I know the folks back in Washington told you to sit tight. But they don't know about the earthquakes … and the tremor. Let's you and I figure out what's really happening. We could be heroes."

"Well," Roy said, "I suppose you could be right. Maybe somebody should take a look underground. No harm in that, I guess. But that's your idea, Hank. Not mine."

Roy looked to Chuck, reached out and gripped his shoulder.

"Right Chuck?"

"Right," Chuck said. "Hank has some fuzzy theory he wants to check out, and the BSS crew agrees to help him this one time. So we can check up on our gages."

Hank was prepared to take all the blame and share any glory that might come from his request.

"Fine," Hank said. "Make the call, Roy. Now!"

Roy walked to his work chair, grabbed a portable radio from its mount on the desk, thumbed the send button, and transmitted the call.

"Don't tell your guys about my tremor story," Hank said. "Just get them underground."

Roy nodded, as a response came in on his radio.

"Hello Johnny my friend. How ya doin'?"

"What? Yeah. You're seein' your clock right. It's barely three in the morning."

Roy flipped on the conference-call switch.

"Sorry to roust you way before sunup. Got a rush rush job for you, though. First thing. Wake two other guys. You pick 'em."

"What the hell for, man?" Johnny said. "It's not even close to wake-up time."

"Come on, just do it. Okay? Maybe you've got a score to settle.

"I want the three of you loyal BSS employees to put on your radiation suits, rubber boots and air tanks. You're gettin' dressed up to go on an underground adventure."

"Is this one of your mountain-boy pranks, Roy?"

"Nope. This is for real. You're goin' on a discovery trip. Somethin' to spice up your dull job."

"This better not be a joke. Or your ass is coal and I'm a book of matches."

The guys at the CO heard a loud whistle followed by the shout of "up-and-at-'em."

Johnny and five other BSS employees lived in a small house near the Jackass Flats airstrip. Like the men who worked at the CO, security team crews cycled through for Yucca duty every six months. Normally, they patrolled the area for possible trespassers by day.

"I want you guys to go underground and check a couple of gages for me," Roy said. "A few of them are actin' up."

Roy decided to create some incentive. "This shouldn't take you long. BSS folks back east are worried. Maybe you'll be heroes and get a big raise."

"Okay. Okay. But you'll owe us after this," Johnny said.

"Beers are on me next time we're in town together. Let me know as soon as you're underground."

"Will do."

"Over and out."

Johnny explained the situation to Ed and Mel. They donned clothing for entering the mountain, loaded their oxygen tanks in a van, and headed out over Forty Mile Wash. They had done underground inspections before, but never at night in search of possible electronic problems.

Yucca was a thousand-foot-tall ridge, about eight miles north-south and a mile wide. The top sloped gently to the southeast. The west side dropped off abruptly, where the ground was broken along an ancient earthquake fault. The east side sloped gradually toward Forty Mile Wash, and was corrugated with the washboard clefts of tributary stream channels. The storage area inside Yucca was laid out in a rectangular pattern, more-or-less centered beneath the ridge.

The crew parked near a huge pile of broken rock that had once been the solid guts of Yucca. They strapped on oxygen tanks and ran a routine safety check of their equipment.

Entrance was near the north end of the mountain. All three chuckled at the flapping MISSION ACCOMPLISHED banner overhead as they walked toward the steel portal.

Mel freed the lock. Inside, each guy clicked on a powerful headlamp and a hand-held lantern. Mel re-secured the door and the crew began to slog deeper underground.

They were headed due west in a twenty-five-foot-diameter opening called the north adit. Equipment built into their radiation suits permitted them to chat with each other and the guys at the CO.

"Roy. This is Mel."

"We hear you loud and clear, Mel. So you're one of the lucky ones that Johnny woke. Who else is with you?"

"It's Johnny, Ed and me. Gem of a crew."

"What's your status?"

"We're inside headed along the adit. The entry door's locked behind us."

"Good. The NRC thanks you for following security procedures."

"Yeah, right. Like bad guys are always out here waiting to get into Yucca."

The CO guys heard the sounds of labored walking.

"This place is still as miserable as your damn coal mines back in West Virginia," Mel said. "Maybe even worse. It's like being in a sauna. With a wool suit on. Wish I could go naked in here."

"I guess you could do that," Roy said. "You've told me you've got all the kids you want."

The floor of the adit was lined with a set of rusting railroad tracks on which the freight cars of radioactive garbage had been transported to their storage places. Water dripped from the top and walls of the adit, gathered into a small stream along the trough of a channel between the steel rails, and was piped out beneath the entrance door to feed one of Yucca Mountain's many new fission-heated warm springs.

The Department of Energy's science office still claimed to be surprised at how easily water permeated the mountain. But once Nature got around to running her own percolation test at Yucca simply by raining a lot, the rate at which water flowed into and through turned out to be a hundred times what DOE had officially adopted from the results of small-scale experiments run by their highly paid hydrologists. It was another case of misidentifying the elephant by studying only one foot.

Mel, Ed, and Johnny plodded deeper into the mountain. They sweated profusely inside their sealed radiation suits. The crew at the CO heard heavy breathing and the sounds of rubber boots splashing in water puddles.

"Roy. We're about under the ridge crest now," Mel said. "Where the adit turns south."

From that point on, the adit was called the access tunnel, because it gave access to scores of smaller side openings where waste canisters sat on their rail cars. About four miles south beyond the elbow, the access tunnel turned due east and emerged back to ground level at a place called the south adit.

"Okay. You guys are doin' great. See or hear anything unusual yet?"

"Nope. My legs feel a little shaky. I suppose because these old posts had a long workout at the gym yesterday. Everything else seems normal. Hot, wet, humid."

"Yeah. Maybe it is worse down there than in the coal mine where my daddy worked. At least you guys aren't gettin' black lung on the job.

"Go on down the access tunnel a ways and report back. Hank Thomas is here and he'll take over. He's got an idea he wants you to test about the gages and stuff."

"Roger, buddy. Sure looking forward to collecting on the beer you've promised. Could use a cold one right now."

The crew slogged south. A one-of-a-kind digging machine that looked much like a modified diesel train engine had bored the entire gigantic U-shaped path of adits and access passageway. This powerful drilling rig, called the Yucca Mucker, could have played a critical role in a James Bond movie. Its business end was a twenty-five-foot-wide drill bit that spun on a horizontal shaft. The bit's steel teeth chewed their way through solid rock as the mucker crept forward. Chewings passed out the backside of the beast like the digested waste of a giant mammal, and were transported to an outside dump by a conveyor belt. Yucca Mucker was a mechanically minded boy's dream machine. At the moment though, job complete, it sat where it had emerged from the mountain … a useless and unwanted heap of rusting scrap steel bearing a For Sale sign that had yet to tempt a buyer.

A thousand feet underground, Mel, Ed, and Johnny tromped past several sealed side drift doors.

All told, there were forty miles of these storage passageways, each just wide enough to receive railroad cars loaded with high-titanium stainless steel canisters filled with the radioactive waste dispersed within a matrix of brittle glass. Each canister was a cylinder about three feet across and twenty feet long. They looked like an oversized version of the Lone Ranger's silver bullets. Both were deadly.

Three tired guys paused to rest.

"Roy. I think it's getting hotter as we move south. It's hard to tell in these suits, but we're all sweating more. I don't remember any heat like this the last time I was underground for an inspection."

Hank, Roy and Chuck heard the labored breathing of exhausted men coming in with the broadcast of occasional words.

"Mel. This is Hank. Take a short break. There's no need for you guys to walk in any further."

Sighs of relief from underground filled the CO.

"Here's what I want you to do. Pick a side drift where you are. Doesn't matter which one. Open the door and tell us what you see."

Each drift contained several railroad cars loaded with stainless steel canisters. And each was sealed off from the access tunnel by a nearly airtight metal door.

"Just remember," Hank said, "Roy's gage readouts say something unusual is happening down there. Be ready for a surprise. Go slow. Be careful."

A will-do response was followed by the metallic clunk and screech from the door to a drift.

"We're trying to open the door of number eighty-seven," Mel said. "One of those on the west side of the access tunnel. It's stuck."

The hinges were rusted, another victim of Nevada's wet climate.

"Johnny. Ed. Help me pull on this sucker. Together now. One. Two. Three. Heave!"

The door swung open to the whoosh of escaping compressed air that almost toppled the security crew. Mel entered the drift. A piercing hiss, like the tires of a hundred eighteen-wheelers simultaneously deflating, assaulted their ears. He played his flashlight across the floor.

"Jesus!" Mel shouted. "There's an open crack. Just under the front of the canister car! You see that guys?"

Johnny and Ed stepped up beside Mel.

"Yeah. What the? ... Yeah," they said.

"You still listening at the CO?" Mel said.

"Yes," Hank said. "We hear a loud hiss. What's this about a crack?"

"It's a couple inches wide. Right across the floor. Looks like it goes partway up the walls, too. Hot gas is blowing out. It's spitting out chunks of rock.

"The place smells like rotten eggs," Mel added between hacking coughs. "We're turning on our oxygen."

They opened the valves of their tanks, while staring mesmerized by what was happening in the swatch of ground illuminated by their lamps.

"Damn crack's getting wider," Mel said. "Rocks are starting to fall from the roof!"

"Get out!" Hank said. "Get the hell out of there!"

"Let's go!" Mel said. "Head for the mission-accomplished door."

Orange blobs about the size of water balloons sprayed from the crack. Some splashed against the walls of the drift, stuck there, and cooled to a solid iridescent black coating. Others splattered against the underside of the railroad car and fell back into the crack.

The car tilted away from them as the ground swelled along the edges of the widening crack. A solid curtain of orange lava the temperature of molten iron bubbled and spewed from what was now a foot-wide fissure.

Slowed by their cumbersome radiation suits and air tanks, Mel, Johnny and Ed couldn't retreat fast enough to escape.

"Shit! We're toast!" was the final message heard at the CO.

As the drift filled with lava, they were stirred into Vulcan's searing bubbling porridge. If communication hadn't been cut off, the guys in the CO might have heard the loud *psssssst* of three breached air tanks losing their pressurized contents.

"Mel! Talk to me! Talk to me!" Hank repeated to silence. *What have I done?*

By now, Roy and Chuck were believers in tremor and what it meant. Not far beneath them the storage chambers of Yucca were filling with molten rock. The erupting fissure continued to propagate north and south to fill the entire lineup of side drifts. Pressurized lava snapped heat-weakened rusty hinges, spilled from the drifts and flowed along the access tunnel and its adits. When all underground passageways were full, the top of the erupting fissure broke through to the surface.

Unbeknownst to the crew in the windowless CO, by 3:45 AM, full-fledged volcanic eruption was underway on a three-mile-and-growing stretch along the crest of Yucca Mountain.

"What the H is goin' on Hank?" Roy said.

"I'm not sure." A puzzled look decorated Hank's face. "A lot. My computer can't handle all the information coming in. Let's drive down to the north adit and see what we find. Somebody should stay here."

"Chuck, you're on duty. I'll go with Hank. Keep in touch."

"Okay. You guys be careful," Chuck said.

Right then the north end of the fissure opened beneath the east side of the CO. The building slumped into the gaping crack far enough to jam the entry door against a rocky ledge.

"Jesus H Christ! Now what?" Roy said to Hank. "You're the expert professor. You're supposed to know about this crap!"

Hard as they pushed, the door wouldn't budge. They fought for stable footing on a shaking ramp. The thud, whump, whack sounds of something raining down on the roof filled the CO.

Hank stared at his computer screen but wasn't seeing a clear answer to Roy's question. "I think we're caught up in a volcanic eruption," he finally said.

"Think?" Roy said. "Shit man! Give me the radio. Security! Security! This is Roy Bates. Wake up down there. Wake up!

"An eruption's hit the storage chambers. Sounds like it's right outside our CO door, too."

"A what?" a sleepy Ordell said.

"You heard me right. Our professor here says maybe a volcano is erupting right through our mountain. Did you hear the last message comin' from your guys underground a few minutes ago?"

"Naw. We were asleep. Didn't know you had company up there with you, either."

"If the brilliant professor's guess is right," Roy said, "Johnny, Ed and Mel are deep cooked, way more than a Virginia ham. Up here, somethin' keeps poundin' on the roof of the CO. Earthquakes are shakin' the place. The whole building is tilted. The damn door's jammed shut. Seems like the world is coming to an end." Ordell was shaking off sleep with each incredible bit of news.

"My relief guy Chuck is here with me, along with Hank," Roy said. "Get up here fast and see what's screwing up the door. We want out!"

"Oh my god!" Ordell said. "I just looked out the west window toward Yucca, Roy. Oh my god! Hang tough. We'll be with you in a few minutes."

The CO kept shaking. The comfort level of standing on a tilted floor was real low. Roy and Chuck kept working at the door.

"Damn. It's thick solid steel," Roy said. "Why'd they make this thing open out? Somebody even welded the hinges on. Stupid security regulations."

Hank sat with his feet propped against the east wall. He watched the chaotic seismic symphony being played out on his computer's screen. He was processing the fact that the eruption was an extremely low-probability event, but being trapped inside the CO was a poignant reminder of Nature's almost limitless possibilities.

Roy and Chuck spent the next few minutes processing thoughts of self-preservation.

A little later they heard: "CO crew. This is Ordell. Mark and Virgil are with me. We're nearby, but we can't get close to your building. Lava's erupting a couple hundred yards to the south. Chunks like footballs are falling all around the CO. That's the noise you hear on the roof. Most of the stuff is blowing away, though.

"You'll have to sit it out for awhile. You're okay as long as the main lava stays south. It seems to be holding there. Mark and I are going after a jackhammer so we can bust a hole through a wall when it's safe. That'll be faster than using a cutting torch on the steel door."

"Yeah, should be," Roy said. "We'll be here waitin', won't we. Call my wife and let her know what's goin' on. Hurry! Hank wants to talk to you."

"Ordell. Hank here. Please contact my wife. And watch for my science partner Barney. He's on his way from Santa Barbara, driving."

"Will do," Ordell said. "We'll be back soon with the jackhammer. Virgil will stay and keep you updated on what the eruption is doing."

By 10 AM, the families of the BSS employees had been advised about the possible fate of the underground crew and the situation of the men trapped in the CO. Wanda sent the two kids off to Puckney and caught the first available flight to Nevada. Bonnie and Barney waited with the jackhammer crew, a safe distance north of the CO.

Eruption continued unabated, with no hint of letting up.

9

MEDIA MANIA

*"**You can observe** a lot by just watching."* Yogi Berra

August 15, 2027:

While the CO crew sat trapped, wondering if they would ever be rescued, President Forty-Six activated the security forces of the entire nation. He withdrew that order when his science advisor pointed out that terrorists could not have triggered a volcanic eruption.

Locally, Nevada's Civil Defense was on full alert. There wasn't much to do but keep a safe distance, observe the eruption and be prepared to react if necessary.

There was no hiding from the public the fact that something terribly unusual, and perhaps dangerous, was afoot. An eerie red glow, dancing along the bottoms of drifting rain clouds, was clearly visible to motorists driving along US 95 some ten miles to the southwest of Yucca Mountain. Calls from curious travelers to the Nevada Highway Patrol received an honest answer.

"It seems a new volcano has decided to erupt at Yucca Mountain. No. It's not a nuclear explosion. Just a volcanic eruption."

The Conklins, Christianssons, Bradys, Cransons and others who happened to be traveling the information highway learned of the eruption early in the day. Normal commerce tanked nationally as radio, Internet and TV ratings soared.

Equally early, word spread from on-site observers. Motorists phoned family and friends, who phoned family and friends and friends of friends, rapidly building a tall Ponzi pyramid.

Parked cars created a traffic hazard along the highway. Frustrated with trying to maintain order, Nevada troopers, themselves curious about what was happening at Yucca, decided to chaperone caravans along a dirt road that crested at a place called Steve's Pass. There, folks had an unobstructed view of the eruption, at a safe platform several miles from the action.

They saw a long surging blade of orange lava slice thousands of feet into the nighttime sky. Small blobs at the top of the blade solidified in flight and drifted downwind to the southeast as a cloud of hot gray grit billowing ever higher. Most of the lava splashed back to Earth and spilled down the flanks of Yucca in thin flows. Encounters with water produced prodigious clouds of steam.

"Looks a lot like what I saw on the Big Island last year," a young man said. "Add a few coconut palms, Pacific surf, a mai tai and I'd be reliving that honeymoon trip. The out-of-bed part anyway."

"Change that tropical scene to one of barren lava fields with a huge glacier looming in the background and this could be what I saw in Iceland two years ago," another observer added. "Raw nature at its most exciting. Chance of a lifetime to see new land created. Beautiful."

"Yeah but there's only one Yucca Mountain in this world," a thinking realist said. "And we all know what it's being used for. I don't think anyone could find beauty in an eruption here."

Members of fringe religious sects sermonized on how their god was punishing the American people for the sins of moral lapses and material excesses. "Why else would this disaster happen on the Sabbath?" Parson Herby Kinsley preached from a rocky podium at Steve's Pass. "Repent. Make amends. Ten dollars for my prayers will start you down the path to righteousness."

Before long mainline media began to converge … first by helicopters, then by vans and small trucks that carried the equipment needed to broadcast live stories. Normally this lonely spot might see one vehicle per week, driven by a quirky rock hound. Steve's Pass now grew into a parking lot and helipad for hundreds of excited viewers and reporters.

Once the sight of a steady lava curtain and its ash cloud became predictably commonplace, reporters fanned out across the region in search of information to flesh out human-interest stories. They dug deeply into personal lives, broadcasting tales and displays of human angst and potential grief where privacy would have been tasteful.

The nation learned about three men named Mel, Ed, and Johnny presumed dead, trapped underground with the radioactive waste, at about the same time the victims' families were notified.

Another story reported that three men were trapped in a concrete observation post near the eruption.

"Can those men be rescued from a prison we've been told is known as the CO?" TV personality Brad Billings asked, wearing his most sincere look of concern. "The earth has already opened and partly swallowed that building. Will the

CO disappear underground? From our perspective here at Steve's Pass, the situation looks grim."

CO became a widely recognized acronym in the American version of English.

As daylight arrived, so did a fleet of catering vans and a flotilla of two-bits-a-visit chemical outhouses. These were accompanied by a sewage-pumper tank truck, whose block letter logo announced YESTERDAY'S MEALS ON WHEELS.

The profit-seeking commerce of free enterprise had discovered beauty in the Yucca eruption.

10

FROM CURTAIN TO CANNON

Maximum violence for steam explosions happens when magma and water mix in the weight ratio of about 1 to 5. Whatever the ratio, if they don't mix, they can't go kablooey. From Barney's class notes the day of the phreatomagmatic lecture.

August 15, 2027

Outside the CO, Barney, Bonnie, Ordell, Virgil and Mark watched from a sheltered upwind spot as the eruption dealt out a sequence of devastating hits in what proved to be a losing blackjack hand for Nevada. Barney described the action into a voice recorder as the eruption evolved. Bonnie listened in, waiting for words of comfort and hope that she could radio relay to Hank.

"It's 10 AM local time. I'm near the CO at the north end of Yucca Mountain, watching an eruption that is reported to have started at about 3:45 today. Basalt is fountaining from a fissure that runs along the crest of Yucca. I guesstimate it's several miles long. Can't see the whole thing from here, though. It's a classic Hawaiian-style curtain of fire."

Images beamed down from satellites would later show Barney that the curtain was five miles long.

"The lava is extremely gassy. It's rising up a couple thousand feet at least. Vulcan's out-of-control champagne bottle at its most violent."

Bonnie withheld that description from Hank. "How are you doing lover?" she asked. "Barney says we're seeing a curtain of fire eruption along Yucca. It's staying south of the CO."

"I'm okay Bonnie. Don't worry about me. I can tell a lot of what's happening from watching my computer. And the noise on the roof tells me the eruption isn't too far away. Just so it stays south. Please be there when I get out."

"Of course!" she said. "You'll get the biggest hug of your life."

At first Barney couldn't see details of what was happening along Yucca for all the steam produced as lava flowed down wet streambeds on the flanks of the mountain. But as molten lava cooled to solid rock, channels filled with basalt. Higher up, the sources of warm springs were plastered over with more basalt, stopping the normal release of groundwater from the saturated mountain. Steam abated. As Barney would later hypothesize in print, the leaky mountain sieve became sealed in a cocoon of lava flows, setting the stage for especially spectacular phreatomagmatism.

Shortly before noon, the curtain of fiery lava sputtered and broke into a line of steam-powered cannons. Satellite images later showed a half dozen of these artillery pieces firing their projectiles straight up into a wind that continued to blow strongly to the southeast.

"It's noon," Barney said into his recorder. "Within the past ten minutes, the eruption has evolved from a frothy lava curtain into a phreatomagmatic phase. Magma's finally mixing with groundwater efficiently enough to fuel incredible steam blasts."

"What's phreatomagmatic mean?" Bonnie asked.

"It's a fancy word for something pretty simple. When magma mixes with the groundwater of Yucca, kapow! Steam blasts happen."

Barney extended the fingers of both hands as he raised his arms to simulate a blast. Then he pointed toward Yucca.

"Look. You can see what's going on. There's the light-colored stuff of old Yucca Mountain blasted to smithereens and mixed in with the new black basalt ash. The orange lava curtain is history."

"I see what you mean about the color change," Bonnie said.

"Yeah. And the grit comes out in surges of rocky pellets," Barney said. "Something like blasts of pellets from a shotgun. What we see as color change, Hank'll see as powerful earth shakes on his computer. He'll know what's happening."

"What about the CO?" Bonnie said. "Will it stay safe?"

"There's no way to be sure. All we can do is wait and watch."

Barney wanted to offer hope for Bonnie, without stretching the truth. "If the main action stays south and the wind keeps blowing away from us, the CO should be okay. Tell Hank I'm optimistic. Give Ordell and his guys an update too while I jot down a few notes."

As satellites and the CO vigil watched, six surging rocky plumes played their phreatomagmatic game. The prevailing wind gathered their grit into a single tongue-shaped cloud headed straight for Las Vegas.

With each blast, the erupting cannons excavated pits deeper and deeper into the mountain. Rocks dislodged from the walls of pits tumbled downward to become buckshot for the next blast. Each mouthful of the crumbling mountain was spit out piecemeal, like a child violently upchucking its first few tastes of spinach.

Within a couple of hours, the steam explosions had drilled to the depth of the underground side drifts, stuffed with their inventory of radioactive garbage.

Barney watched expectantly. "Jumping Jesus!" he said. "Now the canisters are coming out."

"What are you talking about Barney?"

"Look for the glint of silvery things Bonnie."

He pointed south. "Look there. I see two shiny objects in that blast debris. They crash against each other like billiard balls. Going up and down like lotto balls in a wind tunnel. It's classic phreatomagmatic drilling into the ground. Classic!!"

Bonnie was increasingly worried for the safety of her man. She kept a conversation going with him, as she eavesdropped on Barney's words.

To avoid upsetting her further, Barney quietly recorded the fact that he thought he saw the pinwheel outline of a human body mixed in with canisters, rocks, and ash.

At Steve's Pass, anchor Betty Rich of TV's OBN network held her Zhumell binoculars very steady on their monopod stand and recognized what was happening to the canisters. She instructed her cameraman to zoom in on the nearest part of the lineup of erupting cannons and to highlight shiny metal things. She fluffed her hair and practiced her smile.

"Okay. Start a new live feed nationally," she said.

"Hello viewers. This is Betty Rich of OBN, broadcasting only the best news. You've already seen plenty of the eruption going on at Yucca Mountain. For a change of pace, I'm going to take you to a mega drawing being held here in Nevada. Remember, we're just outside of Vegas. The gambling capital of the world. Get your tickets ready to see if you're a lucky winner."

The picture went to split screen, Betty on one side and the eruption on the other.

"Watch closely for the bouncing silver balls on the right side of your picture."

She steadied her binoculars and focused briefly on the eruption. She lowered the heavy Zhumells and turned to gaze directly into the camera. "The first ball is plutonium," she said. "That would be Pu on your ticket."

She went through the binocular routine once again.

"Ball two is uranium. Look for a capital U.

"Hang in there folks. Here comes another. Yes. Ball three is polonium. That's a Po for memorable old polonium 210.

"And now the bonus ball. It's that patriotic americium, the big Am."

The screen reverted back to just Betty. She looked squarely into the camera and smiled. "This drawing has been monitored by an independent watchdog agency called the Nuclear Regulatory Commission, sponsored by the U.S. Government. Good luck. I hope that someone out there is a winner."

Government officials were not amused.

Two years of groundwater seeping into the storage drifts had rusted pits into the walls of the canisters, fatally weakening the once strong and pristine stainless steel alloy containers sheltered beneath umbrellas of titanium-rich metal. True to a carefully thought out design, each umbrella diverted liquid water seeping through the roof of a drift around and away from its canister. But once converted to sauna-house humidity by the heat of a drift floor, the vapor rose to coat and corrode its way into the once seemingly indestructible metal.

The addition of magma's heat was more than any corroded steel could long withstand when crazily crashing about in the buckshot debris of a steam-blast cannon. Canisters and their glassy radioactive contents shattered into a gazillion pieces. Fine grains of radioactive dust mixed with the non-radioactive products of eruption and joined the growing wind-driven plume. Within an hour of the first appearance of a canister, the nation's entire one hundred forty thousand ton inventory of high-level radioactive waste was part of the gritty debris headed toward Las Vegas.

It's hard to believe what I'm seeing, Barney thought. I've got another ground-breaking ... yeah, I'll use that pun ... tale to tell on the pages of a journal.

He continued recording notes for the tome to come.

Security observers were helpless to do anything but watch and warn police and politicians in Vegas that the eruption plume headed their way contained much more than volcanic ash.

To fill time, media mouthpieces reminded their audiences of past major battles between volcanoes and people ... the Mediterranean's Santorini versus the Minoan culture, Italy's Vesuvius versus Pompeii and Herculaneum, the Caribbean's Mt. Peleé versus St. Pierre, Columbia's Nevado del Ruiz versus Armero, and on and on.

Nuclear accidents at Three Mile Island and at Chernobyl were stirred into the story mix, although thinking listeners realized that volcanoes had nothing to do with these power-plant mishaps.

11

DEATH AT THE CO

"There was a bright red-orange glow and a wave of heat hit my face. The molten lava engulfed my legs, and I sank rapidly to a depth around my knees."* Excerpt from a story written in 1991 by geologist George Ulrich, who six years earlier had barely escaped being enveloped by a lava flow at Kilauea Volcano, Hawaii.

Sunday, August 15, 2027:

Wanda joined the group at noon, following a commercial flight from Washington's Reagan International Airport to Reno and a BSS-chartered helicopter connection to the rescue crew near the CO. Ordell gave her a brief update and handed over a radio.

"Roy! Roy!! It's Wanda. Are you okay in there?"

"God honey it's good to hear your voice. I've been worried sick about you and the kids."

"The kids are fine. They're with family in Puckney. We need to worry about you, not us. I can't believe what I'm seein' out here Roy. It's like … like the world's comin' to an end.

"I'm really afraid Roy. Afraid like we were back home when miners got trapped underground. Remember? Never knowin' if they were still alive, buried down there in a dark dungeon."

"Yeah. I surely do remember those times Wanda. But we're not part of that anymore."

"Well at least I can talk with you. Know you're alive. Even if I can't hold you. I can see the CO, and I know you're alive in there."

"Now don't you fret sweetie. Ordell and the crew will have us out of here soon as it's safe to get closer. They'll hammer a hole in the wall in no time. You just stick with them and watch.

"Think good thoughts. Say a prayer or two for good results … like we did each time you were gettin' ready to have our kids. The man upstairs has taken good care of our family so far. I don't think he's about to let us down now."

"I've got the faith, Roy. I've got the faith. I'll be right here when you escape from your crypt."

"Good. That's my girl. One more thing Wanda. Let's you and me do a drive-in movie when I get out. For old time's sake. That should put a smile on your face."

"Yeah. It's already workin' Roy. It's workin'. You're my rock. And my roll."

There wasn't much anybody outside could do but wait and watch … and keep the guys inside apprised of the situation.

Around six o'clock the character of the eruption made another quick about-face. By then, magma mixing with the water-saturated rocks of Yucca Mountain had dried out the ground … had used up all the water in the rocky sponge. Within a period of minutes, steam explosions evolved from out-and-out violent, to *I think I can*, to *I thought I could*, to *I'm all pooped out*. Barney faithfully recorded the progression and timing of these events.

At the same time that the phreatomagmatic cannons ran out of their steam propellant, the magma literally ran out of gas. The cork-popping introduction to the eruption party was over. The vintage champagne had gone flat. But there was still a whole lot of champagne in the bottle, and it spilled out to make an incredible hot-and-sticky mess of the landscape. Barney continued recording his observations.

"Eruption's now quiet. No more steam blasts. No more fountaining. Lava's oozing out. There's a line of churning lava lakes. Probably one in each crater. They're filling fast."

As Barney spoke, satellites captured images of a scene that mimicked a row of six round ingot casts being filled with pig iron.

With the change in eruption style, the BSS security crew recognized that a rescue mission could get safely underway.

"Roy. This is Virgil again. How are you guys doing in there?"

"We're okay. There's plenty of food and water in the kitchen. But we surely would prefer a meal of tasty honey-baked Virginia ham to cold cuts and Coke. And tryin' to find a comfy way to stand on a tilted floor is for those Swiss milk cows with two short legs. What's goin' on out there?"

Unflappable, Hank continued to reassure Bonnie that he would be okay. "We just need a lull in the eruption so a jackhammer crew can punch a hole in the wall of the CO," were the words of the ever-analytical scientist, not fully in touch with the seriousness of his situation.

Hank now noticed the lack of whump thump whump thump volcanic fallout on the CO roof.

"Virgil, this is Hank. It's very quiet in here. No more drumming on the roof. Does this mean what I think it does?"

"Yup. The eruption has settled down. All the action is way south of us now. We've all moved up to just outside the CO. You guys should be free in no time. The jackhammer crew is getting their compressor and tools in position as I speak. It's gonna get noisy inside there again. But I don't think you'll mind the sounds this time."

"If I remember correctly," Hank said, "these walls are eighteen inches thick. I examined the design plans once when I was thinking of locating one of my seismometers here. There are two layers of rebar that sandwich heavy gage mesh steel wire for added strength. You'll have to cut steel as well as concrete."

"We know all about that, Hank. We've got the building specs here and have all the equipment needed. You'll soon be hearin' the rat-a-tat-tat-tat of jackhammers and the sizzling hiss of steel-cutting torches. Hang tight."

Hank focused his attention back on the performance of the seismic symphony displayed on his computer screen as the noise and vibration of creating an escape hole filled the CO. He was seeing nothing but the signal of throbbing tremor, and lots of it, the seismic sign of magma on the move ... the heartbeat of a volcano. A few of his seismic instruments in the field had been destroyed by the eruption, but his orchestra still had enough functioning players to provide the vibrations that were music to his eyes and knees.

By half past six, lava had completely filled the six steam-blasted pits. Overflow spilled out onto what was left of Yucca Mountain, covering the wounded ridge with thickening shimmering layers of black rock called basalt. Surge after surge of overflow created a stack of solid rock that had the shape of an overturned soup bowl. As the top of this hump-backed landscape grew higher, the distal edges of the growing volcanic mountain extended incrementally outward in all directions. A race was underway between lava advancing to the north, and jackhammers creeping inward at the CO. Barney watched this classic Hawaiian-style shield volcano in the making.

"Barney," Wanda said, "what do you call that black stuff pilin' up on Yucca? It looks a lot like coal. Shiny as anthracite. I didn't think Nevada had any of that stuff."

"Looks the same as coal alright," Barney said, "but this is basalt. It's red and hot as burning coal when it comes out of the ground. Then it cools and hardens to a black rock. Kinda the opposite of what happens with coal I guess."

Wanda looked confused.

"It's good what's happening now, Wanda," Barney said, placing his hands reassuringly on her tight shoulders. "The eruption's settling down. The guys should be out of the CO soon."

Barney could feel some tension ebb, as her shoulder muscles relaxed.

"Talk to your man. Tell him it's looking up out here. I want to take some notes."

Barney turned away from Wanda and spoke into his recorder.

"We're now into a shield-building phase. Lava keeps oozing out quietly. By now all evidence of the phreatomagmatic craters is gone. Covered with sheets of lava. I wonder how much more of this hot stuff will erupt? How long will the new volcanic mountain continue to grow?"

Whatever answers might develop for Barney's questions, getting through the CO wall was taking longer than anyone had anticipated ... or wanted. Ordell was on the jackhammer, working up a hell of a sweat. Bust concrete and cut steel. Bust concrete and cut steel.

Lava started to lap at the south side of the CO as Ordell worked frantically on the north side. He stumbled momentarily as the tool made unexpected sudden headway.

"We did it, guys! We're through the wall."

As the steel tooth of the jackhammer penetrated to the inside, lava began to creep along the west and east walls of the CO. Roy, Chuck and even Hank let out a cheer, at Ordell's *did it* shout, unaware that a photo-finish race to possible death was underway outside. Nobody there wanted to let the inside guys know about the contest.

"Stand back in there so I can enlarge this opening."

In his peripheral vision, Ordell saw lava begin to seep around the corners of the building as he shouted to the CO prisoners and concentrated on making a wider opening, He guessed he had five minutes, max, to make the hole man sized.

Wanda and Bonnie watched in horror, unable to help.

"Jesus! What a time to hit another piece of that damn rebar," Ordell said. He exposed enough of the bar to push with one foot and bend it inward, jackhammer thrown to the side. There was no time for more hammering or using the cutting torch. Fiery red-orange lava was oozing toward him along the base of the north wall from both sides.

"Okay. Who's first? Come on. Come on, damn it. We don't have much time."

Not knowing how close lava was, Roy and Chuck deferred to higher education. They helped push Hank into the hole, head first with arms extended in the streamlined posture of a high diver. A body would have to slip through this way, or not at all.

Barney huddled with Bonnie and Wanda, keeping them back, out of the way of the rescue team.

"Virgil. Come here and grab a hand!" Ordell said.

Feet braced against the north wall, Ordell and Virgil pulled on Hank's outstretched hands, while Roy and Chuck pushed on Hank's feet. His small body was halfway out … and stuck.

"Shit, Hank. It's that damned computer of yours that's the problem," Roy said.

The CO boys pulled Hank back in far enough to release his belt and get rid of the machine. Then it was back to tug and push, tug and push. This time the waistband of Hank's khakis caught on the protruding prong of bent rebar. Pants and boxer shorts ripped off as Hank's slender body finally passed through the opening. Blood from a rebar gash along his left thigh streamed down a naked lower torso. As Hank was helped away from the hole, he shouted "Have Roy throw out my computer."

"Forget that thing professor!" Ordell said. "Bonnie. Come here and take your man. Tell him he can buy a new computer later, for Christ's sake."

Ordell and Virgil passed Hank to Bonnie barely in time to avoid contact with fingers of lava advancing from the sides.

"I've got him," Bonnie said. "Go after the other guys."

Bonnie cradled a silent Hank as a mother would a child, and moved further from the CO and its advancing hot lava embrace.

The rescue crew turned back toward the hole and stood helpless, looking through at Roy getting ready to go for his try at escape. They had to retreat from the intense heat radiating from the oozing flow that was now only a few feet from engulfing the ground along the north side of the CO. The smell of singed hair flavored the air.

"Guys! Guys! We can't get you out," Ordell said. "The damn lava is right here, rising to the level of the hole." Intense eye contact through the hole registered primal fear in Roy and Chuck and helpless sympathy from Ordell.

Wanda broke free from Barney and raced forward. "Roy! Roy baby. You gotta get outta there. Come on! If you're not comin' out, I'm comin' in."

Ordell grabber her. "It's too late Wanda. Nothing anybody can do. Stay back or you'll get burned."

Roy and Wanda stared at each other, barley ten feet apart. Both were crying, unable to think of anything sensible to say. Ordell pulled Wanda back as lava deepened against the CO wall.

None of the outsiders could think of useful chatter as they watched lava rise to the level of the hole and enter the CO, an uninvited but insistent guest. Roy was caught trying to slither out as lava slithered in. He instantly withdrew, cursing as he flailed away at his burning shirt with blistered fingers. He looked through the narrowing hole where Ordell clutched Wanda.

"Wanda. I love you so much."

Roy had to back up as lava spilled in. "Take care of yourself and the kids."

He stepped to one side, away from lava and out of sight. "I'll be seein' you all upstairs. Later."

Wanda sobbed hysterically, and went limp as Ordell carried her back, away from the searing heat radiated from the lava.

That was the last anyone saw of Roy. But those on the outside heard from him and Chuck as they first cursed and then screamed in pain as lava enveloped them in a black cocoon of hellish temperature.

The living stayed long enough to be absolutely certain that the CO crew had no chance of surviving … then left the scene to maintain a safe distance from the growing volcano.

By the time eruption ceased, at seven o'clock the next morning, the CO was buried beneath one hundred feet of hot basalt, glistening in a cloud-free Nevada sunrise.

The families of Roy and bachelor Chuck later agreed that their loved ones should stay where they died. A marker of remembrance was erected over the buried CO. The CEO of BSS eulogized the two as *brave captains going down with their ship*. As if they had any choice!

The package of financial compensation was substantial for widows of BSS employees lost in the line of duty. Wanda would never need a paying job and would be able to send her kids to any university in the land. She planned to stay a widow. No man would or could replace Roy Bates in her life. She moved back to Puckney and volunteered for social and educational activities in his name. Roy Bates was chiseled into the Puckney granite monument where the names of all those lost to the black death were memorialized. A footnote mentioned that basalt rather than coal was Roy's killer.

"Thank you Roy," Wanda was heard to sob behind a black facial veil while standing at the empty coffin at his memorial service in Puckney ... well, not quite empty. Before the lid was secured, she had tossed in a single square crinkly packet with an obvious hole scuffed through one side. "I'll always have a little bit of you with me through Troy and Helen. You're our hero. You've taken such good care of your family, and we do love you."

Wanda hosted a potluck dinner that night with four special friends, her fellow cheerleaders from their Puckney High days. There was a lot of reminiscing about whom all five agreed was a very remarkable man.

12

THE LIGHTS ARE ON BUT ...

4:00 PM, Sunday, August 15, 2027:

"Beep! Beeeep!! Screach!!!

"Hey buddy. Move it! This ain't no picnic we're all goin' to."

As usual Las Vegas was in churning chaos, but this time not in the pursuit of pleasure and profit. Law enforcement officers and a cadre of hastily deputized helpers were trying to evacuate the city and its suburbs as quickly as possible. Highly radioactive dust and grit were settling out from the wind-drifted eruption plume, building up a blanket of stuff that sent scintillometer readings off-scale.

Experts in human exposure to radioactive material assured officials and the public that they wouldn't get a life-threatening dose of radiation if they wore simple painter's masks, and if they were able to empty Vegas in hours rather than days. Serendipitously, a convention of paint manufacturers was meeting in the city. Plenty of masks were available. It was critically important to not breathe in radioactive dust. Particles could lodge in lungs to fission out a variety of deadly half-lives before a person could live a full life.

Hotel managers broadcast an evacuation order throughout their buildings. "Ladies and gentlemen. Your attention please. The city of Las Vegas is being covered with harmful dust. This is not the benign grit of a desert windstorm. This is bad stuff. You don't want to breathe it. You don't want to walk in it. You don't want to have anything to do with it."

The same message blared loudly in casinos, trying to rise above the din of gambling bells and whistles. Overhead, the message rang from bullhorns in helicopters that flew back and forth across the metro area.

Initially, the jolting news didn't penetrate minds that were conditioned to see and hear anything highly unlikely as just another act in Las Vegas's hyped-up non-stop entertainment.

"A violent volcanic eruption is underway at the Yucca Mountain storage site for radioactive waste. That's eighty miles northwest of us. The eruption has blasted the waste into a dust plume that's being blown here by the wind. If you don't believe this step outside, take a look at the sky and listen to the crunch of new grit underfoot."

The idea of radioactive dust started to grab the attention of gamblers and local residents alike. Maybe this wasn't just another glittery Las Vegas stunt.

"Leave town immediately. Do not go north. That's where the problem's coming from. And do not go south. That's the way the wind is carrying the dangerous dust. Leave via Interstate 15, either eastward in the direction of Utah, or westward toward southern California. If you don't have an automobile, jump on any bus on the streets. All have been ordered to load and get out of town.

"Don't even think of flying. The airport is closed. It's not safe for aircraft engines to suck in dusty air."

That lesson was learned early on when the city's helicopters began falling from the sky in power-off forced landings. Ingested gritty ash quickly ruined the internal workings of an engine.

By this point in the announcement, those not drunk, drugged or otherwise physically and mentally impaired were moving toward motorized ground transportation.

"This is not a drill. I repeat. This is not a drill. This is the real thing. Anyone refusing to leave will be forcibly hauled away. If you value your life, get out of town. Now!"

The warning was repeated non-stop in all hotel rooms and gaming parlors. It was blasted from the bullhorns of patrol cars cruising city streets. It ran continuously on all local radio and TV stations. Casino marquees replaced the mugs of their floorshow crooners and exotic dancers with the warning. One would have had to be blind and deaf, if not dead, to have missed the message.

The fastest growing city in the nation had passed the three-and-a-half million population mark a year earlier, a landmark of great civic pride and boasting by developers and politicians at the time. Including adjacent communities, the wannabes that inevitably germinate and grow to surround a vibrant core city, the population was flirting with four million. Shallow thinking at all planning levels was buoyed by the American notion that bigger is always better. The bread-and-butter infrastructure framework of roads, law enforcement staff, schools, and an adequate supply of potable water barely kept pace with the exploding number of citizens.

A worried Mayor Ben Lamici wished that Vegas was still the small cow town it had been in the 1950s. Herding a few tens of thousands of people away from the invisible danger of radiation would have been easier than a Chisholm Trail cattle drive. Now, millions of doubters had to be convinced that mortal danger lurked within the dusty air, and then persuaded to leave town immediately without packing personal possessions or playing one more hand of blackjack or betting on one more athletic event underway on a huge TV screen. The mayor's task was more like herding cats than cattle. Traffic was snarled, horns were honking, fenders were bending, and panic-driven road rage was rampant.

Improbably, by early the following morning greater Las Vegas was as ghostlike as a played-out mining town, save for coyotes, rattlesnakes, lizards, spiders, abandoned family pets and a few human transients who had been passed out or just hidden away in storm sewers and dingy basements, effectively insulated from the broadcast warnings. Highways leading to Los Angeles and Salt Lake City were clogged with the traffic of escapees. Unlike the 2005 experience of evacuating New Orleans in the wake of hurricane Katrina, this traffic moved at a respectable and steady pace. All eight lanes of I-15 carried outbound vehicles.

Once evacuees were safely out of town, they followed instructions to burn the clothes they were wearing and bury the ashes. The final step in personal decontamination was a long shower.

Ingvar Christiansson managed to catch a bus that dropped him in Salt Lake City. From there he flew to Minneapolis. He helped his father on the farm until he enrolled at Hamline College in the relatively safe upper Midwest the next fall.

When the sun set on the scintillating dust-covered city, thousands of clock-controlled switches flipped to the on position. In a city known for its profligate use of electricity, the lights were on … flickering, flashing, creating garish repetitions of art nouveau through sequential illumination.

But no one was home.

13

TESTES TINGLE

Millirem (shorthand for "milliroentgen equivalent man"): *A standard unit of measure for the effect of radiation on man.* From "The Nuclear Waste Primer" of the League of Women Voters Education Fund.

Three hundred sixty millirem: *The annual amount of radiation exposure to the average person in the United States.* From a U.S. Department of Energy Fact Sheet.

3:30 AM, August 16, 2027:

"Oooooh. Man I hurt."

A supine Billie Parker woke slowly, in the grips of a painful headache. The sack surrounding what passed for his brain seemed to be squeezing ever harder. He'd really tied one on last night and was now paying the price for drinking so much cheap beer and wine in so little time. He stroked his scruffy beard of four-days growth, scratched a crotch in bad need of a shower, stretched and yawned. He'd been in the same clothes for a week.

Earlier yesterday, he'd also hit the fifty-dollar jackpot on a one-armed bandit for the first time in his life, using a quarter he'd found in the gutter outside Murrah's Hotel and Casino. And he'd celebrated this highly improbable event by drinking fifty dollar's worth of the cheapest booze he could find. With all that money in hand, he'd considered looking up his soul mate Joel Bratskey to share in the riches. But Billie decided to just treat himself this time. He didn't have the moola to do this very often. Who would know where Bratskey could be found anyway? That guy was not dependable.

The beer … Dusky Derby, Billie thought he remembered it being. He regularly bought that brand for ten cents in Los Angeles. Somehow the rotgut seemed to have migrated to Vegas, where it was even cheaper. Maybe the beer he had over-imbibed was just the liquid version of the dark-colored stuff that littered the track at the end of the real Derby. His mouth surely tasted that way.

"Oooooh. Dusky Derby all right," he moaned as he rolled onto his side and pulled a sharp-edged empty can from under his left shoulder.

And the wine. He saw the Stormy Weather label on an empty screw-top bottle at his feet. The distinctive logo of a dark roiling thunderhead reminded him of how his head felt. A deep-pitched hangover noise kept reverberating from ear to ear across what was a pretty empty space.

The rumblings of real thunderheads were what Billie heard when he stood on wobbly legs, walked to the upper end of the water-runoff tunnel he'd been asleep in and emerged to peer into the neon-lit night of Vegas. The rain-cloud gods sounded extra angry tonight. City lights briefly flickered as a shaft of fiery electricity from Thor's quiver flashed across the night sky. Giant raindrops splashed around Billie's feet.

Billie stood motionless, enjoying a free shower while standing in ankle-deep water. Next came the ominous sounds of a bowling-ball rumble from upstream. Though Billie wasn't bright, he knew that a gully-washing flash flood might be headed his way, channeled down the concrete-lined drainage ditch that had been his bedroom.

"Time to make tracks if I don't wanna end up dead in a Vegas ditch," he said to his awakening imagination.

During the past few years, he had lost more than one inebriated friend to Vegas flash floods. Drainage ditch bedrooms were free, but dangerous.

He scrambled on hands and knees up the steep slippery wall of his bedroom trench and headed for the shelter of the nearest casino lobby.

"Huh? What the hell's goin' on?" he wondered aloud when he noticed that he surely was making tracks, nicely defined shoe-print tracks in a layer of wet sandy grit inches thick.

"Where the H is everybody? Where's all the traffic?" Never mind that it was not the conventional rush hour of a big city. Vegas had the deserved reputation of never slowing down, never experiencing a non-rush hour. The streets were empty … the sidewalks too. But all the marquee lights were ablaze.

Billie was alone.

Puzzled but still too tipsy to reason out what might be going on, a childish personality kicked in.

"I haven't had a sandbox this big since I was growing up on the beaches of LA. I won big money yesterday. Now I'm gonna play big time right here in the streets of Vegas. Yippie!" he said with a slight slur as he kicked off sandals, dropped his jeans and drawers, plopped down into a lotus position, and scooped damp sand over his legs and around his lower body until he was covered to his waist within the moat of his version of a castle.

Billie didn't know it, but that moat was no protection, especially not from getting the worst kind of dose a person could contract, in a state famous for its brothels and the possibility of a VD dose. His gonads and scuffed legs were covered with the strange sand of the night. A silent-and-invisible Greek alphabet of radiation was wreaking havoc with his reproductive system and other tissue as he sat motionless, wearing a silly grin. The three strikes of alpha, beta, and gamma rendered Billie out of the offspring-producing game at the speed of light. He was absorbing thousands of millirems, enough to produce a fuzzy, warm and ticklish feeling that prompted a satisfied *aaaaah* of pleasure.

Forty-one years earlier, a radiation victim at Chernobyl had described this feeling as a sensation similar to experiencing hundreds of needle-and pinpricks ... tingly and not unpleasant.

Sand play finished, Billie walked to the nearest hotel. He found an open room (it seemed that almost all rooms were open), took a long soapy shower, shaved with toiletries someone had left behind and took advantage of clean clothes in the closet.

He scooped up a bundle of cash left on betting tables in the gambling parlor and walked outside. He found an unlocked BMW at the curb, with keys in the ignition. He started the engine and slithered off toward Reno on the slippery sand coating US 95.

"This is my day," mused a man whose health would soon slip down the toilet faster than the gully washer that hadn't quite claimed him on this fateful night. "Maybe I'll have even better luck in Reno."

Ten minutes later, police turned Billie back at a roadblock and told him to head toward either LA or Salt Lake City.

Like folks in Vegas, residents of Henderson, Boulder City and other suburbs had been warned of impending disaster drifting in on the evening breeze. They had fled pell-mell westward and eastward like rats deserting a sinking ship.

Shortly before the onset of the rain that had showered Billie, the leading edge of the radioactive eruption plume had drifted a bit beyond Vegas. The sharp dividing line between this deadly and the non-lethal clear sky was hanging directly over Hoover Dam when descending raindrops began to wash grit from the air. Satellite images of what was happening recorded Nature's wind-powered version of a conveyor belt, carrying solid and gassy highly radioactive garbage from Yucca Mountain to its most distant dumping-off targets of Las Vegas and Lake Mead.

Evangelist Herby Kinsley, who continued to follow the unfolding eruption, was now absolutely certain that his god had created the eruption to punish the Sin City fallen for their wicked ways.

When all was said and done, when all was quiet on the southwestern front, the one hundred forty thousand tons of radioactive waste that had been blasted sky-ward had mixed in with volcanic ash and now covered the ground in a teardrop-shaped blanket that originated at Yucca and looped around Hoover Dam and Lake Mead. Areas further downwind in Arizona were the beneficiaries of heavy rain, which kept Nature's conveyor belt from distributing the killer radioactive poison beyond Hoover and its lake.

A crew on duty in the guts of the dam, operating and maintaining the turbine generators and various other water works, were ordered to stay put. They were protected from radiation by massive concrete walls and by an air filtration system that effectively removed even the finest of dust. No one else was in the fallout zone, unless a few more Billies were wandering the empty streets of Vegas and surroundings.

What happened in the teardrop area was truly a crying shame. But as many a realist and optimist would soon observe, "It woulda been worse, without that rain to clear the sky."

14

FRUSTRATION

Magma: *Molten rock located within the earth. Magma contains dissolved gases (sounds like my favorite beer!!), sometimes several percent by weight (Prof says this means lots of potential fizz!). Magma is called lava when erupted onto the surface of the earth.* From Barney Shanks's notes taken as a student enrolled in Introductory Geology.

Basalt: *Name applied to magma that forms when the earth's mantle begins to melt. The name is also applied to the erupted magma and the rock that forms when that lava solidifies. Basalt is the most common type of volcanic rock on earth.* More information from Barney's notebook.

August 17, 2027:

"Good morning students. Let's get underway. There never seems to be enough time to cover all the topics I want to.

"During our last session I described the different magma types and the volcanic rocks that form from them. You should remember the names rhyolite, rhyodacite, dacite, andesite and basalt. They're sure to show up in tests."

Note-scribbling students put an asterisk beside that entry.

"Today I'm going to concentrate on basalt.

"Why?

"Because basalt is the world's most abundant magma and volcanic rock. And it's fair to say that basalt is the parent of all the other volcanic rocks. We'll get into how this happens in a later lecture.

"For now, let's look at the big picture to help us understand why basalt is so common. We'll start with the special exercise I assigned to Barney Shanks at the end of our last meeting.

"Barney. Are you ready to tell us about the relative volumes of the three principal zones of planet Earth?"

"Yes sir."

He walked to the blackboard at the front of the room, grabbed a piece of chalk and drew a large circle that he labeled Earth. Inside he drew a concentric circle, about half the diameter of Earth. He thickened the circumference line of Earth and turned to face his classmates.

"You'll have to think in three-D. I've calculated the volumes of the core. This small inner circle. The mantle. This wide ring around the core. And the crust, shown by the wide outer circumference line. I used the dimensions that Professor Compton gave us last session.

"Then I converted those volume numbers into relative percentages."

Barney wrote *core*, *mantle* and *crust* in a vertical column on the board. He checked a cheat sheet of notes and added a volume number opposite each entry.

"By far the biggest part of Earth is the mantle, even though it might not look that way in the drawing. Mantle is about eighty-five percent.

"Next biggest is the core. It's about fifteen percent. I've rounded the mantle and core numbers to the nearest percent.

"That leaves less than one percent for the crust. The outer shell that we live and die on."

Barney turned and looked expectantly at Professor Compton.

"Well done Barney. Please be seated.

"Students are often surprised at how little of our planet is made up of the rocky layer of crust we live on. We mine it. We reshape and use it in many other ways. Here and there we even drill right through it into the mantle. But really the crust is just dust on a big ball, at least when it comes to how much of Earth civilizations occupy and use.

"Here's another way to visualize how insignificant the volume of *Homo sapiens* and their life trappings are. If the planet were scaled down to the size of a volleyball, the crust would be the thickness of a sheet of paper. Mount Everest would be a wrinkle so small you couldn't see it without a powerful microscope.

"Recall that all but the center of the core is a mixture of molten iron and nickel. The surrounding mantle is a solid and very hot rock called peridotite. That's another name you should remember.

"To melt part of the mantle, all it takes is a minor positive nudge in temperature caused, say, by heat moving up from the core, or maybe a small reduction in confining pressure applied by the weight of Earth's rocky lid overhead. There are other ways to trigger some melting, too. We'll deal with them later in the semester.

"But the key point for today's lesson is that this eighty-five percent part of the planet can be tweaked from below or above, or both, and whenever this happens the peridotite starts to melt and the product is always basalt." Compton wrote that word on the blackboard.

Avid note takers put a double asterisk opposite basalt.

"This magma doesn't always get all the way to the surface to erupt," Professor Compton said, "but as many geologists in the volcano game say, *basalt makes it happen!!*"

Barney awoke and stirred, mumbling *basalt makes it happen, basalt makes it happen, basalt makes it happen, basalt makes* ... He'd practically lived in his bean-bag chair since getting home once the eruption stopped, leaving only to visit the fridge and the john. Deeply felt frustration tinged with anguish magnified those days into what seemed like weeks.

Restful sleep was elusive. Dreams kept taking him back through his geologic education in a search for clues as to why he and Hank hadn't recognized that a lot of basalt magma was headed for Yucca. Asleep or awake, his search remained fruitless.

He rolled out of his chair and checked the time. He was due at Hank's Cal Tech office in four hours. He took a quick shower, shaved, dressed in his best denim clothes and headed south on Highway 101.

"Hi Hank," Barney said, as he opened the door and pushed his head through. "Bet you're surprised to see me on time, no?"

"No. Not this time Barney. I think even you'd agree that we've got serious pressing business. Come on in."

Hank stood and met Barney halfway to shake hands. He limped from the pain of the rebar gash to his left thigh ... a reminder of his near death at the CO. Barney noticed that he wore loose-fitting pants to accommodate a thick bandage.

"That bulge sure shows, doesn't it. Bonnie stops by to change the dressing several times a day. Can't be good for her law practice to be away from the office so much. Don't know what I'd do without her."

In the privacy of their home, Bonnie cradled the wounded Hank in her arms and carried him about like a mother tending a helpless baby. She had almost lost her dearest possession.

"If you want to find out how much somebody loves you, have a near-death experience."

The only lady friend I've heard from since the eruption is Heather, Barney reflected.

"How do you like my cane? It's a gift from Bonnie."

Barney took the prop as Hank steadied himself on the edge of his desk and handed over the walking stick.

"Very fancy, partner. Hickory shaft?"

"Only the best," Hank said. "From an eastern hardwood forest."

Barney held both ends, slowly twirled the cane, and stopped. "Carved ivory handle. And your name etched into this small brass plate. That's a very thoughtful lady you're married to."

Barney passed the cane back to Hank. "Here. Looks like you could use this."

"Bonnie bought me a new computer, too," Hank said. "Has a handcrafted leather holster with my name branded in."

Hank withdrew his new hi-tech machine then quickly reholstered it. "She had this engraved with a message that I'm a little embarrassed to show others. Hey. Enough about me. How are you handling the fact that we blew it? That we didn't see the eruption coming until it was too late to do anything useful about it?"

"It bugs the hell out of me," Barney said. "I can't get any decent sleep. I'm surprised the NRC hasn't been knocking on our doors already. Asking what they got for all the lavish funding they've been sending our way."

Hank nodded his agreement and motioned Barney to follow him into his lab. There, the two world-class scientists covered a large table with maps and charts that summarized the results of their studies and began brainstorming about what had gone wrong. Maybe a few things had even gone right. Either way, they knew they would soon face intense questioning. The world was clamoring to find out what had gone wrong at Yucca.

They started with a series of maps that showed changes in land elevation through time. Barney had been responsible for this part of their study ... the old "Yes Sire. I'll bring the data of InSAR" part of the project.

"Take a look at these figures, Hank. There's no hint that some kind of magma-caused blister of elevation increase was forming in the Yucca region ... nothing for the entire three years of our data."

Barney paused and pointed to the location of Yucca Mountain.

"The ground did bulge a little here since we started measuring, but that's what we expected from the rocks heating up and expanding when the radioactive waste got into storage."

"Agreed," Hank said as he stroked his computer holster.

"And look at the regional picture around Yucca," Barney said. "There were some small ups and downs but nothing like the broad domal uplift we would expect if a huge volume of magma was collecting beneath the crust.

"There's no way we could have predicted this eruption from the elevation maps."

Hank and Barney nodded heads in shared agreement.

"I suppose uplift might have been cancelled out because Nevada's crust is constantly stretching and sagging," Hank said.

"Yeah. Maybe. Maybe if we'd had more than three years of data we would have noticed something different in the Yucca region," Barney said.

They set the elevation maps aside and covered the table with maps that showed where earthquakes occurred.

"Barney."

Hank was holding his new computer as though expecting to see the wavy signature line of a quake arrive on its screen at any moment.

"We've both gone over these earthquake plots before, month by month, and couldn't see any pattern to the distribution of the shakes. They're all over the map. Not concentrated beneath or even very near Yucca. And none of them fall along a line that might represent a new fissure for magma to flow up on its way to Yucca."

"We've got nothing but classic widespread Nevada shaking as the crust continues to stretch east-west."

They once again nodded heads in shared agreement.

"I suppose our seismometers could have recorded telltale signs of magma gathering at the top of the mantle under Yucca," Hank said. "You know, swarms of small quakes in a sea of tremor. Sure can't see that pattern on our maps, though.

"Maybe the mantle under Yucca is so damn hot that it behaves more like pudding or putty than solid brittle rock."

"Yeah. Ain't hindsight great," Barney said.

They sighed as Hank rolled up the earthquake maps and replaced them with maps of soil temperature.

"Here we go again partner," Barney said. "We've got satellite images of the infrared energy radiated from Earth's surface for every two-week period since we started our project. We're smothered in data. But like the elevation study, all we see is an anomaly centered right over Yucca."

"And how many times have we done the math," Hank said "to show that this is exactly what is expected because of the heat generated by Yucca's radioactive garbage."

Both nodded heads in silent thoughts of *where have we gone wrong?*

"Maybe we shouldn't be surprised to not see mantle magma affect the surface temperature," Hank said. "If that heat rose just by conduction, it wouldn't have had time to reach the surface unless the pot of magma had been sitting at the top of the mantle for a *very very* long time."

"Yeah," Hank said. "And we don't have enough information to know when the magma pool formed."

No telltale elevation changes, no unusual earthquake activity, and no unexpected heat flowing across Earth's surface to drift off into space. Even Professor George Paine, PhD of the Massachusetts Institute of Technology and their harshest professional critic and constant gadfly, had agreed with the "all quiet" conclusion of the periodic reports that Hank and Barney had submitted to the NRC.

But once the undetected growing batch of magmatic syrup had become so voluminous that its gathering buoyancy could no longer be contained by the strength of the brittle rocks of the crust overhead, the considered conclusions of the best in academia didn't mean spit. All hell broke lose as Nature once again demonstrated how myopic human understanding can be.

Near midnight on August 14, 2027, magma broke through its rocky lid and began to stream upward rapidly towards Yucca Mountain, with the determination of a cork released at the bottom of a tub of water. That's when Hank's seismometers began to shake enough to wake him from an anniversary-night sleep in Bonnie's embrace. That's when the crew at the CO noticed some strange signals coming in from the storage tunnels. By then the die was cast. Humans could be nothing but spectators for Nature's extravaganza. Not only had a highly improbable event occurred, but cutting-edge science hadn't been able to give much advance warning to those who were in harm's way when the holocaust came.

Hank's secretary Brenda entered the room, an opened letter in hand. "You'd better go home and think about what to wear in Washington D.C., Dr. Thomas. You too, Dr. Shanks. Senator Jack Manics of Nevada requests your presence at hearings he will chair on what has happened at Yucca Mountain. The first session is in three days."

"Merde," mumbled French-savvy Barney.

"Mierda," was Hank's south-of-the-border version of their shared sentiment.

Brenda understood no foreign words but got the message from tone and body language.

15

FLOOD GATES OPEN

I guess we'll finally give the Mexicans their legal share of Colorado River water. The difficult decision of USA President Forty-Six when faced with what to do about the highly radioactive water of Lake Mead.

Wednesday, August 18, 2027:

Never thought I'd live to see the day this would be happening. God, what a mess the whole Yucca Mountain thing has got us into here.

As foreman, a troubled Alan Martinez was about to brief his crew, deep in the maw of Hoover Dam. Moments earlier he had received an order from U.S. Bureau of Reclamation Headquarters, Washington D.C., to "open all valves" and begin to draw down the water level of Lake Mead until the reservoir was nothing more than a piddling puddle.

"Look Alan," John Sharky, the head of the Bureau of Reclamation, had said during their phone conversation, "our expert advisor has told us that flushing out the reservoir is the only sure-fire short-term way to get rid of that highly radioactive lake of yours. She suspects that high doses of radiation are already causing unwanted mutations in the lake's aquatic life, animals and plants both, to say nothing about the birds and land animals that dine and drink from Mead. In her opinion, the lake and its surroundings will become a home to populations of corpses and freaks if the concentration of radioactive material isn't diluted way down. Soon."

As he listened, Alan had to admit that it was hard to disagree with Sharky's logic … so far.

"The only feasible solution we see back here in D.C. is to send the tainted water downstream and into the Sea of Cortez where it can mix with enough of the Pacific brine to be diluted to a safe level. We can refill the reservoir with uncontaminated upstream inflow after we deal with the radioactive sediment on the lake floor.

"So do your job, man. You guys stuck down there in the guts of the dam are considered national heroes. President Forty-Six plans to present each of you with the National Civilian Medal of Honor when this is over. Don't disappoint an admiring public now."

"Yes sir. We'll get the draining underway ASAP." Martinez's tone of voice didn't reflect the certainty and immediacy normally carried by the ASAP acronym. He had several misgivings about the wisdom of his marching orders.

"Sir," he said, "what about the flooding of downstream towns when all the outlet gates are opened? Full-bore water release is sure to flood agricultural lands along the river. It'll probably spill into low-lying nearby towns, too. Some of that bottom land is probably already starting to fill up with snowbirds."

"Those problems have been taken care of, Alan. Evacuation orders have been issued. There won't be any RV campout jamborees along the river this year. And yes, a few vegetable patches will be washed away. But hey, there's nothing for you to worry about. Just get those valves opened up."

In spite of Sharky's reassurances, uncertainty gnawed at Martinez's conscience.

"What about Davis, Parker and the other small dams downstream? They'll be overwhelmed when we max the outflow."

"Already taken care of," Sharky said. He had an instant answer for all of Alan's concerns. "Those dams will be opened, too. And they're engineered to withstand over-the-top flooding. If it happens."

One last problem was tugging at Alan … something very personal.

"Okay. Yes, Mr. Sharky. But one more thing. Aaaah … what about our Mexican neighbors? That flat ground beyond where the Colorado River crosses the border … where it empties into the Sea of Cortez … is a wide delta. All that land will be flooded with radioactive water. There's a lot of farming, vegetable growing that goes on down there. The farmers live there."

"Sure. Sure you're right, Alan. But like I keep saying. Don't concern yourself about downstream effects. They've been taken care of by those of us back here.

"Trust me on this. President Forty-Six himself has alerted Presidente Lobo of our plans. He pointed out that environmentalists of both our countries have bemoaned the lack of annual floods across the river delta for years. So providing this flood is actually doing people in both countries a favor."

The words *arrogant bastard* crossed Alan's mind. But he had no more arguing points. It was his job to carry out orders, or it wouldn't be his job anymore. He, his wife and their eight children needed the steady income.

"Yes sir, Mr. Sharky. Consider the valves open."

"Alan. Be sure to send my secretary daily reports as you empty the lake. I want to be able to update President Forty-Six whenever he asks."

"Will do, sir. Is that all?"

"Yes. Goodbye and good luck. Think how proud your family will be with that Medal of Honor decorating the house wall."

An immigrant from Mexicali, Alan had gained U.S. citizenship and worked his way up through the Bureau of Reclamation ranks to his present position. This was an accomplishment of great pride within his Mexican family on both sides of the border. Controlling the flow of water through the dam to generate electricity and sustain downstream waterworks had been a rewarding experience. Now he was under orders to be the cause of evacuating the entire river valley corridor and its floodplains for what might be months, years, or even decades. The flood might even poison uninformed Mexican campesinos, some of them likely to be his kin. This was not the stuff of building pride in one's career. His voice sounded dead, yet deadly serious as he gave the rest of the in-dam crew its marching orders.

"Let's get to it, guys. We've been ordered to drain the lake. This may break our hearts, but if nothing else I'm sure we'll become famous for drying up Lake Mead. Dry for the first time since the dam went into service back in 1935."

Alan's coworkers, Christian George, Duane Zimbel, and Conrad Trestle, were career employees of the U.S. Bureau of Reclamation. Al, Chris, Duey and Conny had worked as a team for a couple of decades. In-house, they were called the AC/DC gang in recognition of their job to keep electrons flowing from the dam's turbine generators into transmission lines connected to places like Las Vegas and the southern California coastal megalopolis. The team's task today would grate against all of their instincts.

Within an hour, intake valves were fully opened to the turbine generators. Ditto for valves to outlet tubes that fed water straight through the dam without harvesting energy along the way. Alan occupied his unhappy mind and broken heart by retreating to the relative quiet of his office to recheck some earlier calculations, while the rest of the AC/DC crew sulked.

"It took about six and a half years for the reservoir behind the dam to fill to the brim, once water started to impound there in 1935," Alan said to himself as he punched numbers into a calculator. "That full tank held almost twenty-nine million acre feet then. That's where we are today."

He suddenly stood ramrod erect, saluted an imaginary superior and shouted "full up and ready to rumble, sir," as though he was PFC Martinez responding to a command from Four Star General Sharky. He expressed his true feelings with a dual bird flip.

The rumble Alan alluded to was the sound and feel that filled the bowels of the dam when all turbine generators were spinning at maximum capacity. Earmuffs were recommended. When standing still, a person could feel the concrete floor quiver. More than once over his years on the job, Alan had fantasized that turbines at full power might shake the dam apart. Today would be the last time for months or years that he would get to initiate that physical feeling of power being created. He sat and returned to mumbling and number crunching.

"Let's see. Now that we have all drain valves opened, water is leaving the reservoir at about one-point-seven acre feet per second."

Click, click, click, click. He punched that figure into his calculator, multiplied by the number of seconds in a year and read the result.

"So, we're releasing water at a rate of about fifty-two-point-seven million acre feet per year.

"During the past couple of years, water's been flowing in from upstream at an average rate of about twenty million acre feet per year. Fifty-two-point-seven minus twenty is thirty-two-point-seven.

"So. We're drawing down the reservoir at about thirty-three million acre feet per year. Full reservoir is twenty-nine. Should take a little less than a year to drain Mead and get rid of the radioactive stuff."

He left his office and found his coworkers in the turbine room. This was a cavernous space in the maw of the dam, where water fed in was converted to useful energy, a bit like the way a human stomach harvests energy from food.

"Hey guys, listen up. It'll take most of a year to drain the dirty water from our bathtub. Let's hope the boss will give us some vacation time before the job is done."

A dirge-like moan from the constricted and unhappy throats of the AC/DC quartet nearly damped out the rumble of spinning turbines.

16

DIRTY BOMB

*A **dirty bomb** is in no way similar to a nuclear weapon. The presumed purpose of its use would be therefore not as a Weapon of Mass Destruction ...* From a U.S. Nuclear Regulatory Commission Fact Sheet.

August 19-20, 2027:

On August 19, Hank and Barney flew non-stop from Los Angeles International Airport to Dulles International in the D.C. area. Barney partially numbed his fear of flying with three quick margaritas as soon as drinks were offered in flight. Hank passed the time watching his hand-help computer, monitoring earthquakes still shaking the Yucca area.

They touched down at 5 PM and caught a limousine to the Ritz Hotel just off the D.C. Mall. Before registering, they dined simply in the hotel restaurant. At check-in they decided to share a room so they could discuss what might transpire at tomorrow's hearing. An hour on that topic, once their bags were unpacked, resulted in heavy eyelids. They were about to hit the sack when the phone rang.

"Hello."

"Good evening, sir. This is Morgan at the front desk. I'm sorry to disturb you at this late hour."

"It's okay. What's up Morgan?"

"Nevada's senior senator Jack Manics is calling for Dr. Henry Thomas or Dr. Barnabus Shanks."

"This is Shanks. I'll take the call."

"Very well. I'll connect you."

"Go ahead sir."

"Hello. Barney Shanks here. I understand Senator Manics is calling."

A deep-pitched gravelly voice answered. "Speaking. Howdy Dr. Shanks. How are you tonight?"

"Hello Senator. I'm just fine. You too I hope."

"Yup. Feeling great. Ready to start some important business tomorrow. And you Dr. Shanks and your colleague Dr. Thomas will be critical witnesses."

"If you don't mind sir," Barney said hesitantly, "I prefer to be called Barney. I've never felt comfortable hearing that doctor label attached to my name. It just doesn't fit."

"Okay. We both know you've got the credential. I'm guessin' that you think like me. You know that folks who insist on using the fancy titles are often a bit insecure. With good reason, for some that I've met.

"I appreciate dealing with a person who doesn't beat around the bush. So let's forget the formal Washington and academic BS. I'll call you Barney. You call me Jack. We're both folks who grew up far from the banks of the Potomac. As some like to say, even snobs put their pants on one leg at a time. But I think people like you and me have a better way of doin' it."

That introduction broke the ice sufficiently for an open conversation to flow.

"Well Barney, I apologize for bothering you tonight. But I want to get acquainted before the formalities begin tomorrow morning."

Hank was in bed, snoring peacefully.

Barney walked into the bathroom and closed the door to continue the conversation. He listened as Manics continued his cowboy-style chat. He had never before talked with a U.S. senator, or even a state politician for that matter. His one political contact, a continuing friendship with Iceland's former president Gutrudsdóttir, grew out of a shared love of volcanoes, hardly the stuff of Washington D.C. politics.

"First of all Barney, welcome to D.C. For those of us who are true westerners, as I know you and your colleague Dr. Thomas are, even a brief visit to the seat of our government can trigger culture shock."

"So I've heard, sir. I've never visited Washington before. I haven't had time to react one way or the other."

"Please Barney. None of this sir stuff. It smacks of the East Coast class system."

"Okay Jack. But my folks taught me to respect elders, even if I thought they were a bit … different."

"They gave you good advice. But between you and me I want it to be Jack and Barney. Except when on the formal record. I hope I don't come across as … strangely different."

"Oh no. I didn't mean any disrespect," Barney said. "I guess I thought that all senators were like the ones I see on TV. I've never talked with one before."

"Relax Barney. Relax. I think you and I will get along fine. In and out of committee.

"Now, if your time here rubs you raw, like breakin' in a new saddle can, just remember that you'll soon be back home. I think the business of the Yucca Mountain hearing will wind up in just a few days at most."

Barney open the lid and sat on the toilet stool, as Manics continued talking.

"The reason I called tonight is that you're gonna be involved with the opening session of that hearing tomorrow morning. I want you to understand ahead of time the basics of what'll happen. Give you a leg up so to speak, rather than let you try to mount this beast alone. It's foolish to try to tame your first bronco before talkin' with a horse man who's got the experience."

"You're on target there, Senator ... errr Jack. I'd really appreciate some guidance. I'm definitely new to this kind of meeting."

"Okay Barney. You're gonna get an earful of the noise of naked power politics. As chairman of the hearings, you'll hear me aggressively attack certain witnesses. And I anticipate there'll be the defensive sounds of meadow muffins thrown back at me. This'll be partly for show. And partly because that's the way even serious business is done around here. I suggest you tune out this shootout drama stuff. Unless you want to soak up a few entertaining stories to share back home around a Pacific beach fire."

Manics heard a soft chuckle from Barney.

"What I'm countin' on from you and your partner Dr. Thomas is to explain the nuts and bolts of the geology behind the Yucca disaster. You know. Like what caused that mess from a purely scientific point of view. You two are the experts who have been studyin' the area. The guys with their feet firmly on the ground. You were there at the beginning of the eruption and right on through to the end.

"So, when I ask you to tell us what happened, give us the straight scoop in language that us non-geologists can understand. Forget the highfalutin' lingo. Tell your story in a way that certain past Presidents we can think of could even understand. That's the sort of low-ball target to aim for.

"Are you with me?"

"Yes sir!" Barney said. He was developing a warm feeling of shared politics and other values from Senator Jack. This man would be a welcome addition to a surfer's beach party.

"Come on now. Save those sirs for the hearing. One more thing. Then I'd better let you get some shuteye. Is your colleague listenin' in on us?"

"Nope. Hank dozed off just before you and I started to chat. He's taking pain pills for a bad gash on his leg. You probably know about that accident from the national news. The pills make him drowsy.

"He's a true-blue scientist though. Last thing he did before going to bed was watch the tracings of earthquakes on his computer screen. Those wavy scenes are a soothing symphony to him. Yucca's still shaking you know."

"Hank sounds like a fine, devoted man," Manics said. "I've got lots of old cowboy buddies who have a hard time getting to sleep without the sounds of cattle mooing in the background. We're all products of what we grew up with.

"Now I don't mean to insult anyone with what I'm about to say. But my sources tell me that you're a better public spokesman than Hank. More charismatic in politician talk.

"Don't get modest and interrupt. My sources also say that Hank is one of the world's brightest earthquake experts. It's just that he seems more at ease with his high-tech tools than with people. So, I'm thinkin' that you should be the main speaker when it's time to tell the volcano story. If you agree, I'll guide the hearing in your direction when science is the topic."

Barney said that would be okay with him and that he thought Hank would understand and agree.

"Truth be told," Barney said, "Hank would much rather be home in the care of his doting wife. You'd enjoy meeting her."

Barney and Jack reminisced for a few minutes about how superior life back in the West is compared to the stuffed-shirt prissy East Coast. They were soul mates preaching to a two-voice choir. It was ten o'clock by the time they ran out of West Coast tales, said lights out, and hung up.

The next morning over breakfast, Barney briefed Hank on most of his conversation with Senator Manics. They hailed a cab at 8:15 and at 8:45 arrived at a gray limestone building a block off the National Mall. They decabbed onto a sidewalk crowded with people moving toward a matched pair of oversized glass entry doors. Inside, a hallway led straight to stairs that descended one floor to the hearing room.

A sign posted there announced, "Lead-off session of the joint Senate-House committee to review the recent and ongoing events at Yucca Mountain, Nevada." Above the door was a brass plate with the name A. Gore Conference Room etched in black bas-relief. The room was crowded and abuzz with reporters and concerned citizens. The mood seemed tense.

Hank and Barney identified themselves to a uniformed guard at the door and headed toward the front. A large digital clock on the wall displayed 8:50 AM.

They found their name cards mounted in clear plastic stands on a long curved table, open to the front. They sat, facing another gently curved table on a raised platform across the front of the room, where the congressional delegation was assembled. The symbolism of Congress looking down on everyone else was obvious. Barney and Senator Manics exchanged a smile and wave of recognition. Handshakes and an introduction for Hank would come later.

A cadre of reporters occupied a shallow oval-shaped well between the politicos and witnesses. Several hundred observers occupied rows of uncomfortable folding metal chairs at the back of the room.

At exactly 9:00 AM, the staccato Whack! Whack! Whack! sounds of an oak gavel impacting the chairman's oak table brought the meeting to order.

"Ladies and gentlemen," Manics said, "please take your seats and be quiet."

A subsiding din ebbed from the room as myriad conversations wound down. Late-arriving observers jockeyed for the few remaining seats.

Whack! Whack!

"I can't emphasize enough that we're here to discuss a matter of grave, immediate and developing concern to the nation. And to the world. Let's try to maintain orderly quiet and civilized decorum for the duration of this hearing. We have a lot of ground to cover."

Seventy-five-year-old Jack Manics was the aged version of his earlier years. An unruly shock of gray hair topped a head whose tanned and weathered face was that of what had been an honest-to-god cowboy until he decided to serve his state as a politician. Bowed legs spoke of many more hours across the broad back of a quarter horse than the typically pampered career airline pilot might log in the cockpit of a plane. Given the cushy work hours of those pilots, during his thirty-five years on the range, Manics and his steed may even have outdistanced a typical flyboy. Manics still bore the muscular frame of someone who had worked cattle and fences for years. While in D.C. he worked out at the Congressional Gym.

He was joined at the head table by part of Nevada's congressional delegation—Senator Seymore Luchs and Representatives Nancy Billings and Ned Pepper. Given the location and nature of the event to be discussed, Nevada held the majority of committee seats. Senators from Wyoming, Vermont, New Mexico and North Carolina rounded out the panel, mostly for show. This was going to be a Nevada shindig, with Manics leading the roundup.

The committee was charged with the task of ferreting out the what, how, and why of the disaster that had occurred at Yucca Mountain only days earlier. There was also the thorny issue of the long-term impact of radioactive fallout. Their report would help shape policy on how to deal with the Yucca disaster.

The mountainous new lava hump covering old Yucca remained hot to the touch, like a festering blister. The nation was reeling from the fact that the entire stockpile of high-level radioactive waste once stored there had been pulverized and spread over Las Vegas and surrounding real estate. The President and every concerned citizen wanted some answers, some explanation to soothe the nation's troubled psyche.

Three years earlier this President had promised the nation that the Yucca site would be secure for at least ten thousand years. He was up for reelection in one more year. Damage control was the Administration's prime concern. Would the Nevada congressional delegation cooperate, given the nearly four-decade history of several administrations, including the present one, wanting to shove the nation's radioactive waste down Nevada's throat at Yucca Mountain? The President had ample cause for concern about the findings of the Manics committee.

Facing the congressional committee were representatives from the Department of Energy and the Nuclear Regulatory Commission, along with Barney and Hank.

After his chat with Manics the night before, Barney expected to field most of the technical questions from the congressional inquisitors. That would come later. On this first day of hearings the secretary of the Department of Energy was present at the insistence of Manics. Politics would trump science as the leadoff topic.

Newsprint and electronic reporters, photographers, and commentators for broadcast media huddled in their bullpen space. They kept themselves and their equipment low enough to be out of the line of sight between the congressional questioner and a respondent.

Whack! Whack! Whack!

"Ladies and gentlemen," Manics said, "I believe we all know exactly why we are convened here today, so I won't waste a lot of precious time describing background details. Those will come out as we proceed. But first let me explain how I'm going to run this hearing. My ground rules may surprise you folks of the Fourth Estate.

"I will not allow other members of the congressional panel equal time to question each witness. You know. The old traditional structured agenda. If one of my colleagues up here wants to butt in, I'll entertain a request. But I hold the gavel. And it'll fall whenever I think it's time to move on. After years of us Nevada politicians being pushed to the back seat whenever Yucca Mountain was the order of D.C. business, we're now going to run the show. It's time for our voice to control the conversation.

"A terrible, terrible disaster has befallen our nation, my home state of Nevada, the good citizens of Las Vegas and Boulder City, and the entire patch of innocent desert that surrounds these affected areas. Even as we meet here today, experts in the field of radiation exposure are trying to determine how to minimize harm to people and other living things from the blanket of radioactive dust over the blighted ground.

"The volcanic eruption that spread that lethal blanket seems to have gone to sleep. Permanently we hope. But the nation's problems are far from over."

Manics paused to scan across the audience, knowing that judiciously timed silent moments would enhance the impact of his words.

"The fundamental question that we will address is 'How could something so intensely studied, so carefully planned, so lavishly funded, so meticulously constructed and so religiously guarded come to such a disastrous end?'

"Is our country and its cadre of experts as incompetent as the facts would seem to indicate?

"Did past Administrations hurry the evaluation and approval process at Yucca Mountain for political reasons, rather than being patient enough to let science find solutions to recognized problems?

"Was Yucca Mountain selected even though safer storage places across our vast nation might exist?

"Was that site simply a sacrificial lamb, a place that the political establishment back east considered expendable because my state is sparsely populated and the Yucca Mountain area was already tainted with radioactive wastes left behind from decades of testing atomic weapons there?"

As Manics paused between spitting out his string of damning questions, reporters scribbled notes, tape-recorded and photographed the scene. Nevada politicians had fought to keep the nuclear waste out of their state from the very beginnings of the nation's search for a safe repository. Now they had a genuine gripe to air. A preachy *we told you so* was high on the committee chairman's agenda.

"As a concerned citizen, a senator, and a life-long resident of the great state of Nevada, I expect some very thoughtful answers to these and other pertinent questions that are sure to arise during our deliberations. If I'm not satisfied, I guarantee you that fur will fly. The way it should have when our government first harmed its innocent citizens with radioactive debris from the Yucca area.

"Don't forget the massive downwind kill-off of sheep and the unusually high incidence of cancer in our brethren Utahans, all linked to radioactive dust that originated with nuclear testing just a few miles from Yucca Mountain in the

1950s and 60s. Let's not try to sweep government responsibility under the rug again, as was done back then."

Manics paused to read notes from an outline he had prepared for the day.

"First I want to emphasize a simply incontrovertible fact. In light of this fact, I hope that all the officials who over the past couple of decades worked so hard to put the nation's nuclear waste in my back yard are thinking about eating a little crow. No, I *insist* that they eat crow. Not that this will do my constituents much good at this point. But by whatever higher power you may recognize, we who have always opposed storage at Yucca Mountain have been proven right, and we damn well want to be sure that the entire nation and the world know this."

Ever hungry for conflict over serenity, the media and public were eating up the harsh words. There was nothing like a national scandal for entertaining the masses. Manics wore the most serious and threatening facial expression he could muster as he continued. He ran his fingers through his hair, leaving it even more menacingly unruly than usual. Back in his home state, he could legally have had a pair of pearl-handled revolvers strapped around his waist, as the cowboy mentality lingered on interminably in remnants of the Wild West. It took little imagination for people at the hearing to add that six-shooter accoutrement to the man speaking to them today in tame-and-genteel Washington D.C.

"The fact I speak of is this: For two and a half decades, ever since nine-eleven of the year two thousand one, our national leaders have chased after so-called terrorists suspected of planning to attack our good citizens and institutions with portable weapons called dirty bombs. And with what results? A litany of failures to apprehend someone, anyone, using a dirty bomb. I believe the chase has been sterile.

"Meanwhile …"

Manics paused and scanned the room with his stern wrinkled-forehead cowboy expression.

"… Meanwhile, it seems that these same so-called leaders helped create the world's ultimate dirty bomb, stored it in my back yard, assured me that it would be safe there for thousands of years, and then stood by helplessly as it spread its poison over the nation's most vibrantly growing city. Such incompetence is astounding. It's unforgivable! I demand an explanation of how such a terrible mistake, if that's what it was, could have been made!"

His suggestion that what had happened at Yucca Mountain might be less than an innocent accident prompted a concerted buzz in the room.

"But first. First I want to be sure that everyone in this great nation of ours knows what a dirty bomb is. No sense talkin' about and me complainin' about a dirty bomb unless we all know what it is."

He stopped talking long enough to change facial expression from confident to confused.

"I can't speak for others, but I've always been confused by this label. I mean, if there's a dirty bomb there must be something called a clean bomb. Right? Or has my cowboy logic gone astray like a lost dogie?"

This brought a few chuckles from the audience. Manics stared straight at the contingent from the DOE.

"I'm sure that our Energy Secretary, the honorable Richard Heade, can enlighten us on this apparent repetitious, on the one hand, and oxymoronic on the other hand, labeling of bombs. I've always thought that all bombs were so dirty that they didn't need a slippery modifier attached to help listeners know the filthy truth about them."

Manics focused on Heade.

"However, Secretary Heade, for purposes of our hearings I accept the silly notion that a bomb might be clean. As the man at the top of the Department of Energy, please, educate us on what a dirty version of a bomb is. Since your DOE facility at Yucca has proved to be one, I'm sure you can easily answer my question."

Richard Heade cleared his throat. He looked horribly uncomfortable, as he focused his attention on Manics. His flesh was soft and plentiful. He sported a military crew cut atop a face covered with pasty-white skin, the antithesis of Manics's appearance. He stood five-foot-eight on tiptoes.

Cameras were rolling. Heade was on national TV, live. He had been selected for his position by President Forty-Six, after rising through the political ranks in typical good-old-boy smoky backroom manner, first as mayor of Miami, then as governor and finally as Senator Heade of Florida. In the recent past, he and Manics had butted heads more than once on opposite sides of senatorial issues. At the moment, Manics was enjoying the fact that Heade was in a very hot seat.

Heade had no training pertinent to issues of energy, other than the fact that he had begun his professional life as a patent attorney. As such, he had helped several clients secure patents for doodads and widgets that claimed to, and sometimes did help the nation conserve a little energy. But to career civil servants of the DOE who were genuinely concerned about national energy issues and trained to do something useful about them, the man was an incompetent embarrassment. Behind his back, they likened his meteoric rise in DOE to what happens in an open sewer, where the biggest turds typically float to the top. They took great delight at informal settings in referring to their boss as Dick Heade, with a strong vocal emphasis on the first name.

Heade looked toward Manics and the rest of the congressional panel and began describing his version of a dirty bomb.

"Distinguished panel members. I thank you for inviting me to your hearings. I look forward to explaining the DOE role in what has transpired at Yucca Mountain, both the earlier planning stages and the following run-up to actually storing nuclear waste there. I think I can convince you that all feasible care was taken along the way. That all possibilities were analyzed and assessed to conclude that storage there would be safe."

Though listening attentively, Manics scanned here and there around the room as if bored with Heade's opening remarks.

"Later in these hearings, when we come to the science involved, you will hear from the experts with me here at this table. The nation's brightest, who can describe the technical details. But first, let me address Senator Manics's concern about bombs by explaining what we at DOE mean when we talk about a dirty bomb."

Heade shuffled through some papers until he located a fact sheet that had been prepared by his staff, in anticipation of the dirty bomb question. He scanned it quickly and looked up to address the congressional panel.

"At the DOE we call this type of weapon a Radiological Dispersal Device. That would be an RDD in technical lingo."

Representative Billings raised her right hand and Manics nodded.

"Mr. Secretary," Billings said, "let's not use confusing acronyms during these hearings. We want plain talk so all interested citizens will understand. Let's call a dirty bomb a dirty bomb. Not an RDD or even a DB. Continue please."

"Well since we want the masses to understand, let me begin by pointing out that a dirty bomb is nothing like the mud ball that a Johnnie might throw at a Julie. Or vice versa," Heade said, seeing a frown grow across Nancy Billings's face.

"The dirt of the dirty bomb is radioactive waste. Typically it's low-level material that can nonetheless cause serious health problems to living things if ingested or simply by being present in an environment with living things."

This time Representative Pepper got the Manics nod to interrupt.

"So, radioactive waste is a necessary part of the bomb. Yucca Mountain surely had that bad stuff aplenty."

"Yes, Mr. Pepper. Yucca Mountain contains … that is it used to contain … tons of radioactive waste, one hundred forty thousand tons to be quantitative. I'll get to Yucca eventually and explain why it was never, and I repeat, *never* a dirty bomb."

"We'll see about that," Pepper said. "We'll see."

"Now," Heade said, "a bomb is something designed to explode. But. And this is a point I want all listeners to understand. The radioactive material of a dirty bomb does not explode. We are not talking about a scaled-down version of what took out Hiroshima and Nagasaki.

"The explosive material that is part of a dirty bomb would be something non-nuclear. Perhaps plain old dynamite. The job of the dynamite would be to disperse the radioactive material. To spray it over an area, maybe something as small as a train depot, an auditorium or a football stadium. To poison the space and to fall on and be breathed in by the people there."

The senator from Wyoming asked for and got permission to speak. As a man loyal to the current Administration, he was sympathetic to the Energy Secretary.

"Thank you for your excellent description of a dirty bomb, Secretary Heade! Very clear and concise. I doubt that anyone else could give a better explanation of the weapon."

"Enough back patting from Wyoming," Manics said. "Let's keep moving. Continue Mr. Heade."

"Let me reemphasize a key point about dirty bombs with reference to some recent history. All of us who lived through the wars with Iraq during the late nineteen-nineties and early two-thousands will surely remember the meaning of WMD."

Hearing another acronym prompted an audible groan from several panel members.

"Wait a minute," Heade said. "Just a minute. I have an important point to make with regard to the WMD acronym.

"Dirty bombs are also often described as WMD. But they have nothing to do with weapons of mass destruction. They are weapons of mass *disruption*. The key notion is that any harm caused by a dirty bomb would be relatively minor and very local … simply disruptive in nature. There would be no atomic explosion, only the inconvenient effect of sprinkling radioactive powder over a small target area."

Heade looked pleased with himself. He smiled toward the panel, and relaxed back in his chair.

Manics allowed enough quiet time for Heade to think he had satisfied the panel. *Now I'll put this sleazy varmint in his place.*

"So Mr. Secretary," Manics said, "you say that a dirty bomb is relatively harmless in the greater scheme of bombs. This is all very interesting and educational. Could you please describe some specific incidences to help us all better understand what you mean? For example, tell us in detail what happened when a dirty bomb exploded in a stadium, in a theater, or at some other place of public gathering."

Heade looked confused. He put a hand over his microphone and turned toward the DOE attorney next to him. They whispered back and forth animatedly.

"We're waiting, Secretary Heade," Manics said.

Heade turned his attention back to Manics.

"Senator Manics, I'm afraid I can't cite a specific time or place when and where a dirty bomb was deployed."

"I beg your pardon? How is it that you can describe these bombs in such detail if you don't know of any examples?"

"Senator, if our homeland security forces had verified the use of a dirty bomb, we would certainly all remember the news of that attack. But I think we'll all agree that there have been no such public reports."

Panel members and people in the general audience nodded heads in apparent agreement.

"Now on the other hand," Heade said, "might there have been an occasion or two when a dirty bomb was used on our citizens but didn't make the evening news? It's hypothetically possible. But counsel advises me that any such attacks would be top secret information of national security."

This hint of government secrets triggered a murmur of disapproval across the room. Manics spoke for the masses.

"As you know Mr. Heade, many of us in this freedom-loving Republic dislike the dangerous policy of so much of your Administration's information being kept secret. This is an abomination in a truly open democratic society.

"But, I rather like hearing your public admission that no dirty bombs have been reported in our country. That this weapon of mass disruption, as you call it, is nothing more than a hypothetical object dreamed up by the overactive imaginations of those who seem to like to govern by fear."

Applause arose from the audience. Manics leisurely gaveled the room back to silence.

"Let the record clearly show that the DOE's weapons of mass disruption are in the same category as the Iraqi weapons of mass destruction of recent national experience. Both are hypothetical, imaginary things that didn't exist then and don't exist now."

The hearing room filled with the noise of audience conversations and media equipment recording the scene. Secretary Heade tried to speak, but was gaveled to silence by Manics.

"Quiet, ladies and gentlemen. You too Mr. Heade. Please. Everyone be quiet."

Manics checked the time.

"All this talk about hypothetical things has given me an appetite for something real. We'll take our lunch break and reconvene promptly at two."

Whack! Whack! Whack!

Whack! Whack! Whack!

"Now that we're properly fed with real solid stuff, let's move on," Manics said. "Next I want to examine where the radioactive waste that was stored at Yucca Mountain fits into the *scheme* of the DOE definition of a dirty bomb. Having just learned that no dirty bombs are known to have been used in our nation … not that one won't appear someday … the public alarm about them that has kept emanating from certain Administrations does impress me as a scheme."

Manics and Heade glared at each other briefly.

"Let me continue by comparing the characteristics of the DOE definition of dirty bomb to the situation that has unfolded at Yucca Mountain.

"Mr. Heade. You say that a necessary feature of a dirty bomb is that the radioactive material involved does not itself explode. Some other non-nuclear material provides the oomph to spread the radioactive stuff over an area. Am I correct?"

"Yes, Senator. You are correct."

"Then what happened at Yucca Mountain just a few days ago fits this part of the DOE definition."

"Yes. Yes of course," Heade said, "it satisfies the no-nuclear-explosion limitation. But surely you aren't suggesting that Yucca Mountain was blasted apart by dynamite or a similar conventional explosive, are you?"

"We'll get to the details of the answer to that question during hearings scheduled for tomorrow."

Manics and Barney shared a glance.

"I believe you'll find the forthcoming testimony of Dr. Shanks to be extremely interesting and illuminating on this point."

Manics looked back at Heade.

"Meanwhile, let me simply state that the principal punch that shattered Yucca Mountain … this would be the dynamite of your story … came from something like the pressure cooker Grandma used during canning season. You do remember those historic times, don't you?"

"Of course I do. But the steam blasts reported at Yucca Mountain were nothing like those of an overheated stovetop pressure cooker. How can you justify even suggesting a comparison?"

Manics grinned. The Fourth Estate watched and listened closely.

"Mr. Heade. Mr. Heade. Mr. Heade. To paraphrase a well-known actor turned politician: There you go again.

"Can't you think big? If I may add a personal observation for the record, the entire Administration that you're part of seems to have an aversion to thinking …"

Manics paused noticeably.

"… big."

He stared directly at Heade and voiced his next thought slowly and deliberately.

"What happened at Yucca Mountain was nothing more than a scaled-up version of Grandma's exploding pressure cooker."

Manics's memory retrieved the many nights he had spent sleeping on the ground during cattle roundups.

"I reckon what happened at Yucca is also the scaled-up version of the unopened can of beans left too long over a cowboy's campfire. Those were messy mistakes some of us made out on the prairie. Talk about a dirty bomb! Beans may be the source of flatulence, to use the polite term in present company. But at least they aren't radioactive."

Manics let his criticism of Heade's lack of imagination be further absorbed by his audience before continuing.

"So. We have now established that the Yucca Mountain event … can we on the panel agree to call it an event?"

Heads nodded in agreement.

"The event was the deployment of a dirty bomb as defined by the DOE."

Heade stood. Blue arteries bulged through the soft fatty flesh of his neck. "I strongly object. Very strongly. Even if I were to concede that the Yucca event was an example of radioactive waste being dispersed by simple steam blasts, that event was not the product of human planning. Dirty bombs are weapons used by evil people. By terrorists. By cowards who are unwilling to try to solve problems with words and logic and reason, who instead use brute force and ignorance. The Yucca event was not, I repeat, was not the work of such people."

Manics let Heade's emotional outburst echo around the room, and then carried on in a rational and quiet manner.

"Thank you, Secretary Heade, for reminding us about what the focus will be during the third day of our hearings. The why of this event. Why it is that Yucca Mountain was selected for radioactive-waste storage, leading to the tragedy still underway in my home state as we sit safely here in the nation's capitol.

"Today, we have satisfactorily completed addressing the what part of the agenda. We on the panel, and the media observers here with us, can confidently report that the Yucca event was a spectacular example of a dirty bomb as defined by the DOE.

"Tomorrow we will explore the how issue. I may have somewhat simplified how the event unfolded with my comparison to Grandma's pressure cooker. Scientists will fill in pertinent details.

"Meanwhile …"

Manics looked up and down the panel's table for any indications of objection, fully prepared to ignore them.

"… this panel is in recess until 9:00 AM tomorrow. Sleep well and be prepared for a lesson about how volcanoes behave when hot stuff meets water."

Manics and Barney shared a glance and a nod.

The single Whack! of oak on oak preceded Manics's "Until tomorrow."

As the room began to empty, he motioned Barney and Hank to come forward. Firm handshakes were exchanged.

"Dr. Shanks. And Dr. Thomas. Nice to meet you experts in the flesh. Thanks so much for agreeing to attend my hearing."

"Our pleasure, sir," was the simultaneous reply of a tenor and an alto.

"We hope we can provide useful input," Barney said.

"Tomorrow will be your first chance to do just that. I plan to devote most of that session to getting on record an explanation of the eruption and how it was able to cause as much havoc as it did. I recommend a good night's sleep before taking the stage tomorrow. See you then pardners."

With a farewell handshake and a wink to Barney, they went their separate ways.

17

MAARS AND MARS

Homophone: One of two words that sound the same but differ in meaning. For examples: Maars(Mars) want(wont) to(too, two) burrow(borough).

Saturday, August 21, 2027:

When Hank and Barney entered the A. Gore Conference Room at 8:45, Senator Manics waved them to the front. They weaved their way through a challenging obstacle course of people milling about before business got underway. At the front table, Manics reached across. The grip of his heavily callused hand was firm.

"Mornin' Barney. Hank."

"Good morning sir," they said.

"Have you two adjusted to the bustle and opportunities of Washington overnight?"

"We opted for a good night's sleep, thinking we'd want to be alert today," Barney replied.

"That was a darn good decision. When we get started, I'll give a bit of introduction. Then I'll call on you to explain the geology behind the Yucca disaster. Remember. Keep it simple. But accurate."

Barney and Hank nodded.

"I'll begin with you, Barney, for the volcano part of the story. If I think we need to get into what earthquakes had to do with the mess, I'll call on you Hank."

Another dual nod.

"Okay. Take your seats. It's time for the gavel."

Barney and Hank crossed the Fourth Estate dugout and sat, while Manics looked up and down the length of his table to be sure the entire congressional delegation was present. A glance at the witness table revealed familiar faces, with one obvious change. DOE Secretary Richard Heade was not present. Apparently his tender fanny needed a rest after yesterday's sizzling experience in the hot seat.

Further back, the public part of the room was filled to the brim. Today's proceedings would appear live on a big screen for other concerned citizens at a large nearby D.C. auditorium.

Whack! Whack! Whack!

"Good morning ladies and gentlemen. I realize that it's a bit unusual for Washington politicians to work on a weekend. But our business cannot wait on such artificial propriety. As we cowboys say on the range, 'cattle don't give a damn what day it is.' So, like responsible cowboys we're going forward on a daily basis until we've covered all the ground, rounded up any stray bits of pertinent information, and hogtied the core topics.

"Radioactive clocks are ticking in that new blanket of grit draped over the Las Vegas area. The water of Lake Mead is a lethal fissioning soup. So lethal that President Forty-Six decided to drain the reservoir. The plug at Hoover was pulled three days ago. To no one's surprise this triggered extreme political tension with Mexico. Our nation is dealing with a real-time disaster, not a piece of dusty history.

"Now to focus on our part of this business. Today we'll hear about the science behind the eruption that created all these problems. I think we all want a clear explanation of how our nation's nuclear waste became strewn across much of my beloved home state. To help us understand how this could happen, we'll hear from one of the world's foremost volcano experts. He's sitting right there."

Manics pointed at Barney, who waved a Churchillian V with his right hand.

"Let me give a brief biographical sketch of this man for the record."

Before beginning, Manics glanced at notes that he had nearly memorized the previous night.

"Barnabus Shanks was born in Huntington Beach. A coastal suburb of Los Angeles. It's been rumored that his mother thought her son came with webbed hands and feet, because he seemed to literally swim right out into the bright lights of the delivery room. One of the quickest and least painful births on record, apparently."

This personal note triggered a titter across the room.

"It should come as little surprise, then, that as soon as he could heft a surfboard, youngster Shanks was in the Pacific Ocean, trying to catch all of those mystical seventh waves. If you're interested, you can find a summary of his record as an international top-flight surfer in the Huntington Beach Surfing Museum. There are some pretty unusual accomplishments recorded there."

The senator from Wyoming harrumphed and waved his hand.

"Yes?" Manics said.

"Do we really want to waste valuable time listening to a homily about Dr. Shanks?" Castor said. "I suggest we stick to the serious business of Yucca."

"Yes. Yes of course, Senator. We should and will concentrate on the advertised agenda for this hearing."

Castor and Manics stared icily at each other as Manics said "My divergence into Dr. Shanks's watery early years carries a pertinent point."

Castor's visible exasperation softened a bit.

"The talented young surfer was not only about play. By his late teens, he came to realize that life would be incomplete without a challenging professional career. His adventuresome personality led him to the study of volcanoes.

"The kind of volcanoes that interact with water," Manics said slowly to add emphasis.

"Water, Senator Castor, is a key theme in this man's life. And water is extremely important to our understanding of what has transpired at Yucca Mountain.

"To keep a long and captivating story short, to the benefit of Senator Castor's patience, in 2003 Mr. Barnabus Shanks enrolled at the University of California at Santa Barbara. There he obtained a Doctorate of Philosophy in Geology, with high distinction. In a record time of three years, mind you."

Manics lifted the table microphone he was speaking into and retrieved a sheet of paper pinned there.

"The title of his dissertation is *Styles of Eruption at the Hopi Buttes Volcanic Field, Arizona*. And yes, Senator Castor, the Hopi Buttes area was a wet place when those volcanoes popped off."

Manics's words were accurate, but Barney was uneasy for all this laudatory attention. Barney understood that establishing the credentials of those giving testimony was important to the impact of Manics's eventual committee report. Still, if Barney knew how to blush, he would do so now.

"While obtaining his PhD, Mr. Shanks studied under Professor Ward E. Toomé, who was recognized as one of, if not *the* world's leading expert in the field of volcanic eruptions that occur in a wet environment."

Manics looked down the table at Castor.

"Here's that water theme yet again.

"Dr. Toomé is no longer with us. But we'll get the benefit of his brilliance through Shanks.

"Thesis completed, Dr. Shanks chose the private patch for employment. He's been a consultant for the past twenty-one years. His public record of professional accomplishments in this role is unparalleled. I imagine that there is an equally impressive confidential record of achievements in the service of satisfied clients.

"Of special interest to the business of our hearing, in 2024 he began a collaboration with Professor Henry Thomas of the California Institute of Technology. Dr. Thomas is an expert on earthquakes and is also here today."

Manics paused and motioned for Hank to stand and be formally recognized. Hank rose, steadied himself with his cane, did a slow three-sixty, and gingerly sat back down.

"For the past three years, this team of arguably the world's most talented volcanologist and seismologist has been working to keep tabs on the potential threat of a destructive earthquake or volcanic eruption impacting Yucca Mountain. They look for indicators in the field."

Castor loudly cleared his throat. Manics ignored him.

"Unfortunately, by the time their instruments showed reason for alarm, it was too late to do anything but try to minimize the damage. As I believe we all know, lives were lost underground at Yucca. Also in the surface outpost called the CO. Dr. Thomas himself was almost lost in the line of duty there."

Manics briefly glared at each of the panel members whose political party had pushed through final approval for waste storage at Yucca Mountain.

"Now, fortunately for those of us trying to understand the event that took those lives and destroyed the storage facility at Yucca, Dr. Shanks was on site, standing outside the CO with Dr. Thomas's wife Bonnie, from almost the very beginning of eruption.

"That was just six days ago. Feels like a century to me.

"He'll tell us what happened in language we can all understand. Even a cowboy."

Manics looked up and down the row of his panel colleagues for possible comments, though not actually wanting any. This was *his* show.

"So if no one objects. I yield the floor to Dr. Barnabus Shanks."

A hand gesture invited Barney to begin.

He cleared his throat and tugged at a constricting shirt collar. He was uncomfortable in a suit and tie but had been told that such attire was de rigueur at the hearing. Even Manics was suited up, his throat cinched by a bolo tie. Barney cleared his throat again and leaned closer to his microphone.

"First, I want to thank you Mr. Chairman for the opportunity to testify before your panel. It's quite an honor for a beach boy turned scientist to be in the presence of so much fame and wisdom.

"Second, and I hope I'm not out of line here, but I prefer to be called Barney. Barney Shanks. As the panel gets to know me better you may come to understand why my closest friends refer to me as old BS. I assure you, though, that my discussion of the science behind the Yucca eruption will not be BS."

Another wave of titter washed across the room. Barney was succeeding in getting most of this serious crowd relaxed.

"As I describe how the eruption at Yucca Mountain did such incredible damage, which we've all read about and seen photos of by now, I'll try to keep it as simple as you've requested. If that offends some of my learned academic colleagues, and it may, so be it."

Barney paused to organize his thoughts. He popped open the top button of his shirt, tugged at the knot of his tie for easier breathing, grabbed the wireless mike from its stand, stood facing the panel, and began.

"Think about champagne and maars."

Before he could utter a follow-up word, Senator Ruiz of New Mexico, who was a member of a congressional committee that oversaw the government's program of interplanetary-space travel and exploration, piped up.

"You can be sure the nation will be celebrating with champagne when our manned lander sets its pads on Mars."

Now that a human colony was established on the moon, putting people on Mars was in the crosshairs of the Buck Rogers gang. Barney gently interrupted.

"I'm sorry, Senator. I'm afraid I've caused some confusion. Your word and mine sound the same. But mine has a completely different meaning. I'll try again."

Barney spent a few more seconds in silent thought.

"Here we go. Think about the batch of molten rock that erupted at Yucca as a very very very large bottle of champagne that's been bouncing around in the back of a delivery van on its way to a celebration."

Barney outstretched his hands to illustrate the girth of a large container.

"Visualize a jeroboam of unimaginable size."

A brief pause helped listeners assimilate this information.

"Next, think of that bottle as being so hot that if it comes into contact with water, the water would instantly become steam."

He looked up and down the congressional panel.

"We know this wouldn't happen in real life. None of us would treat a bottle of champagne this way. But put your imaginations to work."

Nodding heads seemed to indicate that Barney was hitting the proper level of explanation.

"We know what would happen if that hot bounced-around humungous bottle was uncorked, don't we. Champagne would be spewed all over the place. Someone might even get a black eye, if he or she happened to be in the path of the cork missile."

Nodding heads again suggested that Barney was getting his message across.

"Okay. Now imagine what would happen if that way-hotter-than-boiling gigantic bottle of champagne was uncorked *while* immersed in a tub of water."

Barney waved his arms enthusiastically, tie now pulled so loose that curly chest hair peaked out the top of his shirt.

"We'd not only end up with champagne sprayed all over the place, we'd also have jets of steam shooting and hissing out of the tub! It would be a double whammy of a show. I guarantee that you wouldn't want to be standing close by, and not just because of a cork in wild flight."

He took a drink of water and gathered his thoughts about how best to segue from hot champagne in a tub of water to the eruption at Yucca.

"The situation at Yucca was similar. There were many cubic miles of molten rock called magma that represent the sizzling hot bottle of champagne. Both were saturated with gas. Magma always contains some gases. One is carbon dioxide. The same bubbly that gives champagne its fizz. Magma has others, too, that add to the fizz power of eruption.

"The innards of Yucca Mountain were wet with the rainwater that steadily percolates down into them in Nevada's present climate."

To help clarify the concept of percolation, Barney raised both of his arms, fingers extended up, and slowly lowered his hands while wiggling the fingers.

"So. Put gassy magma into the mountain, and we have a version of hot champagne in a rocky tub of water."

Barney kept sentences short and paused between them to help his verbal images register in the minds of his listeners.

"By the time the magma rose into the storage tunnels of Yucca, its gasses were fizzing off fast. The cork was just about out of the champagne bottle.

"When magma erupted at the surface, that cork was gone. As one of my volcano friends would say, Stand back! It's kablooey time!!"

He raised his hands overhead, extending fingers on the way up in the fashion of an expanding explosion.

"Graphic, Barney. Very graphic and understandable," Manics said. "You've given us a lot of information to think about. It's going on eleven and some of my best thinking is over a platter of victuals. I declare a lunch break. I want you to continue your story from the point of kablooey at exactly one PM."

Whack! Whack! Whack! "We are adjourned til then."

Barney and Hank found a bench on the National Mall where they sat to eat bag lunches brought from their hotel. Tourists strode by, business-like with guide books in hand, intent on visiting as many of DC's monuments and museums as possible before having to return home. Barney spotted the distinctive roofline of the Smithsonian Castle across the Mall, a building he had seen in photos. He thought about spending a few leisure days there after the hearing.

Nearby, teens played Frisbee on expansive plots of Mall grass, athletically dodging piles of dog poop left by inconsiderate pet walkers. Leaves on deciduous trees rimming the Mall showed hints of fall colors. Though a sunny August day, a chilly breeze carried the notion of an early end to summer.

Barney swallowed the last bite of a ham sandwich and wiped mustard from his chin. "How do you think it's going Hank?"

"Earthquakes are still shaking Yucca," Hank said as he studied information coming in on his computer. "But I'm pretty sure they're just the kind of small shakes that taper off after the end of any big eruption." His lunch sat uneaten.

"Forget that toy for a minute," Barney said. "What I *mean* is how do you think the hearing is going? You know. Am I getting the story across okay? Am I forgetting important stuff? Lecturing to Congress is kinda challenging. And heady! What's your take?"

Hank looked up slowly from his computer screen. "My take is that you are doing fine. That Manics is delighted with your testimony.

"My take is that I don't know what the H I'm doing here. Except that an invitation from the senator is a command performance.

"My take is that I'm more than ready to go home."

"Wait a minute," Barney said. "What's your gripe? It's not like I'm trying to monopolize the science testimony. Manics asked me to speak. So I did. I'd happily yield the floor to you. But that's not my call."

Hank was again watching his computer screen.

"Put that thing away would you," Barney said.

Hank complied. "Look Barney," he said, "you seem to enjoy what's happening. I'm happy for you. And you're doing great at describing the eruption story, judging by the reactions of the panel and public observers. But my passion is with pure science with all its precise technical terms. Giant jeroboams. Kablooey. Are you kidding?

"And I prefer teaching motivated graduate students. I do not enjoy diluting science with partisan politics. Sure. That happens and maybe it has to sometimes. But given a choice, I'll always opt out of that sewer."

Hank looked at Barney with a sad-puppy expression.

"I'm serious about being ready to go home. My leg hurts, and believe it or not, this monogamous guy misses his one and only human love."

Barney laughed. "Touché Hank. You may not believe *this*, but I'm starting to understand what you mean about a one and only."

Barney threw an arm around Hank's shoulder and hugged. They shared a friendly smile.

"Hey. We'd better get going. The gavel is scheduled to fall in fifteen minutes."

Whack! Whack! Whack!

"We'll get back underway with testimony from Barney," Manics said. "We left his volcanic tale of this morning with hot gassy magma moving up into and through the water-saturated rocks of Yucca Mountain. The word kablooey comes to mind. Please continue from there Barney."

Barney stood. "The eruption story gets more complicated now. At the risk of seeming silly beyond hot champagne, I'll take you to your mother's kitchen where she has laid out the ingredients for a dynamite dish."

Barney heard a soft sigh from Hank, but continued with his home-spun version of the eruption.

"Senator Manics just reminded us of the two starting ingredients for the eruption. And from that short and simple list you might reasonably expect a single uniform result. But no way! Like mother's delicacy about to be assembled, our eruption went through very different phases as the ingredients became more thoroughly mixed together and had time to interact."

"Here we go again Senator Manics," Castor said, without asking for the floor. "I came here to be educated about the science of the volcano that destroyed Yucca Mountain. Not about the culinary practices of family kitchens."

"You may have a point," Manics said. "I'm not sure what trail Barney is taking us down. But I'm going to follow him until I find it of no use to our panel.

"Barney. Proceed."

"Thank you Senator Manics," Barney said, flashing a quick grin in his direction.

"The recipe for my eruption hot dish involves three sequential phases that result from how the ingredients behave as they intermingle and age.

"Phase one is called a *curtain of fire*. This was the time when lava spewed from a fissure along the crest of Yucca Mountain. It surged up about two thousand feet. Most splashed back to earth and gathered into flows that spilled down gullies on the flanks of Yucca.

"The lone ingredient for phase one was gassy magma. The fiery curtain was powered entirely by gas fizzing off into the air, carrying lava with it. I have a picture to show you."

Barney turned to the back of the room. "If the projectionist would please show the first image."

Lights dimmed and an oblique aerial photograph appeared on the white wall behind the congressional panel. Predictable ooohs and gasps were heard from people who had never before seen such an eruption scene.

"This shows Hawaii's Kilauea Volcano erupting in nineteen seventy-one.

"The crest of Yucca Mountain looked like this just six days ago. The hot curtain held steady for nine hours. Until about noon that day. Lights please.

"Then another ingredient got into the act. Ordinary water. The stuff that the mountain was saturated with. When this water *mixed* with magma, powerful steam bursts began to blast Yucca to pieces.

"This is phase two. The technical term is *phreatomagmatic eruption*. It's simpler, easier to pronounce, if we call it the *steam blast phase*.

"The blasts worked like a giant drill, breaking the ground by fits and starts. Burrowing deeper and deeper into Yucca. Eventually, the canisters of radioactive waste got caught up in the action and were blown out with lava. When they broke, their deadly contents were carried away by the wind blowing straight toward Las Vegas."

Barney's arms were aflutter in animated lecture mode. He paced about and spoke as much with various body parts as with his voice.

"I'm not sure why phase two began hours into the eruption instead of sooner. Could be that it took that much time for magma surging through the mountain to break up the guts of Yucca enough for the groundwater and magma to mix in explosive proportions. That's my best guess. Whatever. Steam blasts happened."

As he spoke, Barney recalled the dry desert of Nevada that early European settlers had discovered and had to live with for centuries before climate change provided much more of the scarce ingredient for an easier life. Easier, but now deadly.

"Isn't climate change a bummer!" Barney said. "If the mountain hadn't been saturated with groundwater, the eruption might have been far less destructive.

"Finally, after six hours of the steam blasts, the eruption entered its third phase. Lava started to ooze out like syrup slowly squeezed from a tube. It built up layer upon layer of lava flows that eventually covered what was left of Yucca Mountain. Even the CO outpost.

"Project my second image please," Barney said. "This photo was also taken at Kilauea. Just a garden variety lava flow adding one more layer to an already thick stack of basalt.

"The switch to quiet lava flows at Yucca happened because the water ingredient of the eruption recipe was all boiled away. No more steam blasts. At the same time, the magma literally ran out of gas. No more fizz."

Barney sat, feeling too fizzed out himself to offer a comprehensive concluding wrap-up of his story, rather than ending with: "So that's what we think happened."

"Thank you Barney," Manics said. "I think your explanation of the eruption and how it evolved is clear enough. I hope my colleagues up here agree. Any questions from my committee colleagues?"

"Yes. I have one for Barney," Senator Ruiz said. "You mentioned that if today's climate in Nevada wasn't so wet the eruption might have been less destructive. I got the impression that we might not have this current mess on our hands if Yucca Mountain was still in the middle of good old Nevada desert. Is that what you meant?"

Barney feared that the past three decades of the politics of climate change were about to rear their ugly head. Political science versus honest science had simmered and boiled over repeatedly during those times … times when global warming was underway, yet irregularly enough for the long-term trend to be arguable. Barney had little interest in replowing that old field today. He also didn't want to leave the senator's question unanswered.

"I wish I had a short pat answer for you, Senator Ruiz. But the honest answer is that I can't be sure what would have happened if the mountain had been dry. The reason I'm not sure is because really gassy magma started the eruption at Yucca.

"There are places around the world where geologists have discovered chaotic volcanic formations called pipes. These are basically the throats of volcanoes that are filled with busted up rock. Geologists believe these formed by the explosive degassing of bubbly magma. Some of the pipes are thousands of feet deep.

"So you see with such gassy magma at Yucca, the eruption might have drilled down to the canisters even if the mountain hadn't been water saturated. We'll never know."

Ruiz nodded, ready to move on.

"Let's go back to the maars I mentioned earlier," Barney said.

He leafed through his prepared statement and held up a page.

"If you haven't read my testimony, you won't know that my maars is spelled *m a a r s*. It's German slang for lake. In geology it refers to a certain kind of volcanic crater that's partly filled with a lake. As Senator Manics has correctly pointed out, water is an important theme today."

"What's a German lake got to do with our business?" Castor said, again interrupting without first asking Manics for the floor. "Barney is sounding like a slick lawyer on a diversionary tangent."

Manics ignored Castor and motioned Barney to proceed.

"There's a place in Germany called the Eifel District where volcanoes with crater lakes dot the landscape. Decades ago, geologists concluded that violent steam blast eruptions were responsible for making the craters. It's where this kind of volcano was first recognized and named maar."

"This is interesting if you're a geology student," Castor said. "But we are here to discuss the tragedy at Yucca Mountain, not to listen to a primer on volcanoes of Germany."

Manics weighed in. "Yes. I agree Senator. But I want Barney to continue. I suspect that what seems off the point to you will help us better understand what happened at Yucca."

Manics nodded to Barney.

"The connection is that phase two at Yucca was a maar eruption. That's the phase that excavated the canisters and caused all the grief."

"Oh?" Castor said. "Where's the crater? Where's the lake?"

"There was actually a line of several craters active at the same time," Barney said. "Phase three of the eruption filled and buried them. So of course we can't see any craters or lakes.

"Let's go back to the idea of eruption ingredients. Each eruption at Eifel ran out of magma before it ran out of water. So groundwater seeped into the Eifel craters.

"At Yucca, eruption ran out of water before it ran out of magma. And we're damn lucky it did, or all the action after the curtain of fire might have been incredibly violent. Instead of changing to the pretty benign phase that produced the large mound of lava flows."

Barney traced the shape of the new volcanic mountain with a gently arching lateral sweep of his hands. Manics spoke before Castor could interrupt yet again.

"Barney. Let me recap some of what you've told us so far to be sure we understand. You've given us an awfully big mouthful of oats to chew on.

"My notion is that if I were to visit the Eifel today, what I'd see would look entirely different from Yucca Mountain. Yet you tell us that the very same kind of eruption occurred at both places."

"Yes. And yes. And you've described one of the biggest challenges faced by geologists," Barney said. "Being expected to assemble an entire picture when pieces of the puzzle are missing. It's true that the Eifel landscape looks nothing like that at Yucca. Another difference to keep in mind is that no one watched and took notes during the Eifel eruptions. What happened there has been cobbled together through careful study of the products of the eruptions."

A surge of déjà vu swept over Barney. He was back at UC Santa Barbara defending his PhD research to a group of skeptical professors.

"Is there any uncertainty in the geologic explanation for the origin of the Eifel lakes? Of course. Many pieces of that puzzle are missing. But top-flight volcano experts stake their reputations on what I've described for you.

"Now. If a geologist who knew nothing in advance about the eruption at Yucca were to visit a decade or two from now, he or she might conclude that the eruption had been nothing more than a calm extrusion of magma that built up that big mound of basalt that covers the mountain. Talk about missing puzzle pieces!"

Barney sensed that he was losing his audience in technicalities important only to geologists. It was time to get back to basics.

"Anyone could discover the Yucca maars if they drilled at the right spot. Still, I hope you understand my point about the difficulties of assembling a completely accurate picture of almost any geologic puzzle."

Senator Castor was becoming increasingly interested in Barney's testimony as the notions of *hypothetical* this, *maybe* that, and *my best guess about* cropped up. Castor was still pissed about the embarrassment Manics had heaped on Secretary Heade yesterday by pointing out that Heade could not cite one instance of a dirty bomb being deployed, even though the DOE was happy to provide a very detailed description of this weapon. It was time to throw the hypothetical crap back into Manics's lap, with Shanks doing the pitching.

"If I may be recognized," Castor said. "I want to follow up a bit before Barney moves on."

Manics nodded. "You have the floor."

"Barney has provided us with a very detailed description of a maar volcano. How it erupts and what the landscape looks like at the end. But it strikes me that this is all too hypothetical. It seems that understanding a maar volcano comes from studies long after the eruptions. As Barney has emphasized, there's substantial uncertainty in assembling the complete picture with pieces of the puzzle missing.

"So, to paraphrase the Chair's question posed yesterday to Secretary Heade vis-à-vis a dirty bomb. Could Barney please describe a specific example of an observed erupting maar volcano to corroborate his description of the ideal, but hypothetical version?"

Castor's gotcha feel-good facial expression lasted barely halfway into the first sentence of Barney's reply, and quickly turned into an inward groan.

"I can provide detailed information, written and photographic, of a nineteen seventy-seven maar eruption," Barney said. "It happened near the tip of the Alaskan Peninsula. At a place called Ukinrek. I forgot to show a photo of this to illustrate the action of phase two at Yucca. Let's do that right now."

The image of an angry dark eruption cloud billowing up from a deep circular crater turned a flat white wall into a portrait of hell.

"The photo was taken by Richard Russell from a small airplane. A steady wind kept the ash cloud away from his plane."

"A couple other maar eruptions occurred during the nineteen fifties. One in Chile and another in the western Pacific, for example. All it takes is that potent mix of magma and water."

Manics and Barney exchanged an innocent-looking loaded glance as Barney continued his description.

"The lives of a few grizzlies were probably disturbed at Ukinrek. But the eruption site was so remote that no people or buildings were harmed."

Had it been audible, Castor's reaction of disappointment could have come from the throat of a wounded grizzly.

"Two craters were blasted out. Groundwater seeped into one to form a lake, exactly as the hypothetical model developed at the Eifel maars said would happen. It's still there today if anyone wants to visit.

"Please project the last slide."

The image of a pristine emerald lake appeared. Its calm surface and clear-air setting belied the lake's violent origin.

"The other crater was too shallow to intersect the water table. It's just an empty hole in the ground."

"Excellent! Excellent, Barney," Manics said. "It's evident that, unlike DOE's version of dirty bombs, maar volcanoes and the character of their eruptions are in the record of human observations, rather than some hypothetical construct of political convenience. Do you agree Senator Castor?"

"Yup."

"Then I propose that we wrap up today's session by revisiting my suggestion of yesterday that the phase of the eruption that spread radioactive dust over the landscape was like Grandma's pressure cooker gone out of control. Barney. I'd like to hear your thoughts about my analogy."

Barney stayed seated and spoke slowly.

"I think the comparison is valid, Senator Manics. But as you pointed out yesterday, one must *think big*. I'll try to do that now.

"To steer back into that murky realm of the hypothetical, let me speculate that were it not for the fact that Yucca Mountain was saturated with downward percolating rainfall, the eruption *might* have left all of the canisters right where they were in the system of storage tunnels. It *might* have helped seal them even more securely by enveloping them in a tight wrapping of hard solid lava, once the magma ran out of gas.

"In other words, if not for the new wetter climate of the region, which has likely been caused by the huge increase of carbon dioxide added to Earth's atmosphere since the onset of the industrial revolution in the late nineteenth century, the eruption at Yucca Mountain might not have created the problem that beleaguers our country today."

Barney had hoped to stay away from this politically charged topic, but he was now talking about his utmost passion as a scientist and as a concerned inhabitant of planet Earth. After assembling all available pieces of the complex climate-change puzzle that he could find, he had concluded years earlier that humans were major contributors to what was happening weather-wise. But he also understood the considerable uncertainties behind his conclusion. After all, Earth was known to have gone through many wild climate swings, long before any individual of the arrogantly self-named *Homo sapiens* variety of life had arrived on the scene. Barney wanted to tell the world what he believed from this highly visible platform, but he didn't want to come across as just another rabid preacher.

"I'm not talking about an effect of climate change as bizarre and unlikely as the story told by that two-thousand-four movie, *The Day After Tomorrow*. No serious and competent scientist believed that story line. But I am talking about an effect of climate change that might have been considered very highly improbable when experts were assessing the potential for a volcanic eruption to impact Yucca Mountain. What we have seen is that highly improbable events can and do occur. It's a lesson to remember and pass on to future generations."

Fourth Estate folks soaked up Barney's closing words about climate change, rain, eruption at Yucca Mountain and improbable events. Some would report that Barney's string of cause-and-effect building blocks created a structure that is the result of decades of unbridled and uncontrolled human interference with Nature's atmosphere. Others would report that the activities of humans had nothing to do with climate change. Uncertainties in both story lines would keep the debate lively for decades into the future.

"Barney, I have one last question for you," Manics said. "Simply put, why now? Why was there an eruption at Yucca Mountain on August fifteen of this year? If there had to be an eruption there, why couldn't the darned thing have waited for a few generations, thousands of years or longer? The way mankind treats Earth, there might not be any people around to be bothered by then."

"I don't know the answer," Barney said without hesitation. "And if any geologist claims to know, that person is a liar. Volcano experts are pretty good at recognizing signs of unrest at volcanoes. Things like telltale patterns of earthquakes. How the surface of the ground swells when molten rock pushes upward. And so forth. But these are symptoms of an eruption that is already on its way. Not one that might happen at some inconvenient future time.

"It's useful to know about the signs of unrest so folks can be advised to stand clear. This kind of eruption forecast has saved a lot of people and their possessions. But it's a different challenge when you are asked to predict an eruption for a place that shows no signs of unrest. Especially if that place is a mountain like Yucca, which has never been the site of a volcanic eruption. There have been some a few miles away, but not right at Yucca.

"He_ _ ... that is heck, I'm not even sure that my airline flight will get me safely back to California later this week. And we know a whole lot about what makes a plane safely airworthy. So how could I possibly know that an eruption will or won't occur at some spot tomorrow, to say nothing about thousands of years in the future?

"I must sound defeatist. But I won't pretend to be able to do something I know I can't. In a sense my entire career has been a failure. I've spent much of my adult life trying to unveil the secrets to eruption prediction, and have failed to do so."

Manics had heard enough for the day. "Thank you Barney for your illuminating explanation of the eruption at Yucca," he said. "We have now covered the what and the how bases of our agenda. I want the record to show that magma-engendered steam explosions destroyed the Yucca storage site and in so doing unleashed a very large and deadly dirty bomb.

"Tomorrow we will explore the question of why this situation was allowed to happen. Specifically, why was Yucca Mountain selected as the site for burial of radioactive waste if it was thought to be even slightly prone to volcanic eruption. And a maar type of eruption at that."

Whack! Whack! Whack! "We stand adjourned until nine o'clock tomorrow morning."

Manics beckoned to Barney and Hank as the room began to empty. "Very nice job, Barney. Sorry we didn't get into the earthquake part of the story, Hank, but it didn't seem necessary after Barney's volcano stuff."

"That was fine with me sir," Hank said.

"I think you two should get out and enjoy the sights and tastes of Washington tonight. Tomorrow's hearing will be my show. You can relax."

In their hotel room that night, Hank told Barney that he was returning to California on the earliest morning flight that had space.

"Give Senator Manics whatever excuse you want for my departure. Tell him my leg hurts. My dad had a heart attack. Whatever. Truth is I detest being part of this science for politicians show. I'm an unnecessary witness for providing the information Manics wants. I feel like a dunce, just sitting there, and he's not going to call on me anyway."

Barney started to say something about that situation, but was cut off.

"Like I told you at lunch," Hank said, "no hard feelings between us. We'll huddle when you get back west to figure out if we might have a future project with the NRC."

"Okay Hank. Go home, relax, and don't worry. I'll give Manics a convincing explanation for your absence. He said he plans to do most of the talking tomorrow anyway.

"More important—give Bonnie a hug for me. Tell her I'm starting to admire the relationship you two have."

When Barney awoke at sunrise the next morning, Hank was gone.

18

WHY YUCCA MOUNTAIN?

***"No one** lives on Yucca Mountain."* A reason that Yucca Mountain was selected for long-term storage of the nation's high-level radioactive waste, as explained in a U.S. Department of Energy Fact Sheet.

Sunday, August 22, 2027:

Barney entered the conference room at 8:45 and waved for Manics's attention. They huddled in a front corner.

"Mornin' Barney."

"Good morning Jack," Barney replied. He extended a right hand, prepared for a finger-crushing grip.

"Where's your sidekick? Did you two paint the town so bright last night that Hank's head is throbbing?"

"Nope. Nothing that exciting. Instead, we had a heart-to-heart chat. Hank said he was going home."

"Home?"

"Yeah. Home," Barney said. "As in Pasadena. He's probably somewhere over Colorado right now."

Barney looked down at his feet, hesitant.

"I told him it was okay. That you would understand."

Manics nodded.

"Sure. Enough said. I want both of you to critique my panel's report before it goes upstairs. But that can be done in California. Hope I haven't made an enemy of Hank."

"No, it's nothing like that. He wants to get back to pure science within the comfortable halls of academia. He misses his wife a lot, too. They're the original joined-at-the-hip velcro couple."

"Good for them. This country could use more behavior like that. We've got too damn many folks who think they should ride a different mount every day. I can tell you from personal experience that a regular smooth ride is priceless. I've had one wife and four horses in my life."

Manics's smile went taciturn. Barney thought he saw tears forming.

"Would have been just one horse too. A beautiful sixteen-hand pinto named Torlof. If only those animals lived as long as a human."

Manics took a deep breath and exhaled a sigh.

"Give Hank and his wife my best when you see them. Meanwhile, it's time for our business. Relax and watch. I hope to have some serious fun today."

They took their seats.

Whack! Whack! Whack!

The sharp crack of oak on oak brought the third session of the Manics committee to order promptly at 9:00 AM. The head of DOE was present as requested. The pit for the Fourth Estate was full of anxiously waiting reporters. Public rubbernecks filled the back of the room and the remote auditorium where proceedings would again be shown live.

"Good morning ladies and gentlemen," Manics said. "Welcome to our third, and I anticipate final Yucca Mountain hearing.

"In our earlier two sessions, we covered the *what* and *how* of the disaster. In brief, as a reminder for anyone with a weak memory, the *what* is a dirty bomb. The *how* is the vivid description of what our volcano expert Barney calls an incredibly explosive phreatomagmatic eruption."

Manics briefly looked at Barney.

"I reckon that *phreatomagmatic* has become and will remain a word common to most personal vocabularies a long time into the future. When I start to hear it around cowboy campfires back home, I'll know it's become a truly American word."

Manics shuffled through some papers.

"Today we will deal with the *why*. Why was Yucca Mountain selected as the storage site for the nation's high-level radioactive waste? There's a long convoluted history behind choosing that place. I'll be including pertinent government documents in the official file of our hearings to document that zigzag path to Yucca."

Manics spoke slowly and deliberately. He was in no hurry. He anticipated hearing testimony that would provide ammunition for many *I told you so's*. He planned to be sitting on a bundle of new political capital by the end of the day.

"Nevertheless," he continued, "I think it's important that we all hear an oral summary of the decision-making process. To know the benchmarks that led to the selection. We can now say the *unfortunate* selection of Yucca Mountain.

"I've asked DOE Secretary Heade and his counterpart at the NRC to provide such a summary. I'm advised that Mr. Heade will do the honors. Without further ado, I yield the floor to the DOE Secretary."

Heade looked as ill at ease as he had two days earlier during his bumbling exposé on dirty bombs. He planned to fare better personally today. He had excelled at memorizing key dates of history as a college student. Julius Caesar crossing the Rubicon with his army in 49 BC; issuance of the Magna Carta in 1215 AD; the congress of the thirteen colonies adopting the Declaration of Independence on July 4, 1776, and so forth. He was well prepared today with a list of historic government actions and when they occurred to explain how Yucca Mountain had been selected.

"Thank you, Senator Manics, for the opportunity to describe the steps in this selection process. My prepared statement includes a timeline plot that identifies government actions that led the nation to Yucca. I'll speak to a graphic of this projected on the wall."

Lights were dimmed and the image appeared.

"Here are the key events in the order they happened. Left to right."

Heade remained seated as he began what he hoped would be an acceptable, to Manics, dry litany. He highlighted item one with a laser pointer.

"The Nuclear Waste Policy Act became law in 1982. This established the nation's plan for the disposal of spent nuclear fuel and other high-level radioactive waste. The roles of the Department of Energy, the Environmental Protection Agency, and the Nuclear Regulatory Commission were spelled out in that legislation.

"With Senator Manics's permission, I won't bore everyone with the details of how these three key agencies interact. Complete information is in my prepared statement."

Manics nodded his assent.

"There was early consensus for establishing an underground geologic storage repository. Initially, multiple sites were considered. For example, places in Washington State and New Mexico were on the list, in addition to Yucca Mountain in Nevada. Preliminary studies of all sites got underway."

Heade adjusted the aim of his pointer to the next label on his timeline.

"Congress amended the Nuclear Waste Policy Act in 1987. The most important change was that DOE was directed to evaluate only Yucca Mountain. All other candidate sites were removed from consideration."

"Much to the relief of folks in Washington and New Mexico," Manics said.

"Yes, I suppose so," Heade agreed.

"Amen," Senator Ruiz added.

"In my state, this change is known as the 'Screw Nevada' bill," Manics said.

Heade quickly moved the laser beam to the next event. "In 1992," he said, "Congress passed the Energy Policy Act. This directed the EPA to adopt specific safety standards for Yucca Mountain. The standards were established by panels of experts in the National Academy of Sciences. DOE-sponsored studies would evaluate Yucca in terms of these standards. The NRC would be the judge of whether the standards were met before issuing a waste-storage permit."

"Mr. Heade," Manics said, "you've reminded me of a point I forgot to make yesterday. Both Barnabus Shanks and Henry Thomas are members of the National Academy of Sciences. If it wasn't already obvious, these two are among the nation's brightest. We're fortunate to have their input to our proceedings.

"Excuse me," Manics said as he checked the time. "I need to make a couple of calls. We'll reconvene in twenty minutes."

Manics was impatient with Heade's testimony. The information so far was important for the record. But it wasn't material that could be thrown back at those responsible for approving Yucca. He would direct Heade onto a more useful track after a break. He disappeared into a private office and dozed in a comfortable reclining chair.

Whack! Whack! Whack! reverberated across the room twenty minutes later.

"Mr. Secretary. Your excellent summary has led us to the point where we are anxious to hear about how the safety standards were evaluated. How this process resulted in the issuance of a license to store waste at Yucca. Tell us about the DOE studies that justified that license."

Heade cleared his throat and moved to less firm footing in his presentation.

"Well, there are basically three potential hazards that all parties to this approval process agree must be addressed."

He paused, remembering a fourth hazard. "Actually, there's another hazard. The potential for terrorists to compromise a storage site. If we can agree that this hazard exists anywhere storage might occur, I suggest we consider only the natural hazards. These are the factors for which the EPA has adopted standards."

"That's fine," Manics said.

"Number one is corrosion-caused leakage of waste that would percolate downward and contaminate the regional groundwater resource. Number two is physical damage that might cause leakage of waste as a result of earthquakes. Number three is damage and potential leakage as a result of volcanic eruption."

Heade was moving to the topic that Manics wanted to explore.

"Nearly three decades of scientific studies showed that EPA standards were met for the first two hazards," Heade said.

"Agreed," Manics said. "Now what about the hazard that brought us to this hearing?"

Heade continued by pointing his laser to the year 2000. He spoke more slowly and deliberately. "The results of the studies addressing the volcanic hazard were somewhat problematical. Problematical but not serious enough to derail the project."

"Explain what you mean by problematical," Manics said.

"I just mean the results were not as clear-cut as those for canister corrosion and earthquakes."

"Stop right there," Manics said. "I know that the volcano results did not meet the EPA-adopted standard. That fact is in print. It's in the public domain. A panel of the nation's top volcano experts, ably guided by Dr. Vincent Gordon, found the volcanic hazard to be greater than the EPA standard."

Heade wrinkled his nose and tugged on an earlobe.

"Yes. Technically. Strictly speaking you are correct," Heade said.

Manics's gut tightened in a surge of energy. "Technically? Strictly speaking? What kind of weasel response is that? You know that an EPA standard for the volcanic hazard exists. The public record shows that the Yucca site does not measure up to this standard. And you seriously propose that some technicality can contradict such a clear undisputed conclusion?"

The Fourth Estate hummed to life as Heade stumbled and became defensive.

"The nation desperately needed a storage site," Heade said. "The finding of the volcano panel was so extremely close to an acceptable result that my predecessor at DOE quite reasonably recommended to President Forty-Three that an application for a storage license at Yucca could go forward. It was for the good of the country."

"Quite reasonably?" Manics said. "So close, you say! We're not playing horseshoes are we?"

"No, but ..."

"Let the record show that I see nothing whatsoever reasonable with this action by Secretary Heade's predecessor. This story sounds like the fiction that a lady can be just a little bit pregnant. You know. So close to not being pregnant that no one should worry about the consequences to follow."

Manics formed his best philosophical facial expression. "If this was an act for the good of the country, I shudder to think what an act of malice might be."

"Senator. If you'll grant me the courtesy of continuing."

"Go ahead with your fairy tale," Manics said.

"In light of the DOE recommendation, notwithstanding the results from the panel of volcano experts, President Forty-Three concluded that the Yucca site was potentially suitable for waste storage. As expected, the governor of Nevada objected to this conclusion. The political process was played out when the Senate voted sixty to thirty-nine to override Nevada's objection. So you see all necessary steps were followed."

"The *political* steps were followed," Manics said. "At the expense of science."

"License was granted to DOE by the NRC," Heade said, "and the nation's high-level radioactive waste was safely stored within Yucca Mountain by the year 2025."

"Safely? Do you really think that *safely* is an appropriate word given what has happened to my dear state of Nevada?"

"Not in hindsight. No. But at the time the storage chambers were filled and sealed, safely was an accurate description," Heade said, lapsing into thought.

Maybe history is more than a litany of sterile isolated facts. I never was good at interpreting the significance of historical events. I got the dates right, but when it came to essay exams, my blue books came back with a large red shovel drawn across the lead page.

Maybe the EPA safety standard for a volcano threat was like the Declaration of Independence … a clear statement not to be loosely interpreted? I guess Caesar was worried about more than wet feet when he crossed the Rubicon. Maybe the Yucca okay driven by politics was another risky river crossing.

Manics stood, for the first time at these hearings, to address Heade and the entire gathering. His six-foot-six frame loomed as large as his deep voice.

"The problem I have with your tale, Mr. Secretary, is that the final steps in the process you have described lacked scientific rigor. Also plain old honesty and foresight. Your mention of hindsight is nothing more than a transparent attempt to cover some misguided hindquarters … the butts of those who had apparently decided on an answer before the critical tests of storage suitability had been completed.

"What the nation deserved during the evaluation process was honest foresight. The foresight to have faith in the scientific method. The foresight to rely on the wisdom and knowledge of the nation's best. The men and women who are the National Academy of Science. Those who established a standard that was compromised by the administration of President Forty-Three and a spineless Congress. The foresight to put hard-nosed science above political convenience.

"I've lost my appetite for hearing any more of the sorry story of how Yucca got its license. We'll take a lunch break and reconvene at two."

Whack! Whack! Whack!

Barney returned to his hotel room and placed a call to his Isla Vista home. He was about to give up when her familiar voice sounded.

"Hello."

"Heather," Barney said. "Heather, I was afraid you wouldn't be there. Well, you know."

"Uh huh. But you apparently still don't," she said. "I was in the shower when the phone rang. I've been sleeping in your bed, or maybe I can call it *our* bed, every night since you went back to D.C. You left me here when you headed east. And you'll find me here when you come home."

"I like the sound of that. There's a lot I want to talk about. But not over the phone."

"Like I said. I'll be here. Just show up. How are the hearings going?"

"The hearings are fine. It's interesting to watch Senator Manics operate. He's bright. Knows what he wants. And knows how to get it. We've kinda bonded. I hope you can meet him someday."

"Did you know you were on national TV news last night?"

"Nope. Instead of watching the news, Hank and I had a serious talk. Bottom line is that he left for home this morning. Why don't you give Bonnie a call? You know. Have a woman to woman chat to be sure all is okay. Hank was very disgusted with mixing politics and science at the hearing. I imagine he's happily back in his classroom by now."

"I'll call Bonnie this afternoon. I have to get going. I'm teaching in half an hour, and I shouldn't show up in my birthday suit."

Heather pulled the phone from her ear as a loud animal grrrrrr came through. "See you soon I hope," she said.

"Tomorrow night, I think. Get dressed and wow your students."

While Barney and Heather were whetting their appetites for getting serious, Manics was devouring a sixteen-ounce steak with all the trimmings. He wanted to be fully fueled for a feisty afternoon.

Whack! Whack! Whack!

"It's time to come to order once again ladies and gentlemen. Unless an unexpected surprise pops up in the next hour or so, this afternoon's session will wrap up the hearings of the committee. Secretary Heade's testimony this morning has partly addressed the *why* question of the committee's agenda. As the lead person here I will now add my thoughts about *why*."

Manics stood, tugged on the large silver medallion of his bolo tie and launched into a lecture he had planned from the day his committee first took form.

"Secretary Heade has reminded us of how political expediency trumped science on the road to approving Yucca."

Heade raised his hand and spoke before Manics could continue. "Sir. You are misrepresenting my testimony. I did not say that politics trumped science."

"Not in those exact words," Manics said. "But it doesn't take an Ivy League education to understand the truth behind your explanation of why Yucca was approved.

"Now you will hear my version of the story. I'm going to start with some of the DOE literature that has had wide distribution for many years. For the record, I'll be referring to Fact Sheet DOE/YMP-0026. It's filled with pure propaganda that has been passed off as fact for way too long. The political shenanigans that Mr. Heade has described took place shortly after this two-page document appeared. The DOE was cleared to prepare a license application for the NRC, and the fission express was barreling down the tracks. On its path to a catastrophic wreck."

Manics asked an assistant to project that DOE document on the front wall.

"Look at this pitiful stuff."

His red laser light zeroed in on the first bullet item in the section headed *Why Yucca Mountain*. Manics read the sentence.

"Yucca Mountain is about one hundred miles northwest of Las Vegas, Nevada, on land owned by the federal government."

He turned to stare at Heade.

"The distance to Las Vegas may have been accurate when this rag was printed, if the reference point was the city's south boundary. But there's been a bit of growth in Vegas hasn't there Mr. Heade? It's more like fifty miles between Yucca and Vegas today."

"Yes. I agree," Heade said.

"Of course the reason for mentioning the distance is to make readers believe that Vegas is far enough away from Yucca to be safe from any problem with the radioactive waste. That notion turned out to be pure BS didn't it?"

"Yes. But...."

"I agree that it's convenient that Yucca is federally owned land," Manics said. "But that's hardly a compelling reason to bury the waste there. Last time I checked land ownership maps, the feds owned a lot of real estate around the country. I believe there's a land acquisition process called eminent domain, too."

"Yes. That's correct. But …"

"A little louder with your comments sir," Manics said.

"My answer is yes."

The laser beam and Manics's attention moved to item two, which he read in the voice of someone unfamiliar with English.

"No one lives at Yuc ca Moun tain."

Manics looked down the table to his fellow Nevada legislators.

"Do you agree with that statement Senator Luchs? Representatives Billings and Pepper?"

"As of my most recent visit last month that was so," Luchs said, wearing a bemused expression.

"Ditto," Pepper said.

"I'd have to agree, too" Billings said. "Unless someone was living in the underground tunnels."

"Score one for the Fact Sheet," Manics said. "Truth in advertising. Of course it would seem to be an act of the lowest level of common sense to not construct a dump for radioactive waste within a subdivision. I hope the DOE didn't spend too much of the taxpayer's money to figure this out.

"Besides. No one *could* live at Yucca Mountain if they wanted to. It's part of the Nevada Test Site where all sorts of dangerous military experiments have occurred for decades. Right up to the present. Divine Strakes. Heavenly Strakes. What-will-they-think-of-next Strakes. Do you agree?"

"Yes," Heade said.

A few laughs and groans came from the back of the room.

"Quiet please folks, while I finish reviewing this infantile document."

Manics aimed his laser to the next statement and read.

"The area has a very dry climate." He held out his hands, palms up, as though feeling for the splat of raindrops.

"This bit of information certainly dates the Fact Sheet, doesn't it! I suppose climate has a diabolical mind of its own, to have changed so much during the past couple of decades when certain politicians and a few so-called expert scientists said that it would never happen."

Heade sat quietly as Manics continued his lecture.

"Why does climate matter anyway?" Manics asked rhetorically. "Here's the DOE explanation."

The laser beam moved to the final item on the list. Manics read:

"The dry climate is an important feature because water is the primary way by which radioactive material could move from a repository.

"Hmmm," Manics said, placing his chin on a fist as if in deep thought. "I'm not sure what this statement means. It might lead an average reader to believe that radioactive garbage won't move if you put it in a desert environment. Or maybe it means that waste would first move in water before being sent on its merry way by other non-primary movers. Can you enlighten us Mr. Heade?"

"No."

"Louder, for the record please."

"No!"

"As we heard from Barney yesterday," Manics said, "climate was a key ingredient in the destruction of the repository at Yucca. Water in the mountain was important. But it seems to me that erupting magma, not water, was the *primary* mover of the bad stuff. Would you agree Mr. Heade?"

"Yes."

"I must conclude that DOE has misled the public by distributing thousands and thousands of these fliers. I've brought hundreds of them today in case anyone here wants a copy. They're nothing more than propaganda rags."

Manics motioned to aides who offered copies to the Fourth Estate and people in the back of the room.

Heade couldn't think of a defendable counterpoint to Manics's diatribe against the selection of Yucca.

"Now for the record," Manics said, "I'm going to tell you why I think Yucca was selected.

"First. Yucca Mountain is part of a large tract of federal land that is expendable in the opinion of the myopic folks in D.C.

"Second. Much of that land is already contaminated by radioactive debris from nuclear tests carried out since the 1950s. So, the D.C. thinking goes, why not stack more of this bad stuff in the same place.

"Third. And in my opinion foremost. The arrogant power brokers of D.C. view Nevada as lacking enough political clout to stop anything that the Eastern establishment wants to shove down our Western throats."

Manics paused to wipe away a froth of spittle forming at the corners of his mouth. He took a deep breath to help relax. He didn't want to lose his cool to the detriment of the impact of what would be in his committee's report.

"The conscience of whoever is to blame for the bad decision to use Yucca Mountain for radioactive waste should be haunted beyond death. I imagine that there's plenty of blame that could be spread around to participants of all political stripes in what turned out to be a deadly game of horseshoes. A game that should have been played as a yes or no contest, not one of *close enough for government work.*"

The speech gripped the gathered audience in somber silence. As Las Vegas reporter Sam Donovan had popularized back in the year 2000, "The Yucca project is no laughing matter." Today's listeners agreed. Parts of southern Nevada and its downstream reach of the Colorado River were faced with generations of life-threatening nuclear fission with no known means to short circuit the long-term grief.

Manics was satisfied that he had made his case. He sat. The committee's report to the full Congress, the Executive Branch and all citizens would be hard hitting. Now it was time to wrap up the committee work and get on with life.

"Secretary Heade. I apologize if I've seemed overly aggressive with you, your department, and other administration officials. I hope you understand and appreciate the valid reasons behind my strong feelings. A deep love of my home state has trumped my civility more than once. A cowboy even swears at his horse from time to time."

Heade was in no mood to argue. He simply nodded assent. He knew that the forthcoming committee report would be blistering. That was business for the future.

"In closing, let me add an old cowboy saying. 'There's no making a prize breeding bull from a castrated calf.' Now, Yucca Mountain has surely been castrated. So, what the nation needs to do is to start looking for a new calf with the potential to be a winning breeder, while simultaneously taking care of the one that shouldn't have been cut.

"My thanks to all who have been part of this committee business. I now pronounce a final adjournment."

Whack, whack, whack!

Manics had already outlined his committee's report in his mind. He and his Nevadan congressional colleagues would be the principal authors. Dissenting opinions, if any, would be allotted a page or two in an appendix, although Manics doubted that anyone would have the balls to challenge the Nevada version of the story.

That version would be fair and blunt. It would be especially damning of the Republican Party and its major role in allowing waste to be stored at Yucca Mountain. Manics smiled, knowing that the factual content and overall tone of the report should guarantee that a new repository site would not be in Nevada. It might also garner Nevada many future political "favors" as the business of government played out in its less-than-perfect ways for decades to come … certainly for as long as a large part of the state was off limits because of lingering radioactive contamination. Manics viewed this possibility … hell, a probability in the workings of politics … as his legacy for his home state.

Health willing, he hoped to sit around many a cowboy campfire with rangeland buddies and relive the Yucca Mountain story in retirement, which he planned to start as soon as his committee's report had accomplished its mission. And by god, his MISSION ACCOMPLISHED would ring true.

19

CHERNOBYL TWO?

"The release of atomic energy has not created a new problem. It has merely made more urgent the necessity of solving an existing one." Albert Einstein

The autumn of 2027 through 2028:

When President Forty-Six, his cabinet, their advisors, and selected members of Congress met in August of 2027 to discuss how to deal with containing the large teardrop-shaped patch of radioactive terrain in Nevada, they quickly agreed on who should be in charge of planning and supervising the task. Such agreement, without the usual bickering and eventual compromise that came with decisions made by a mixed political group, was rare in D.C. But when the results of a secret ballot were tallied during the first meeting of this group, there was only one name to list ... Dr. Darcie Chambers.

Chambers was an international icon. She held PhDs in nuclear physics and in inorganic chemistry from Cornell University, and a PhD in population biology/epidemiology from Stanford University. With this impressive array of sheepskins in hand, she was enticed to occupy the honorary endowed Bruggerman Science Chair at the University of Chicago, where she had lectured and researched her way to international fame as a brilliant renaissance scientist whose interests spanned a multitude of narrow specialties. During her sexagenarian decade, she became the world's first three-time Nobel Laureate ... in physics, chemistry and physiology. Along the way, she'd developed fruitful Washington connections that kept her university awash in federal research funding.

In April of 1986, at age thirty, she had watched from afar as the compromised Chernobyl nuclear power plant in the Soviet Union spewed out its deadly radioactive grit and vapor, some of which would travel as far as the eastern seaboard of the United States. Driven by a compelling scientific interest in what this accidental disaster would mean for the future of the plants and animals in the region surrounding Chernobyl and by an equally ardent desire to help afflicted people, she visited the stricken area and subsequently focused her career on the study of radioactivity in all of its forms and impacts. She became a singularly comprehensive encyclopedia on the Chernobyl accident and a source of expert advice to the U.S. government for its programs that dealt with radioactive materials. In this advisory capacity, she carried the nation's highest security clearance.

Now at age seventy-one, yet as mentally and physically active as in her thirties, she was viewed as the nation's most gifted compassionate matron ... a contemporary Florence Nightingale ... who might be able to comfort the country and lead the way to minimizing the long-term impacts of the Yucca Mountain problem. She accepted that image and traveled to Washington when President Forty-Six invited her to the second session of his Yucca Mountain management team.

"Ladies and gentlemen," the president said, "we all know Dr. Chambers and are familiar with her record of scientific achievements and gallery of awards."

The group of eighteen sat around an oval table, with the president seated at the center of one long side. The vice president was at his left. Chambers at his right. Sounds of agreement acknowledged the opening comment.

"We are grateful, Dr. Chambers," Forty-Six continued, "that you are willing to interrupt your busy schedule to advise us on how to deal with the Yucca Mountain mess. We feel that no one is more suited to the task than you."

Chambers smiled a thank you. A smile that was rumored to be warm enough to melt glass when reflected in a mirror. She was as lovely as gracious. She wore a snug blue knee-length skirt topped with a red-and-white short-sleeved blouse ... clothes that revealed firm sleek calves, an athletic torso, and a hint of patriotism. Low-heeled pumps supported a person who enjoyed lots of comfortable walking. Her hair was shimmering silver, pinned up in a bun. She spurned facial makeup of any sort.

In view of her age, the fifty-eight-year-old jowly Forty-Six wondered if her lack of facial wrinkles was natural. He suddenly realized that he was staring at this remarkable woman.

"Well, Dr. Chambers," he said, "we are not at all certain about how to proceed with our task. We understand that we have an unusual and complex problem to address. But we're not sure of how or where to begin."

"Then with your permission, Mr. President," Chambers said, "let me make some suggestions."

"Please. Go right ahead."

The brilliant and well-organized Darcie Chambers had come prepared.

"Gentlemen and ladies. We must first define an exclusion zone to keep people away from ground contaminated enough to pose a radiation hazard to human health. Once this zone is delimited, we must construct an effective barrier to make sure that unknowing and unwanted visitors cannot enter. Even with such a barrier, I recommend human patrols that work every day around the clock, supplemented by various remote sensing devices, to continuously monitor the perimeter of the danger zone.

"I have a plan about how to map out the exclusion zone. I'll explain that later if you wish."

"Fine," Forty-Six said. "What about the situation with Lake Mead?"

"I'm coming to that," Chambers said. "I suggest that we create two contiguous, though separate, exclusion zones. One should extend from Yucca Mountain, the point source of the radioactive fallout, to and including Lake Mead and Hoover Dam. The other would define a corridor along the Colorado River below the dam. The corridor should encompass all areas flooded as a result of draining Lake Mead. Vegetable growers and wintertime snowbirds won't be happy about the downstream exclusion zone, but it's for their own health and welfare."

President Forty-Six looked around the meeting table and said "Agreed so far. Unless someone else has a comment." The silence of nodding heads sealed the agreement. Chambers continued with her train of thought.

"You may recall that the Soviet Union was slow to establish such a zone at Chernobyl. This delay probably led to increased radiation sickness in local populations. We were fortunate to be able to evacuate Las Vegas and surroundings quickly, before people absorbed large doses of radiation. Of course, the Soviets had to deal with a fire and partial nuclear meltdown at the reactor, and that kept them busy at the site, rather than thinking immediately about people at risk in the surrounding region. If they hadn't been able to extinguish the meltdown-ignited fire, their disaster would have been much worse. Thank goodness, our Yucca Mountain situation did not include the possibility of a runaway nuclear reaction, the so-called China syndrome. Not that a volcanic eruption is easy to deal with."

She seemed lost in thought for a moment. "With your permission, I'd like to describe similarities between the Chernobyl nuclear accident of 1986 and what has happened at Yucca Mountain. I think some comparisons with Yucca will help you better understand what we're up against with our own problem."

"Yes. Please go ahead Dr. Chambers," President Forty-Six said. "We're here to benefit from your wisdom. We will listen to whatever you think important to our task."

"As a point of reference," Chambers said, "it's accurate to say that the disasters at Chernobyl and Yucca Mountain were fundamentally the result of steam explosions. This sounds trite and painfully low-tech. But it's true.

"At Chernobyl, the Soviets let fissioning fuel rods run amok with insufficient coolant, to the point of their partial melting. Then, this extremely hot material caused what little cooling water was present to explode in a violent steam blast."

She paused to let her simplified version of the Chernobyl story sink into the minds of her listeners, none of whom was a trained scientist.

"Scientists call this type of event a fuel-coolant interaction. It's a fancy way to describe how the molten nuclear fuel and water mixed to trigger a blast. Once steam explosions destroyed the reactor core and broke the containment vessel, all sorts of mischief followed.

"I understand that Dr. Barnabus Shanks has explained to the Manics committee how steam explosions contributed to the destruction of Yucca Mountain and its radioactive inventory. In that case, molten rock was the fuel and plain old groundwater the coolant. Had the passive innocent bystander—high-level radioactive waste—not been in the mountain, we wouldn't be here today agonizing over what to do with the mess we have."

"Amen!" echoed throughout the room.

"I hope my Chernobyl analogy helps you understand what we're trying to deal with. Let's return to the immediate problem of what to do now that a large patch of Nevada is contaminated. With your permission Mr. President, I'd like to create an outline that we can critique as I talk."

"By all means."

Chambers walked to a message board that covered a wall of the room and began to write notes with a broad-tipped red pen. She labeled *Establish exclusion zones* with a crimson 1. She began a new line with *Establish a program to …* as she continued speaking.

"In addition to the exclusion zones, we should instigate a program to monitor the possible movement of the radioactive debris within the exclusion zones. Flowing water and blowing wind will surely redistribute some of this material. We need to keep up to date on when and where this happens. With time and erosion, it's possible that we may have to revise the boundaries of the zones. Most probably outward."

Chambers paused to adjust the pin that held her hair in a tight bun.

"Whatever the program may be, we should be completely open with the public and the world. The Soviets tried to hide their Chernobyl problem from international eyes. This worked for about a day. The cat leaped out of the bag when employees at the Forsmark Nuclear Power Plant in Sweden noticed unusual radioactive particles on their clothes. They quickly identified these as arriving on winds blowing in from Chernobyl.

"The world already knows about what happened at Yucca Mountain, and we should keep everyone informed about how we are dealing with cleaning up our mess. Unlike the Soviet attempt at secrecy with Chernobyl, I hope we all agree that transparency is the best policy. To act otherwise would promote unnecessary levels of irrational fear until the truth came out."

"Sound and wise policy," Forty-Six said.

"We have a separate problem with what was once a full Lake Mead," Chambers said. "I understand that draining began yesterday and will be completed within about a year. This removes radioactive materials dissolved in the water. And the small solid particles that will be carried away by the river's current.

"But the coarser stuff will be left behind as a blanket of sediment draped over a landscape that was once the lake bottom. I hope that not too many years of rain storms will flush most of this grit downstream. But we need to monitor the progress."

She added item three to the outline. *Monitor erosion of radioactive sediment from Lake Mead bottom.*

"Finally, we should instigate a comprehensive study of all plants and animals in the contaminated zone to document any impacts of radioactivity on what we recognize as their normal growth patterns, life cycles and so forth. I should be able to put my experience with what has happened at Chernobyl to good stead here.

"The encouraging news is that the initial fear that radiation would produce all sorts of plant and animal freaks as the result of exposure to elevated levels of radiation has so far proven to be an overreaction at Chernobyl. Some detrimental impacts are documented, of course, especially to trees and small mammals within a radius of about six miles of the reactor. And an increase in the incidence of thyroid cancer in children seems attributable to increased exposure to radiation. Still, overall the impacts are far less severe than originally anticipated.

"The bad news is that the results of such unintended and uncontrolled genetic damage due to high radiation may not appear for some time to come. Only future generations of humans will be able to document long-term effects."

Chambers wrote one more item, *Comprehensive study of plants and animals in the contaminated zone,* and sat down.

"There may be second-order problems to deal with, later, after we get an initial high-priority program underway. With your permission and funding, I can transform today's recommendations into action within days."

A nod from President Forty-Six precipitated a unanimous "agreed" from all present.

"Coordinate with the director of National Security for whatever permissions and support you need," Forty-Six said. "We will reconvene at least once a month to discuss your progress reports.

"Dr. Chambers," he added, "we have the utmost confidence in you and your plan. The nation is fortunate to have someone of your stature and abilities at this time of turmoil, uncertainty and need."

Forty-Six stood, and all others followed his lead. A presidential thank-you handshake flowed into an extended sincere hug, which would be viewed by a grateful news-watching public that evening. Viewers found comfort in the motherly strength exuded by the woman.

Within a week, Dr. Chambers had fielded a team of well-paid students from her university. Each was outfitted with a radiation suit for protection from the very materials they were being sent to encounter in the field. Each carried an instrument that measured the level of radiation on the ground and contained a global positioning system that automatically plotted the latitude and longitude of a radiation reading with an accuracy of a few inches.

Chambers instructed her student team to map a boundary that was equivalent to five hundred millirems per year. By the end of September 2027, a compilation of the team's efforts delineated a teardrop-shaped exclusion zone. Chambers hung a copy of the map on her office wall and dispatched copies to President Forty-Six and the rest of the group that had chosen her for this important task.

The return email from Forty-Six proclaimed "Well done, Dr. Chambers!!" in a large font that filled the glowing screen of a computer monitor. "I'll notify the director."

The director of National Security oversaw the next step, by awarding his favorite industrial crony a lucrative no-bid contract to construct a twelve-foot-high cyclone fence topped with razor wire. Two months later, two thousand five hundred square miles of Nevada landscape were encompassed by a virtually impenetrable barrier. Beltway Security Systems LLC won the contract to patrol the perimeter, partly in deference to the earlier loss of that company's employees underground and at the CO. Dr. Chambers's primary exclusion zone was secure.

She chose to define the exclusion corridor along the downstream stretch of the river with a boundary that lay one thousand yards beyond ground that was being flooded as Lake Mead drained to the Sea of Cortez. A team of security guards kept people outside this boundary. A cyclone fence, 24/7 security patrols, and remote sensing doodads would appear as soon as the lake was empty.

By the end of 2028, it was not much of an intellectual stretch to call the Yucca Mountain disaster *Chernobyl Two*, in spite of many differences in details. America's detractors relished the public use of this phrase, followed by "those Yankees aren't so damned smart after all." Detractor or not, no rational thinking person found humor in either version of Chernobyl.

20

THE HEALING SLOWLY BEGINS

*"**Time may be** a great healer, but it's a lousy beautician."* Anonymous.

By Valentines Day of 2029, Lake Mead was drained. Once again a river flowed freely through Black Canyon much as it had before the gigantic concrete-and-steel barrier was constructed across this natural wonder. The old cofferdams were once again shunting water through diversion tunnels that had been blasted through pre-dam canyon walls, recreating the situation that provided a dry work place for the dam-building crew of the 1930s. Downstream of the dam, which was now an eerie high-and-dry curved slab of concrete that rose seven hundred feet above river level, radioactive water followed the original course of the Colorado on its way to the international border, and on into the Sea of Cortez.

The subsiding level of Lake Mead revealed an eclectic history of accidental and purposeful trash, hidden underwater since the reservoir was first filled to the brim in 1941. As anticipated, an incredible number of sunken boats, large and small, once again basked in sunlight as shoreline waves etched a series of concentric bathtub rings onto newly exposed lake bottom. The lost and jettisoned trappings of water bunnies and bucks littered rocky ledges and channels tributary to the main-stem Colorado ... oil cans, beer cans, soda cans, other cans; marine batteries, flashlight batteries, radio batteries, other batteries; ice chests, tool chests, medicine chests, other chests, etc, etc, etc. The amount of such trash was a depressingly damning statement about the human relation to its natural environment.

Airplanes, large and small, that had been ditched in the lake for a variety of reasons also reappeared. The largest and most newsworthy to emerge was a B-29 Superfortress ... a WWII bomber made famous during aerial strikes against mainland Japan. Unlike all those lost to the salty depths of the Pacific during that campaign, this particular Superfortress had gone down to a fresh-water grave during a peace-time training mission in 1948.

A story in the *Los Angeles Times* quoted Ranger Max Carpenter of the Lake Mead National Recreation Area: "Isn't it ironic that this airplane lies dead here, covered with muck as radioactive as the stuff spread across Hiroshima by her sister Enola Gay in nineteen forty-five. Maybe there's a mystical connection between B-29s and radioactivity."

As security officials watched the lake level drop, they were somewhat surprised that only one human body was revealed by the time the lake finally morphed into its progenitor river. The fact that the legs, now nothing but stark white bone, of this skeleton were encased to the hip with concrete triggered attempts to match residual DNA to that in the national records of known missing folks.

Job-hunting Lieutenant Marco Martini of the now-defunct Las Vegas Police Department, and not coincidentally in search of publicity that might help him land a similar position in another city, went immediately on record. "I'm quite certain that forensics will ID these remains as belonging to a noted figure of organized crime that we were tracking from our Las Vegas offices." But no DNA match was made, dashing Martini's hopes of padding his résumé by answering the question of what had become of the notoriously unpopular character. Hoffa groupies were disappointed that the mystery of what had happened to the body of James Riddle Hoffa back in 1975 remained a riddle.

Though no human remains were found there, other than bodies still interred in the church cemetery, the entire 1865 vintage Mormon village of St. Thomas emerged at the confluence of the Muddy and Virgin Rivers. Abandoned in 1938 just ahead of the rising waters of Lake Mead, the newly dry place had to remain a ghost town, unsafe for human habitation because of deadly radiation rather than deep water.

Downstream of Hoover Dam, the exclusionary zone of Dr. Darcie Chambers was a chlorophyll-green stripe across an uninhabited corridor of river-with-floodplain all the way to the Sea of Cortez. By presidential decree, inhabitants of towns along the river were forced to evacuate.

Through many sessions of contentious negotiation, President Forty-Six had finally mollified the righteously furious Presidente de Mexico by implementing an extremely liberal immigration law that created a legal sieve-like international boundary ... most especially for those campesinos whose lands in the floodplain and delta of the Colorado River were alive with fissioning wastes.

Northwest of Hoover Dam, the Darcie Chambers exclusionary zone from Lake Mead to Yucca Mountain was an abandoned, albeit an intensely watched wasteland. No one was allowed in unless accompanied by a security guard employee of BSS LLC. Protective radiation attire was required and visits longer than twelve hours were prohibited. Gas masks and oxygen tanks were necessary to avoid breathing in radioactive dust, which would likely lodge in lungs where fission could play its deadly game of knockout punches to healthy cells, setting the stage for genetic change and cancers. Over the course of a few years, salvage crews recovered some readily transportable resources, after decontamination, from Las Vegas and other built-up areas inside the fence.

The metropolitan area remained a ghost town of utterly magnificent proportions. It was an object of curiosity and wonder described by loquacious airline pilots who altered daytime flight paths to offer aerial views for appreciative passengers.

"Ladies and gentlemen, this is Captain Peterson. We're currently at thirty-five thousand feet above sea level, over southern Nevada. The state has long been known for picturesque nineteenth-century ghost towns that came to be when the mineral riches in nearby mines played out. Well folks, now there's a new ghost town that might be thought of as the product of mining that was too successful. Las Vegas wouldn't be what it is today if uranium miners hadn't been so darned prolific."

With that introduction, Captain Peterson dipped the right wing of his plane to begin a broad circle around the abandoned city below.

"If passengers on the right side look out you'll see the ultimate ghost town," Captain Peterson said. "I'll complete a circle clockwise and then counterclockwise to give you all a chance to look. I imagine many of you visited Vegas when it was a thriving center of gambling and pleasures of the flesh. The city's motto is now more appropriate than ever. *What happens in Vegas stays in Vegas.*

"We'll land at Los Angeles International in about an hour."

A desire by many to reclaim this lost culture called Las Vegas was kept on long-term hold by the half-lives of radioactive trash. No one would be allowed to resettle the city until the level of radiation dropped below the equivalent of five hundred millirems per year. The exclusion zones would likely have to be maintained for centuries or even much longer. Even then the areas would remain a radioactive anomaly as the materials with half-lives in the millions of years and longer fissioned on.

Concurrently, biologists watched for radiation impacts on plants and animals within and near the restricted areas. One bit of good news was that much of the radioactive mud lining the walls and bottom of now-vanished Lake Mead was washing downstream to the Sea of Cortez with each rainstorm. Once in the ocean, the briny waters and currents of the Pacific diluted and dispersed the radioactive waste to a low, though detectable, concentration that experts hoped would prove to be harmless to living things.

Outside the fenced-off zones, the inventory of collateral damage was less obvious, though depressingly extensive, and it carried a powerfully negative economic impact whose duration could still only be guessed at. Most of this form of damage had to do with limited water.

With Lake Mead drained to the relative trickle of a "wild" Colorado River, the bottoms of water-intake towers for driving the electricity-generating turbines within Hoover Dam stood high and dry. What had once been a dependable whirring source of two thousand megawatts of vibrating generators was now silent. The good news, if you were such a Pollyanna that you could extract any good news from this silence, is that the lights of Las Vegas were off. Demand for electricity there was down to the few electronic gadgets needed to baby-sit a sealed-off city. The bad news was that what had once been "excess" electricity from the generators of Hoover Dam was no longer available to be wasted by the typically profligate Americans of southern California. No Lake Mead water. No Lake Mead electricity.

Downstream, the lack of river water untainted by radioactivity was a major blow to irrigated agriculture and the continuation of unbridled urban growth in areas once wetted by the mighty Colorado. Until the Darcie Chambers project declared river water to be okay for human usage, the canal of the Central Arizona Project would stay dry. In spite of the new rainy climate, a dry CAP triggered the need for heavy pumping of groundwater across southern Arizona. In what seemed a never-ending journey along a path leading to self-extinction, the rising water demands of a burgeoning population always outpaced the increased level of annual precipitation.

To make up the deficit, intermountain valleys whose sediments hosted voluminous ice-age aquifers yielded their ancient liquid treasures so that agribusiness moguls could continue growing unneeded cotton, alfalfa, and nuts. And so human sun worshippers could lounge beside Olympic-sized backyard swimming pools that functioned mostly as evaporation ponds.

Hydrologists warned that mining groundwater would cause valley floors to settle and crack ... first a few inches, then a foot and soon several feet each year ... as the subsurface volume once occupied by the pumped water was replaced by compacted dry sand and gravel. They were correct. Hairline chinks grew into gaping fissures that swallowed more than one John Deere and its unsuspecting operator.

The fruit and vegetable agri-industries in the Imperial and Coachella Valleys of southern California suffered similar consequences. The All American Canal became a dry trench … a new playground for ATV-driving infantiles … and groundwater pumping ensued. The Salton Sea evaporated to a small pond. Billions of migrating waterfowl had to find new flyways.

As their lack of sufficient water escalated, the governors of Arizona and California pleaded with the president to reactivate their economic agri-aortas to distribute liquid lifeblood to the deserts. With each request, the sitting president passed the buck to Dr. Darcie Chambers, who answered "I'm sorry Governors, but the Colorado River water is still too radioactive for irrigation use. The radiation level of the water *is* dropping a bit each year. Maybe in another decade or so the proliferation of fruits and nuts in the Southwest can resume."

All the while, new nuclear power plants were popping up across the country like mushrooms on a pile of dung. But these new units could never quite keep pace with the voracious appetites of American consumers for more things electrical. Even the most rabid of skeptics had to admit that a new storage site was needed for the nation's hot and growing fissioning garbage.

The team led by a concerned and cautious Dr. Darcie Chambers monitored contamination levels assiduously. At forty-nine years old, the exclusion zones of Chernobyl were still too radioactive for safe human occupation, although many people flaunted the boundaries and moved in at their own risk. Chambers would never allow such reckless behavior for the home-grown Chernobyl baby.

"If Chernobyl's rate of healing is a reasonable guide for Nevada, I'll have to pass the caretaker baton to someone younger before Las Vegas can even think about repopulating," she reminded herself as she hiked along the John Muir Trail of California's Sierra Nevada. "I'm a healthy seventy-nine, and my half-life is already greater than those of pesky strontium ninety and cesium one-thirty-seven isotopes. But plenty of molecules with those elements will still be fissioning away when I'm no more than dust in the wind.

"I should talk to my top student Gladys soon about moving into my role over the coming few years. She's bright, and she can handle stress."

21

A LETTER FROM THE HEART

*"**It is dangerous** to be right when the government is wrong."* Voltaire

October 3, 2028:

The mechanical bird emerged from its house and sang cuckoo three times, its head bobbing with each sound. It disappeared back into its intricately carved dark wooden Germanic hutch to sleep for another hour.

Barney listened and sighed. He sat alone in darkness, slouched down in his beanbag chair, stretching, scratching, and thinking. He was naked, save for his custom-designed silken briefs, whose front panel was emblazoned with a volcano in full climactic eruption. He reached down to remind himself that the elastic waist band was frayed and about ready to fail.

He and Heather had earlier enjoyed grilled burgers, barbeque-flavored chips, and three-bean salad washed down with ice-cold Pabst Blue Ribbon. Then they watched a memory-twig version of Gore's *An Inconvenient Truth*, before playfully enjoying a pseudo-surfing adventure they called riding the crest on a king-sized water bed.

"Gotta get the best out of life before the world comes to an end," they jointly joked each time they romped after viewing an inconvenient truth that seemed to be the damn straight truth as world climate continued to change with global warming.

Heather was softly snoring, zonked on the big bed at the moment. "She'll join me for breakfast," Barney whispered. "It's Tuesday. She has to lecture at eight."

Heather had become a fixture of his life, a life that for years had rarely focused on the same girlfriend for more than a week or two. Trite though the phrase was, variety had indeed been the spice of Barney's female-partner life … the Heinz menu on a fast track of change for three decades. He'd been seeing only Heather for nearly a year. He wished he were sleeping with her right now.

But sleep deprivation had come to haunt Barney shortly after participating in Senator Manics's Yucca Mountain hearings. Since then insomnia had tugged incessantly at his body with increasing strength, as weeks stretched into months and more months. Being sleepless in Isla Vista tonight was a high-probability event in what had become a chronic problem. He scratched an armpit and tugged on an earlobe as he once again tried to make sense of losing sleep over a situation he should be able to control.

The testimony he'd offered to Manics's fact-finding committee had been straight forward and non-troubling to his inner tranquility. He had enjoyed talking about water and its role in that almost magical natural phenomenon called phreatomagmatism, and explaining how seemingly benign water had become an agent of almost unthinkable destruction. He had even introduced the word *phreatomagmatism* into the general public's vocabulary, a feat that professors of the English language often failed to accomplish with far simpler nouns and concepts.

Yet after participating in those three high-octane D.C. days, no matter how hard he willed the significance of them to disappear, he could not empty his mind of thoughts about lessons the Yucca Mountain fiasco should carry for the future.

Will those lessons be remembered and acted on? Or will they go the way of the dodo, to be recalled only when needed to complete a crossword puzzle or an equally mundane board game?

A new site to store the nation's rapidly accumulating inventory of radioactive waste would soon be needed. No one would wish another Yucca disaster on the nation, but Barney worried that the government might pick the next site in a similarly hazardous geologic setting.

He had strong convictions about where that site should *not* be. Still, if politics trumped science the way it seemed to have done for the selection of Yucca, well…. That possibility kept Barney's neurons at high alert day and night.

He had tried several of his old party-life tricks to bring on slumber. But not even an overload of evening beer on the beach could keep him unconscious for several restful hours. Bags were growing under sleep-deprived eyes. The sun-bleached blond hair of a beach boy was graying. The once vain surfer avoided mirrors. He even caught himself thinking he might replace his fraying racy shorts with bland white cotton togs.

His relationship with Heather was further evidence of body and life-style changes. At thirty something, she was his first older lover. This bachelorette professor in the university's College of Arts and Letters was a fascinating foil for a man of science. In bed she enjoyed shouting a Shakespearian "*What ho!*" at the peak of pleasure, not the punny sort of "*Gneiss! Gneiss!*" exclamation that a rock jock might use. Whatever was nagging at Barney's id and corroding his normally sanguine attitude on life, this woman with age, experience and maturity was preferable to the wild instability of young female students.

The science side of his life was also evolving, but toward what end Barney was uncertain. The professional excitement of witnessing the historically unparalleled phreatomagmatic eruption at Yucca Mountain had subsided considerably. The so-called thrill of discovery had worn thin, if not off.

Early on, he had published a technical version of the event in the prestigious *Bulletin of Volcanology* ... yet another feather in his earth-science cap. With all these feathers, though, that figurative cap looked more like a war bonnet than a serious scientist's head cover. His publication record bespoke a near maniacal pursuit of his science, rather than a mellowing and aging of his observations, postulates and theories, like a fine red wine, before uncorking them to be shared publicly.

I should slow down, he often thought. Who needs more publications on record at my advanced age, anyway? I'm gonna throttle back on the professional side of life.

While on the pedestal of the sudden public popularity that came with being the Yucca volcano man, he had sold innumerable non-technical versions of the story to newspapers, magazines, and commercial blog sites. Yucca-man's late night repartee with David Letterman's replacement had been stimulating, but one go at that venue had been plenty. Barney understood that a comedian's lifeline is tethered to laughter, a generally important ingredient in any pleasant existence. But even happy-go-lucky Barney found it difficult to find humor in a radioactive disaster.

The initial flood of requests for public lectures and appearances on talk-radio was finally subsiding. The only currently unanswered invitation was from a college called Carleton, a center of academic excellence whose name might look good on his résumé. But he didn't need more flowers in his professional garden. And southern-California-Barney wasn't sure of the wisdom of visiting Minnesota during February, for any reason.

He limited his international speaking tour to a summer appearance in Iceland as a thank-you for the honorary citizenship that had been bestowed upon him by that island nation when he had been but a graduate student. After his talk he lingered to ride full-tölt on Icelandic ponies across the lush green hillsides near Akranes, to enjoy several soaks in Reykjavik's therapeutic municipal thermal pools, to play a few chess matches on the larger-than-life board built into the main street of the city, and to renew his friendship with an aging Gutrudsdóttir.

Within weeks after the Yucca eruption, three movie studios had approached him about transforming his Yucca Mountain tale into an action film. Each had offered a substantial up-front payment and the position of chief technical advisor during development of the script and filming. Major money almost got the better of his professional ethics, but in the end he declined any involvement with a Hollywood extravaganza about the disaster at Yucca. He had only to recall the absolutely ridiculous *Volcano* and *Dante's Peak* that had earlier drastically diminished the stature of his science in professional and public eyes, in spite of the efforts of well-qualified and well-intentioned volcano experts who were technical advisors during production of those films. Even if Barney had a reputation for being unconventional and practicing his volcano chase a bit loose and easy at times, he wasn't about to prostitute himself and his chosen career for the sake of a few dollars. Not yet, anyway.

A rush of possible book deals followed hot on the heels of Hollywood. These were a tougher call for his conscience. Strange though it seemed to many of his professional colleagues, he enjoyed writing … at an inexplicable visceral level. Several traditional publishing houses offered monetary advances larger than the movie moguls had for "a two-to three-hundred-page book that explains the what, why and how of the Yucca epic."

Barney's initial reticent "I don't think so, thank you" prompted a publisher's phoned counter-offer that invited him to tell his story as either fact or fiction.

"It's your call Dr. Shanks. You might find the story easier and more satisfying to retell as fiction."

This notion captured Barney's imagination. Though publications of his writing career pre-Yucca had been purely of the technical, critically refereed variety, save for those equally technical confidential reports done for commercial clients, his creative juices had long wanted to flow through a pen that was free to concoct whatever tale the muse suggested on a given day. In fact, he had already penned five novellas during the past decade … writings known only to him and his parents. The folks had been very encouraging when he shared his creative prose with them.

"This is wonderful, son" Dad had said enthusiastically, having read a story with a theme that uplifted more than a surfboard, a beer and a skirt. "It's so encouraging to see your interests expand beyond the three Bs." Mother had nodded vigorously in agreement.

That show of parental approval inspired Barney. Bolstered by their encouragement of his inner urge, he had decided that it was time to step out of the harness of technical non-fiction, which was starting to chafe a bit anyway, and also write purely for fun.

"Let me think about the idea of a Yucca Mountain novel," he said to the agent who offered the option of writing fiction. The possibility excited and worried him.

I need to sort through lots of related angles, before going this route. Walking the fiction path could lead me across lots of bumps as well as smooth-cruising stretches.

If I'm going to write about the destruction of Yucca Mountain and the people involved with that messy episode, I don't want to tread on the private lives of real folks along the way. With fiction, I think I could completely avoid this potentially awkward situation. I'd be free to assemble any cast of characters I want. If someone imagines himself as one of my creations and doesn't like what he sees, well ... hey lighten up man. It's fiction.

Fiction also offers a chance to expand on what happened at Yucca. To push the envelope. I wonder though. Would hyping the story, even just a little, upset people who've devoted their professional lives to the Yucca Mountain project for years and decades, and who've taken their roles seriously? Too seriously with some people I know. I want to be careful and considerate about how I describe this sad chapter of our country's history. I don't want to lose friends over a damned silly novel.

But going with fiction is attractive.

"Great! Yes. You think on it Dr. Shanks," the would-be publisher said. "We can provide a talented ghost writer to work with if you wish."

"If I choose to write a novel, the writing will be mine," Barney said. "I'll let you know what I think, later."

Following weeks of chaotic yes, no, yes, maybe, no, yes, he called the acquisitions editor at Vulcan Publishers LLC. "I've decided to accept the offer of producing a fictional version of the Yucca tale."

An approving guttural yes-like sound came from his listener.

"I'm thinking I might do this under the title of *Dirty Bomb*. Here's what a contract must include.

"The science will be accurate, not sensational, no matter what your in-house editors might want.

"I will provide an outline and sample chapter within two months. A complete first draft will follow within four months.

"The copyright is mine and mine alone. Half of the royalties will go to the Geology Department of the University of California at Santa Barbara."

"Done!"

Vulcan Publishers saw dollar signs where Barney saw an opportunity to indulge a dormant desire.

"We'll send an attorney to Isla Vista tomorrow, with a contract for your inspection."

The contract was signed and notarized on the first anniversary of the Yucca Mountain eruption.

Yet, even now, nearly two months later, the opportunity to write fiction for public consumption did little to soothe his restless bothered soul.

"Maybe I should have included publisher-paid sessions of sleep therapy in the contract," Barney whispered, just before the mechanical bird appeared to announce hour four.

He squirmed, creating a symphony of scrunching as plastic beans reorganized around his repositioned buns. He longed for help, comfort and inspiration.

And suddenly he found them. He found them by forcefully squeezing his eyes shut and watching the performance of eyeball floaters that this invariably generated. This was a game his father had taught him as a child. Back then it was a fun diversion when other forms of entertainment had lost their appeal. As an adult, Barney found that the floater game helped him concentrate.

Eyes shut firmly, he saw a seemingly random collage of changing images and patterns skittering in unpredictable directions. If he tried to isolate and follow a particular shape, it scooted to the edge of his eyeball screen and disappeared like an actor leaving a stage.

He opened his eyes to reset the scene by staring through twin south-facing windows toward the moonlit surface of the Pacific Ocean. He closed his eyes tightly again. This time he saw two portrait panels set in a background of black. He concentrated, looking for a message in the shapes.

Within seconds ethereal images of his parents filled the panels. They were standing near the counter in their floral shop, looking to Barney's right. They smiled and appeared to be speaking calmly to a third, unseen party ... perhaps another frantic forgetful husband trying to select flowers for his wife's birthday on the commute home.

The scene reminded Barney that his parents had been the one steadying influence in his and others' lives. Always patient. Always understanding. Always giving yet asking little in return. Their images faded into a variation of the earlier changing collage.

Tears beaded at the corners of his eyes as Barney recalled the day they had died in a freak head-on collision on Highway 101 near Carpenteria two years earlier. The night before, he had dined with them at their modest retirement condo in Ventura. Dad's invitation had included mention of "some family business."

After eating, the conversation had turned from the usual idle laughter-filled chatter of reminiscing to the mirthlessness of serious themes, once a potent Irish coffee had loosened tongues. Dad and Mother had positioned themselves at opposite ends of the sofa. Dad crossed his legs, right over left, and folded his arms over his chest. A relaxed Barney, swinging to-and-fro in Dad's rocking chair, faced them across a coffee table. Dad had been the first to wade into deep water.

◆   ◆   ◆

"Son, your mother and I are getting along in years. Can't live forever, you know. Even you will slow down in a few years."

That sobered Barney. He wasn't one to ponder human mortality.

"We had you over tonight because there's something we want to talk with you about before it's too late."

An awkward silence ensued, with parental questioning eyes focused on their son's expression of surprise. Barney stopped rocking.

Where's this headed? Why now? They're in great health for their age.

Dad continued.

"You're our only child. The only unique living thing your mother and I have contributed to the world."

He smiled as he gushed, "It's hard for us to imagine what the world would be like without Barnabus Shanks."

All three chuckled at that mental image.

"We love you, our creation, for all you've achieved," Dad said. "We're proud of your talents as a volcano expert. And on a surfboard. You've built an enviable international reputation in both fields."

Dad raised a fist for emphasis. "*Thanks to Shanks*, as the media like to report."

As usual, Dad was doing all the talking, with Mother in her role of silent con-spirator, head bobbing in agreement. Barney still wondered what had triggered their desire to have a serious chat tonight.

"But," Dad said with less conviction. "Now don't take this wrong …"

He struggled to find hard-hitting words wrapped in kid gloves.

"… but we want to help you find even more success in your life."

Barney was in favor of that notion. Yet his mind was racing amok. Dad was talking around something Barney couldn't translate.

What surprise is about to hit? I can't think of anything especially outrageous or out of the ordinary that I've been up to lately. Nothing to precipitate this kind of talk.

"Here's the thing son," Dad said. "All through the years as we've watched you grow from a playful child to the precocious teenager into a college student and now a middle-aged professional, it's appeared to us that you've been mostly concerned with your own pleasure. Your own feelings of satisfaction. Your own self-importance."

Dad changed the crossing of his legs and played with a shoe lace, a sure indication that he was feeling stress.

"In a nutshell, you're frightfully self-centered."

Mom's head bobbed yes. Dad blushed from being more direct and emphatic than usual. He leaned back into the arms-over-chest posture.

Barney agreed with what he was hearing. *I've fed a pretty selfish ego as I've chewed my way through life. But I don't think I hurt anyone along the way. Yeah. Number one has always been Barney. And sure. I left a few lovers in tears at the end of a brief fling. So what? I didn't break any promises.*

Dad continued before Barney could further rationalize his lifestyle.

"What would make your mother and me especially proud would be to see you work for the advantage and pleasure of others.

"I was a lot like you as a young man. Then my dad took me to the barn for a man-to-man. He kept his advice simple. Called me a hundred-percent taker. Told me it was high time to learn to be a giver.

"I don't know that my behavior toward others ever completely satisfied him after that bit of advice. But I did try to put the giver idea into practice."

Mother nodded her agreement. Barney had long ago concluded that she had one of the world's most-exercised necks. Dad uncrossed his legs and rested his hands on his knees. He exhaled audibly.

Silence called for a reaction from Barney. He wasn't sure where or how to begin. He had had no idea that his parents so disapproved of his lifestyle. He sensed that this was a defining moment in his relationship with them. But he wanted to steer the conversation onto a lighter path.

"Grandpa Shanks was a caring and generous man," Barney said. "The world would be a better place with more like him, all right. I won't forget that."

Barney stood.

"Umm. Thanks for the advice. I've gotta run. Got a date back at the house. Don't want to keep her waiting. It's Brenda. I think."

Dad and Mother stood.

"We're pleased you had time to listen to us son," Dad said. "Keep taming volcanoes. Be sure to let others know how they can safely live with those powerful creatures. And keep entertaining your lady friends. Just remember that they may have expectations beyond a night or two with the famous Barnabus Shanks."

Barney led as all three moved toward the door.

"You know Barney," Dad said, "we'd be pleased to meet some of them. Maybe someday you'll even find one to settle down with and give your mother and me a grandchild or two to dote over."

What Dad posed as a deeply felt wish, Barney heard as a question. He hugged Mom and shook Dad's hand in farewell.

"Goodnight folks," he said as he pulled the door shut. *Goodbye* would have been more appropriate.

Their deaths less than twenty-four hours later made recollections of that last conversation especially poignant. *Did they know that was their last chance to try to remold my lifestyle?*

◆   ◆   ◆

That last parental advice resurfaced, in beanbag, eyes-closed reverie. Maybe it wasn't too late to become the person his parents had hoped for. Maybe being a giver would help put an end to the sleeplessness marathon. Barney decided to try.

First, he would give the country his advice on how to proceed with selecting a new storage site for the rapidly accumulating radioactive waste. A big question was whether or not the political decision makers would seriously consider his advice. Most politicians seemed to be bad listeners.

"It's worth a try though, Dad," Barney murmured, as he rolled out of the beanbag and headed to the computer keyboard.

Second, he would give Heather time for the meaningful conversation that she had tried to open more than once in recent weeks. No more hiding behind trite phrases and concocted reasons to "have to run." This would be a first for love-'em-and-leave-'em Barney. His SOP was to immediately terminate a relationship if his partner of the moment seemed at all interested in getting serious.

He had viewed those past lovers as desserts … something tasty to be enjoyed at the end of a social evening. He had savored these sweet things and surreptitiously given them names like crème caramel, apple strudel, mousse au chocolat, tarte au pomme, peche melba … and other delicacies.

With Heather he had discovered millefeuille and had worked his way through only the first several layers of this thousand-night treat ... each serving more delightful than the last. He hoped she felt the same desire to continue their relationship.

Barney pushed the on button and opened a blank page for a new document. As he started typing, the cuckoo bird announced hour five. The writing and rewriting of words, sentences and paragraphs came slowly.

October 3, 2028

To whom it may concern:
Re: Thoughts on storage of radioactive waste

As highly radioactive waste accumulates at the nation's many nuclear power plants and at military weapons facilities, a site for the long-term safe storage of this waste will soon be needed to play the role once carried out at Yucca Mountain. In selecting a new site, there are three natural hazards that must be assessed.

1.   Earthquakes violent enough to rupture waste containers and release radioactive materials into the environment.

2.   Volcanic eruptions violent enough to rupture containers and release radioactive materials into the environment.

3.   Chemical corrosion capable of weakening waste containers to the point of leaking radioactive materials into the environment.

A fourth consideration is that the storage site should be far from any moderate or larger population center.

No one can guarantee that any storage site will perform safely for the duration needed to "tame" radioactive wastes with the longest half-lives, whether that period be officially adopted as ten thousand years or longer. However, a single simple precaution can help minimize the long-term risk associated with the first two natural hazards listed above.

That precaution is to select an environment that has *no record of geologically recent earthquake or volcanic activity*, and therefore little if any expectation for such future events, during the designed life-span of storage. By recent I include all of what geologists call the Quaternary Period. This extends two million years back from the present.

Yucca Mountain is within an area that failed this simple safety test for both earthquakes and volcanic eruptions. It also failed a more stringent standard adopted by the Japanese in their search for a radioactive-waste storage site. Even with their landmass being practically nothing but young volcanoes, they rule out any place within ten miles of a Quaternary volcano. There are several Quaternary volcanoes less than ten miles from Yucca Mountain, including that new one that's smack dab on top of the place.

To varying yet worrisome degrees, most of the mountainous West fails the less stringent test that I propose for earthquakes and volcanoes. Nonetheless, there are other regions of our country that have been earthquake and volcano free for many millions of years.

Chemical corrosion: The risk associated with this hazard is more difficult to assess for thousands of years and more into the future. The main corrosion culprit is water. And one fundamental decision is whether to store waste canisters above the groundwater table, as was the design at Yucca Mountain, or within water-saturated rocks below the water table. Experts have put forth pro and con arguments for both settings.

In any event, depth to groundwater changes with climate. And climate can change on the order of centuries. It has changed many times during the Quaternary Period without any input from *Homo sapiens*.

The nation experienced what climate change meant for the Yucca Mountain site, where dry became wet ... leading to violent steam explosions when magma entered the mountain. Similarly, climate change has caused major fluctuations in the groundwater table world-wide during the Quaternary. For example, what would later become the state of Nevada and much of Utah was once the site of huge lakes. Who can say with much certainty that this history won't be repeated in the coming centuries, millennia, or longer as world climate continues to evolve?

These considerations lead me to the following recommendation. A new storage site should be located *somewhere in the High Plains*, by which I mean east of the Rocky Mountains and west of the hundredth meridian. South from the Canadian border and north from the Texas panhandle. There are many sparsely populated locations within this belt of terrain that have been geologically dead in terms of earthquakes and volcanoes for tens of millions of years.

Intense research and development should refocus on the hazard of corrosion caused by water. Recall that before the 1980s, storage below the water table was the preferred environment. Wherever the new site may be, the depth to groundwater there can be expected to change, perhaps repeatedly, during the period of time needed to allow the waste to fission to a safe level of radiation.

There may be no feasible means to stop corrosion. Nevertheless, I firmly believe that minimizing two of the three natural hazards substantially increases the odds that *Homo sapiens* can avert a radioactive disaster of its own making.

Respectfully and humbly yours,
Dr. Barnabus Shanks
PhD, Member of the National Academy of Sciences

As Barney added a few more tweaks to this first draft, the cuckoo reappeared and announced hour six. Document saved, Barney leaned back in his chair and stretched. He started in surprise as firm hands began to massage his shoulders.

"Good morning lover," Heather said. "What are you up to? I woke up in an empty bed again. That's no way to treat your partner."

"You're right," Barney said as he stood and hugged her. He sat back into his typing chair and pulled Heather onto his lap. She was wearing only a gray mini-length athletic shirt.

"It was another sleepless night. But this time I think I've latched on to a way out of the mess I seem to be in. I've got lots of things I want to tell you."

Heather stood.

"And I want to hear them," she said. "But I've gotta run. I have to lecture in less than two hours. I need a leisurely wakeup shower and time to make me look like a serious professor of the English language.

"Last night you promised to cook me a full breakfast," Heather said as she walked toward the master bathroom. "I want my two eggs over easy. No hard yolks. The bacon should be crisp, but not burned. And the hash browns must be crunchy on the outside yet soft but not gooey inside. Whole-wheat toast. Buttered. No jam. Got that?"

"Yes madam," Barney said, headed toward the kitchen. "I'm gonna give you the best breakfast you've ever had. Hey. You forgot to mention the orange juice."

"Oh yeah. An eight-ounce glass. Thoroughly chilled but not slushy. Or I'll put you on a starvation sex diet for the rest of the week."

Heather reappeared a half hour later, looking stunningly beautiful in her professorial slacks and blouse. They began to share a perfectly, according to Heather, prepared breakfast. They watched and listened to Pacific surf through open windows in front of the kitchen table. Barney suddenly turned to Heather.

"Heather," he said through a mouthful of ketchup-slathered hash browns, "I've … I've never said this to anyone before … I love you. I love you very much."

Heather lowered the stick of bacon she was nibbling.

"Barney, I've known that for a long time. I've just been waiting for you to realize it and say so. I never ever want to be pushy. I love you, too, you know."

"You must," Barney said. "Why else would anyone stick with such a selfish ass for more than a week or two? I think we've got something special going. It'll get even better. Soon and fast!"

The sound of the cuckoo announcing hour seven interrupted the love fest.

"Hey, I *do* have to get going," Heather said. "I've got preparation to complete before class. Can I use your bike?"

"Sure. When will you get back? There's lots of things I want to talk about. I've drafted a letter I want you to critique … my live-in English teacher. And there's a research proposal I want to run by you."

"Well," Heather said, "I have student consultation hours after class and then an English Department faculty meeting over lunch. I'll be back by early afternoon."

"I'll be waiting," Barney said, giving Heather a kiss and a long hug on her way out. He stood in the open doorway, watching as she straddled the center bar of his bike.

"Why don't you check out the various meanings of *proposal* in Webster's while I'm gone," Heather said as she peddled away. "You might also consider putting on a few more clothes to cover those ratty shorts."

Barney happily hummed a tune while he washed dishes and tidied the kitchen cooking surfaces. He stopped in mid scrubbing motion when he realized it was the traditional wedding processional from *Bridal Chorus.* With a chuckle, he switched to singing what his surfer's memory could dredge up from Don Ho's English rendition of *The Hawaiian Wedding Song.*

"This is the moment I've waited for. I can hear my heart singing. Soon bells will be ringing. This is the moment of sweet aloha," he sang as he danced his way to the computer and opened the file for his novel. The title page *Dirty Bomb* appeared.

He stopped singing and sat thinking.

Yeah. A serious talk with Heather when she gets back. Meanwhile, damn it, my sample chapter is due at Vulcan Publishers in a week or so. And I still can't even decide how to start the story. Do I let the cat out of the bag right up front? Or do I try to build suspense for the reader and have that feisty feline appear later?

He was about to flip a coin as a way to decide, when his stare at the title page provided the answer.

Shoot. The title and cover photo pretty much say it all. I might as well destroy Yucca Mountain in chapter one.

He thought for a moment about how the bad news initially had been spread across the country on that infamous day in August of 2027.

"You about ready hon?" Barney typed.

22

THE SEARCH

There's a way to do it better. Find it! Thomas A. Edison

Summer of 2030:

The sun about to dip below the distant horizon was nearly blinding him. Sam stopped at an intersection, off the pavement, and studied the map again. He penned an X across Cheyenne County and typed some notes into his laptop computer.

"There," he said to no one in particular, being alone.

God there's a lot of empty space out here. Whoever claims the world is over-populated hasn't seen this part of North America. Course there's probably a pretty simple reason for bein' so empty.

He cranked the air conditioner up another notch in his rental car. He turned left onto Highway 59 and activated cruise control when the speedometer readout said sixty. He asked the computer built into the dashboard to find the nearest motel with air and a pool.

Looks like I'll be stayin' in Lamar tonight. Should be there in about an hour.

He stopped briefly in Eads to draw an X across Kiowa County and enter a few more notes into the laptop.

Later in his room, following a meat-and-potatoes dinner washed down with cold Coors, Sam set up a conference call with the other five members of his team.

"Greetings guys," he said. "I hope you're in nicer quarters than I am. It wouldn't take much to beat this place. I've discovered yet another town to cross off my list of possible retirement havens. Our employer shouldn't object to the expense voucher I'll be turnin' in after this trip."

A simultaneous ditto from five voices followed.

"Okay. Let's get the daily wrap-up. Tom, you go first."

Sam recorded the reports as each of the five described their day's accomplishments.

"Anyone have any unusual issues to add?" Sam asked.

"Well, I'm now acquainted with the Sheriff of Sioux County," Max said. "He wondered why I was snoopin' around his territory til I convinced him I was just a fossil hunter. Turned out we have the same last name, which he found so interesting I had to listen to a recap of three generations of his family tree. So me and Max are solid buddies. Told me where his favorite fossil picking places are. Even warned me to watch for the Feds because they arrest folks taking fossils from their land. Old Max is a true man of the law, that sheriff."

A few chuckles came in on Sam's speaker box.

"Listen to this tale," Steve said. "A rancher pulled up next to me on a back road near Powderville. When he found out I wasn't havin' problems with my car, was just nosing around, he got a bit testy. Started telling me stories about city slickers who roam his range and leave gates open. Turned real friendly, though, when I said I was looking for a good spot to start a major hog raising operation. A spot so isolated that no one would be around to complain about the stink. He was ready to sell me a hundred of his prime acres at a fire-sale price."

"And so it goes when you're a stranger in sparsely settled country," Sam said.

No one else had a field experience tale to tell.

"Okay. Back to business.

"Sounds like each of us needs about one more day to cover our territories.

"Let's see. It's Thursday. Let's plan to meet at the Brown Palace in the big city on Saturday night. We can consolidate our reports there and zing 'em off to our supervisor back east. I think he'll be pleased with some of the options we've identified."

AFTERWORD

*"**Our ignorance** is not so vast as our failure to use what we know."* Statement of M. King Hubbert, world-renowned earth scientist and petroleum expert.

With its principal events set years in the future, most of this novel is indisputably a work of fiction. A few background events are facts of history. Places are real, but characters (with one transparent exception) are the products of my imagination.

Nonetheless, the main story line ... that a violent volcanic eruption totally disrupts a site where the nation's high-level radioactive waste is stored ... even if improbable, certainly is possible, especially if that site is Yucca Mountain in Nevada. As amateur philosophers gleefully proclaim from rear-bumper podiums, *shit happens*. It only has to happen once to be stinkingly real.

The consequences of a volcanic eruption at any site where the nation's accumulated inventory of radioactive waste is stored could be many and varied, from the totally benign scenario of massive lava enveloping the waste in an additional and perhaps even impermeable (to groundwater) protective seal, to the nearly harm-free situation of an eruption causing the release of minor radiation dosages restricted to a small geographic area with few people impacted, to the sort of almost catastrophic situation at the core of the book. Ultimately, the geologic factors that govern which type of drama would play out are beyond human control, just as they often seem to be beyond sufficient human comprehension to allow an accurate forecast of what's to come in terms of a volcanic eruption.

Government officials and their contractors are carefully evaluating possible scenarios of potential natural disaster at the Yucca Mountain site, as they work toward a decision on where and how the nation's nuclear wastes can be stored safely during the period when radionuclides with exceedingly long half-lives (especially when compared with a human lifespan) fission themselves into a harmless state. What cannot be ignored, yet may not be adequately appreciated by the nation's general citizenry, is that once these radioactive waste products are created, they cannot be easily or quickly disposed of. There's no eliminating huge amounts of radioactive debris by burying one's head, or that waste, in the sand. We and many future generations are in it for the long haul.

Those involved in the evaluation and planning stages are asked to create a situation for safe storage farther into the future than all of recorded human history to date. This is a daunting, and some skeptics would say unattainable goal. Given the fact that burial pyramids thought to be impregnable by their Egyptian builders were pillaged shortly after construction, what should we anticipate for the future of a well-known storage site that exists in an international cultural climate of widespread distrust and terrorism and lies smack dab in the middle of a geologic climate of earth-breaking historic earthquakes and geologically young, though pre-historic, volcanic eruptions? No matter how sound and thorough the science, Nature often seems to have the upper hand … a hand teeming with surprises.

Attacking this challenge with the tools of probability analysis is one way to attempt to "out guess" Nature. The application of such analysis is one of the principal tools used to assess the odds that a powerful future earthquake or volcanic eruption will impact Yucca Mountain.

But even if the world's brightest scientists can convince themselves that the probability of a particular event taking place is extremely low, does this mean that it won't happen in a time frame that is inconvenient, and perhaps even deadly to people? If experts conclude today that the chance of a volcanic eruption disrupting the nation's warehouse of high-level radioactive waste is about one in seven thousand for the coming ten thousand years, only to see that an eruption occurs next year, were they wrong? Not necessarily. While rigorously defining the *probability* as being extremely low, they simultaneously recognize the *possibility* of this unlikely event.

That one-in-seven-thousand event could come to fruition sooner rather than later, and the experts could still claim to have been correct in their analysis. This way of being correct wouldn't provide much solace for those in and near the line of fire during that first year. Nonetheless, when the geologic variables are so many and the record of past volcanism is lean, which is the case for the Yucca Mountain site, probability analysis seems to provide the most effective leverage for lifting the veil that obscures forecasting.

And so it goes. Welcome to the dilemma of what to do with the nation's pile of highly radioactive garbage … a pile that is likely to get substantially larger as the United States and other countries seem poised to create more at an increasing rate, in both friendly and hostile pursuits.

It seems fitting if not ironic that the currently preferred (though not by everyone!) storage site is just a few miles up the road from Las Vegas, a burgeoning city built on the premise that "gambling is desirable." If mankind could control

Nature the way a casino owner controls the payout frequency of his games of chance, we could all sleep with less likelihood of radioactive fallout haunting our dreams. However, in spite of the fact that "the house always wins" in a statistical sense, on occasion a gambler beats the odds to prove that extremely improbable events do happen.

I am not intrinsically for or against storing the nation's high-level nuclear waste in Yucca Mountain. Looking beyond the problem of where to store this waste, I am not against generating more of the country's electricity with nuclear fuel, which would create more high-level radioactive waste. I believe that going increasingly nuclear will soon become necessary, *unless* world population quickly stabilizes or decreases (seems unlikely) *or* the per capita appetite for electricity diminishes substantially (seems even less likely), or some combination of these two events occur simultaneously. One "unlikely" plus one "even less likely" equals what? Sounds like another situation for probability analysis!

Petroleum resources are finite and closer to being depleted than to becoming available in increasing quantities for future consumption. Annual production has been decreasing in the United States since the 1970s and is arguably about to enter a similar downward trend globally. This is a troubling status for the so-called petroleum production peaks, first described (and forecast) by the prescient earth scientist M. King Hubbert in 1956.

Natural gas is not the energy panacea that many experts touted it to be only a decade or two ago. Coal is abundant, but its combustion heavily pollutes Earth's atmosphere with carbon dioxide, other greenhouse gases, and such toxic materials as mercury, arsenic, and ashy particulates. Perhaps electricity generated by burning coal should be used to run smokestack purifiers? But then there would be little electrical power left for other uses. Production of carbon dioxide during combustion of coal can never be avoided.

Ethanol made from corn is the current darling of the non-conventional fuels. However, the most thoughtfully thorough analyses of the efficiency of producing ethanol conclude that the bottom line of the balance sheet is a negative number, or nearly so. That is, it takes more (or marginally less) energy to produce a unit of ethanol than that unit contains. This is a bit like burning the house to stay warm on a frigid wintry day.

If ever there were candidates for the grand prize of legislative pork, congressional bills aimed at helping finance the production of even more ethanol from corn are among the top few.

Hydrogen is another fuel described as a significant potential source of energy. Hydrogen is also touted environmentally as a fuel whose product of combustion is nothing more than pure di-hydrogen oxide ... common water. I'm cynical enough to be surprised that champions of hydrogen fuel haven't yet treated the public to pie-in-the-sky plans to bottle the exhaust of hydrogen combustion to sell as competition to Perrier and Evian. Hydrogen, however, does not occur naturally on Earth as a pure substance, so large amounts of some other fuel(s), which is (are) likely to be hydrocarbon, must be consumed to produce hydrogen. Hydrogen is also saddled with a host of problems related to its specific chemical attributes.

It seems that there is no such thing as a free lunch with any of the non-conventional fuels in current vogue. Such alternative energy resources as biomass, geothermal, hydro, solar, and wind can increasingly contribute to the energy equation, but will never themselves be able to completely satisfy demand.

When thinking of alternatives, it's worthwhile to remember that petroleum, coal, and natural gas are the products of solar energy (growth of plants and animals), time and geologic happenstance (a lengthy appropriate temperature-and-pressure environment for converting plant and animal remains into fossil fuels). However, this huge storehouse of solar energy took tens to hundreds of millions of years to accumulate. It would take equally long to create new deposits. This is not a useful timetable for *Homo sapiens*.

Some seers foresee new forms of energy, some ethereal resources not yet recognized, as a solution to removing the growing imbalance in the energy equation. Such imagination embodies the attitude that technology will always bail out *Homo sapiens* when he digs himself into yet another problem pit.

Should humanity risk the future of its standard of living on the promise of an optimistic dream? Whatever the future holds for an energy supply, I recommend heeding Grandmother's advice. "Don't put all your eggs in one basket." A variety of energy baskets and strong incentives to conserve could minimize the potential for self-destruction that comes when eggs are piled too high.

If a large future energy basket contains nuclear power, the question of what to do with radioactive waste with half-lives far longer than human existence will remain a big issue. Can such waste be safely stored? This is a question with no clear answer ... a question steeped in many possibilities and probabilities.

NEWS FLASH!!
(From the May 9, 2005, issue of USA TODAY)

Nevada: Las Vegas—Jo Ann Argyris, a self-employed single mother of two, hit her second million-dollar jackpot in less than a year at a casino last week. Last June, Argyris won her first $1 million jackpot on a slot machine. Several gambling experts said the odds of the same person hitting two $1 million jackpots on the same type of machine in a year's time are *astronomical.* [Italics added].

SELECTED SOURCES OF INFORMATION

Uncertainty Underground: Yucca Mountain and the Nation's High-Level Nuclear Waste, edited by Allison M. MacFarlane and Rodney C. Ewing, A collection of twenty-four articles, published in 2006 by the Massachusetts Institute of Technology Press, Cambridge, MA, 432 pages.

The Long Shadow of Chernobyl, by Richard Stone, National Geographic Magazine, April 2006, Volume 209, Number 4, pages 32-53.

Understanding the Potential for Volcanoes at Yucca Mountain, U.S. Department of Energy Fact Sheet DOE/YMP-0341, November 2003.

Overview: Yucca Mountain Project, U.S. Department of Energy Fact Sheet DOE/YMP-0026, November 2003.

Chernobyl Record: The Definitive History of the Chernobyl Catastrophe, Institute of Physics Publishing, Philadelphia, 2000, 402 pages.

Yucca Mountain as a Radioactive-Waste Repository, U.S. Geological Survey Circular 1184 by Thomas C. Hanks, Isaac J. Winograd, R. Ernest Anderson, Thomas E. Reilly, and Edwin P. Weeks, 1999, 19 pages.

A New Way to Ask the Experts: Rating Radioactive Waste Risks, a review of the results of expert elicitation to determine the probability that a volcanic eruption will impact Yucca Mountain in the next ten thousand years, by Richard A. Kerr, Science Magazine, Volume 274, 8 November 1996, pages 913-914.

The Nuclear Waste Primer: A Handbook for Citizens, written by Susan D. Wiltshire, sponsored by the League of Women Voters Education Fund, 1993 revised edition, 170 pages.

ABOUT THE AUTHOR

Wendell Arthur Duffield holds a BA in geology from Carleton College at Northfield, Minnesota (1963), and MS and PhD degrees in geology from Stanford University, California (1965, 1967). He studied volcanoes for thirty years as a research geologist of the United States Geological Survey, and is now an adjunct professor of geology at Northern Arizona University, Flagstaff.

978-0-595-44203-
0-595-44203-X

Printed in the United States
78520LV00003B/94-120